THE REGENCY LORDS & LADIES COLLECTION

**Glittering Regency Love Affairs
from your favourite historical authors.**

THE REGENCY LORDS & LADIES COLLECTION

Available from the
Regency Lords & Ladies Large Print Collection

PRUDENCE

Elizabeth Bailey.

First published in Great Britain 2002
Large Print Edition 2009
Harlequin Mills & Boon Limited,
Eton House, 18-24 Paradise Road, Richmond, Surrey TW9 1SR

© Elizabeth Bailey 2002

ISBN: 978 0 263 21036 1

Set in Times Roman 15¾ on 17¾ pt.
083-0409-81095

Printed and bound in Great Britain
by CPI Antony Rowe, Chippenham, Wiltshire

Chapter One

The journey, begun at eight o'clock that morning, was becoming interminable. The stage, its progression necessarily slow, bumped unevenly as the coachman swerved this way and that in an effort to avoid the worst of the ruts left by the late snow. Even this early in March, pockets of unfrozen white could be seen about the fields beyond the misty window.

Wedged in one corner, Miss Prudence Hursley wriggled her toes, encased against the numbing cold in a despised pair of eminently sensible black boots. Lifting her mittened hands, she cupped them at her mouth and blew warmth into them.

Like the rest of her ensemble, the worsted mittens were at once warm and sadly unfashionable. The woollen petticoat was of dull grey, as was the short jacket in the pierrot style, closely fitting, with a small frill at the back and long tight sleeves. A plain round bonnet of black completed the picture—one that was to the young lady as familiar as it was unappealing—together with a black cloak that was slipping away from her shoulders and creasing against the aged squabs.

Rubbing her hands briskly together, Miss Hursley thanked Providence for her sheltered position within the vehicle. Or rather, it was less Providence perhaps than the Duck's sense of propriety, reflected Prue. Was not Mrs Duxford rigidly strict upon all points of etiquette? In particular those rules befitting the conduct of the orphaned young ladies in her care. It had nevertheless astonished Prue to have the enormous sum of five guineas placed at her disposal.

'You will take a seat *inside*, Prudence. I will not have one of my girls laid open to that sort of impertinence which may be invited by the circumstance of a female being obliged to travel upon the roof.'

At once alarmed and elated by the sight of the golden coins, Prue had been only half aware of the Duck's further instructions concerning tips to the guard, and the anticipated costs for meals upon the way and her night's accommodation in London. But she came horridly alert when the Duck all but terrified her with a direful warning.

'Do not waste your substance, Prudence, for you will get nothing more until your first wages, and that will not be until the quarter. Any little item you might require in the meanwhile must be purchased from what you have left.'

Prue had made haste to reassure her preceptress. After all, how could she spend so enormous a sum? In the eight years she had lived at the Paddington Charitable Seminary for Indigent Young Ladies, she had never been in possession of half as much money. Small wonder that her fingers had trembled as she had displayed this treasure to her two dearest friends.

She remembered Kitty's round-eyed look. 'Five whole guineas! Has the Duck taken leave of her senses?'

'No, for she says I will use quite half of it for my journey.'

'Pooh! I am sure you could not. Why, you might go shopping in London.'

Dear Nell had laughed at that. '*You* might.'

'Yes, but only think, Nell. Silk stockings at least!'

Prue smiled at the memory. Ever since one of the girls had smuggled in that dog-eared copy of *The Ladies Magazine* in which a gown of spangled gauze had caught Kitty's fancy, to own one like it, and silk stockings to wear beneath it, had formed the main thrust of Kitty's ambition. Poor Kitty. She had as well have reached for the moon!

'What I think,' had said Nell in her prosaic way, 'is that Prue will not dare spend one penny more than the Duck has decreed.'

Which perfectly correct observation had made Prue shudder. 'No, indeed. But, Nell, I am quite terrified. Suppose I should lose it?'

'Lord, yes!' Kitty's horrified gaze had veered back upon Prue, startling her with a dreadful notion. 'Or if some unscrupulous person were to steal it from you.'

She had felt sick at the thought. 'Don't suggest such a thing, Kitty!'

She had been grateful to feel Nell's arm about her shoulders. 'Tuck it securely away, Prue. You must put each guinea in a different place. Then, if you were so unfortunate as to lose one, you would still have the others by you.'

Which had been typical of Nell's good sense. And so it had been that in the flurry of choosing whereabouts in her costume she should secrete the coins, the whole sorry business of taking leave—which all three had dreaded!—had come and gone like a whirlwind.

Before she knew it, she had been well upon the first leg of the journey to London. She had travelled in the stagecoach owned by Mr Miles, the only one to take paying passengers between Paddington and Holborn Bars. It was drawn by one pair of horses and thus, with two stops to rest them, took three long hours to reach the capital.

The fare had been three shillings. How fearful she had felt upon disgorging one of her precious guineas to pay it. And what a relief it had been to receive the change from Miles's boy. Though that had been short-lived. Oh, the embarrassment of his words to the other passengers!

'It's one of they young ladies from Duxford's,' he had informed the two people occupying the forward seat, 'wishful to be going as a governess, like they all do.'

Prue had squirmed. Must she be exposed to the world for her sorry condition? Not that anyone who lived in the area round about Paddington could mistake the distinctive grey costume. The girls were all obliged to wear it when they ventured forth in the winter months.

She ought to be thankful. Well, she was. More so perhaps for the insistence that she learned to ply her needle, unhandy though she was. She had been able to make herself at least a couple of gowns that had not the stamp of Paddington charity. Though had there been no Nell to help her, she dared say the items that made up her meagre wardrobe would have been distressingly ill-fashioned. They were plain and serviceable, made of cheap materials. Linsey-wolsey for winter; linen, dimity or calico for summer. No spangled gauze for a prospective governess!

Kitty had schemed to purchase that desirable commodity secretly, but she could not have afforded to buy it—even had such a frivolous material been available in the village shop that served for the local draper, as well as everything else. Nor were there silk stockings to be had, though plentiful enough were those horrid white cotton hose that adorned all the Seminary legs.

Well, if she looked the part, so much the better, Prue thought stoutly. It had stood her in good stead, for her one night in London had been uneventful. She had met with unexpected kindness from the landlady who had found her a room within her means, with the result that Prue had the best part of two guineas remaining after paying her fare for this last leg of the journey. Indeed, she had been met everywhere with civility and friendliness.

Prue had been surprised, for it was far from the sort of reception she had been led to expect.

'You must look out for yourselves,' had been a favourite saying of the Duck's. 'Independence will be your strength, girls. Remember that a governess is nobody. Do not expect to receive anything but the rudest of treatment, and you will not be disappointed.'

Prue, setting out upon her first engagement, had braced herself to face that lonely independence. Despite the civilities she had received, she felt far less equipped for it today, as the stagecoach brought her ever closer to Rookham Hall. If only Nell were here to bolster her confidence.

The thought threw her into a sudden and unwelcome sense of loss. What was she to do without Nell's sensible guidance? And who would transport her on the wings of wild fancies without Kitty and that vivid imagination? If she had been bereft of family, had she not gained recompense in her two dearest friends? Were they not her spiritual family? They had been as sisters, sharing every waking thought, every secret dream.

Through all these years, they had squabbled and laughed together, and cried upon each other's shoulders. They had known all along that the day of parting must come, but the painful reality was hard to bear.

'We must be strong.'

She remembered Nell saying it, that day when Mrs Duxford had told her that she had been accepted for a post.

Kitty had added her mite. 'Yes, Prue. Remember what the Duck says.'

'Independence!'

They had all three cried it out, and fallen into laughter.

But Prue was far from laughter now. She sank back into her corner of the coach, gazing unseeingly through the window. Could she keep that promise they had all made, not to grieve? She would certainly write as Nell had suggested.

'You must set down all your daily happenings, like a journal. And then send it to us each week.'

Kitty had been sceptical. 'She is going to be a governess, Nell. What do you expect her to write about?' She had put on one of those mimicking voices of hers, as if in the throes of delight. '"You cannot imagine the excitement of my life, my dears. Today I gave a lesson in French. And would you believe it? The samplers are going on very well indeed."'

Prue had shrieked with laughter, but Nell had frowned. 'It's well to make fun of it, Kitty, but the melancholy truth is that there won't be much excitement. We must make the best of what there is.'

'Well, I shan't!' Thus Kitty, mutinous as ever.

'No, for you are always so foolish as to dream of an impossibly wealthy lord, whose eldest son is destined to fall madly in love with you.'

An unlikely contingency, Prue thought dismally.

She did not mind for herself, for she had no ambition beyond the hope that she might find her work congenial. That, and the more pressing concern that she would serve her employment well enough to be asked to remain in the post beyond the first three months. For her employer, a Mr Rookham, had stipulated that the position might well prove to be temporary.

'Doubtless the gentleman wishes you to serve for a probationary period. I imagine your future must depend, Prudence, upon how you acquit yourself.'

Nell had been much of the Duck's opinion. 'I know you will do well, my sweet Prue. Unless these girls are perfect horrors, I cannot suppose they can fail to adore you.'

The remembrance of Nell's fond embrace was comforting, if it did not convince her. Prue sighed in her corner. Perhaps it was better that she thought no more about Kitty and Nell. Let her instead turn her attention to her approaching future.

She must continue to believe herself fortunate. The Duck had said that Mr Rookham's letter had been penned in such a way that she could not suppose him to be other than pleasant and gentle-man-like. The girls in his wardship had not their mother with them, he wrote, and he required a female with a sympathetic understanding to begin upon their education. After such an introduction, how could Prue believe otherwise than that her charges must be angelic little things?

Tired as she was of the journey, however, the nearer she came to its end, the more her conviction lessened and her trepidation rose. She was not, therefore, averse to a slight delay occasioned by a halt in Leatherhead.

Prue had taken a light luncheon at the previous stage in Epsom. The afternoon was not so far advanced that she needed any further refreshment. And surely she must be at her destination within the hour? One of the chambermaids at the Green Man, who had shown her where to find the facilities of the house, had said it was a matter of three miles only to Little Bookham, where it had been arranged that the coachman would make a brief stop to set her down.

Finding the inn stuffy, and not wishing to appear in the coffee-room where she might feel obliged, like other passengers, to accept a cup of that brew, Prue wandered out of doors. It was chilly, but there was no wind to bite at her through the wool of her grey jacket. Though perhaps she would have done better not to have left her cloak in the coach.

It was too tiresome to go back into the yard to

fetch it, and more amusing besides to watch the comings and goings in the thoroughfare hard by. It was a desultory scene for the most part, but busier by far than Paddington.

The fellow on the cob must be a farmer, and the old man in the gig was likely a doctor upon his rounds. And perhaps that woman with the basket and a child at her side was going to market? Yes, for here was a fellow with a flock of geese, driving them through. A delivery boy with a barrow got in his way, and Prue watched with amusement the resulting argument.

Something brushed past her petticoats, drawing her attention. Looking down, Prue beheld a kitten at her feet, intent upon an acorn. A small paw batted the thing, and the nut scurried below her petticoats. The kitten burrowed, and Prue stepped away, stooping down to make friends.

The creature reared back instantly, but Prue chirruped, extending a tentative finger. The kitten, its coat a mongrel mix of brown, white and orange, approached with caution to investigate. Emboldened, Prue stroked it gently.

'You are a handsome fellow! There, now, you need not be afraid.'

The kitten began to purr, and in a few moments was nestling comfortably in Prue's arms, quite at home.

Intent upon her prize, she failed to notice the significance of a growing rumble over the cobbled street. But the kitten began suddenly to squirm. Prue tightened her hold instinctively, and looked up. A carriage was approaching at speed, driven by a man in the drab driving-coat commonly worn by gentlemen. Drawn by four fast horses, it swept down the street in a fashion that caused all in its path to leap circumspectly out of the way.

Indignation rose up in Prue. How inconsiderate! What was he about to be racing through a town in such a way? Unless, perhaps, the horses were bolting?

But the driver was apparently fully in control. For the kitten, no doubt alarmed by the overwhelming noise of the wheels upon stone, all of a sudden leaped out of Prue's unwary hold. Landing, it took off in a panic, straight into the path of the oncoming vehicle.

Uttering a shriek of dismay, Prue leapt unthinkingly to the rescue. She flew into the road, aware only of the blurry form of the suicidal kitten as it raced away. Seconds later, the sound of plunging hooves impinged upon her consciousness, and a violent expletive rent the air.

Prue froze in her tracks and, turning, saw the rearing cattle but a few feet from her. Time stood still as, in terror, she waited for their hooves to come down upon her.

Miraculously, the horses were turned aside. And then voices were in her ears, and hands were dragging her away.

'Mad she is, and no mistake!'

'Was it this you was after, missie?'

Prue stood trembling and bewildered, as a ball of warm fur was thrust into her hands. She took it automatically, and the plaintive mew jerked her back to her senses.

The kitten! Someone had saved it for her. Then she bethought her of the horses. Oh, what had she done?

Turning, she saw that the carriage had been brought to a standstill a little way down the road. The horses were fidgety and protesting, but a man, supposedly a groom by his livery, was at their heads, soothing. There was no sign of the gentleman driver.

'What in Hades were you playing at, you idiotic wench?'

The irate tone made her jump violently. Jerking round, she found herself confronted by a man in a drab great-coat, its several capes making him appear huge. The driver! Prue's throat dried. She had to look up to see into his face, and the fury there made her knees go weak with fright.

'I—I am most d-dreadfully sorry, sir,' she stammered.

'So you should be! A more lunatic performance I have never witnessed! What in heaven's name possessed you, girl?'

Here a fellow behind Prue intervened. 'It were that there kitten, guv'nor.'

'A *kitten*?'

The gentleman's eyes fell to Prue's hands where the multi-coloured bundle was still struggling.

'Ran across in front of your carriage, it did,' volunteered another.

'The missie here went after it.'

Glancing round, Prue became horribly aware that a number of interested spectators were rapidly gathering. A fellow in homespuns and another in a smock seemed to be taking the lead. One of them must have saved the kitten for her. Consciousness deepening, she discovered a couple of boys with trays and an elderly man with a cane standing close, and caught sight of one or two figures moving towards them from across the road. Prue felt her cheeks grow warm.

'Oh, dear. I n-never meant to cause such a stir!'

'A stir? The wonder is I did not run you down! And all for a kitten.'

'I didn't think,' pleaded Prue, turning back to the unwitting victim of her mad action.

'That, my girl, is obvious. Dear God, don't you know better than to chase a cat? It was in far less danger than you. Are you all right? Not that you deserve to be!'

This unkindness served to waken Prue's indignation. She threw up a defiant head. 'That is most unfair! I was in the wrong, I admit, but so were you, sir. You were driving at a shocking pace! And in a town, too.'

Muttered comments of agreement reached her ears, but the gentleman seemed wholly unaffected. Prue received an impression of lean strength, with a jutting nose and eyes of ice and steel.

'Never mind my driving,' said the gentleman shortly. 'I am the more concerned that you have taken no sort of hurt. Have you?'

'I have not,' responded Prue, adding huffily, 'though that is small thanks to you!'

'On the contrary. You may attribute the fact that you are still alive to my skill with the ribbons.'

A general assent from the bystanders made Prue the more resentful, but she felt herself grow hot with embarrassment.

'However,' pursued the gentleman, 'if you are sure you are none the worse for wear, I shall look instead to my horses. And if they have taken any sort of hurt, you had better pray that you never run into me again!'

It was on the tip of Prue's tongue to respond that the last thing in the world she desired was to run into him again, but her conscience intervened. Penitent, she looked up into the strong features above her.

'I am truly sorry, sir. I do hope your horses are unharmed. I know it was wrong of me, but you see, one moment this poor little kitten had been happily purring in my arms. And the very next instant, it jumped out and ran across the road! I am afraid I acted out of sheer instinct, but I see that it was excessively foolish of me.'

A slight quirk of the lips disturbed the severity of the gentleman's expression. But he made no reference to her explanatory speech.

'And what do you propose to do with the animal?'

'Nothing! I mean, it is not mine, you know.'

'Yet you risked your life to save it. I see. I was going to suggest you drown it, but perhaps that advice had better be applied to yourself!'

With which, the gentleman turned on his heel and walked away towards his carriage. Indignant again, Prue watched him confer with his groom, and then jump up into his seat.

In the event she did not see him drive away, for she felt a tap at her shoulder. Turning, she found that those who had remained for the little drama were drifting off about their business. It was the chambermaid from the inn who stood there.

'Miss, I come to tell you that the stage goes in two minutes. The guard is fretting already.'

'Oh, dear, I must run! I cannot afford to miss the coach.' She became aware of the squirming bundle in her grasp. 'Oh, what shall I do with this kitten? Do you know who it belongs to?'

'It's one left from a litter born to our cat, miss. Missus tried to chase it away, but it won't go.'

Dismayed, Prue held the kitten close to her chest. 'What will happen to it?'

'Likely the missus will have it drownded.'

'Oh, no!'

'You'd better hurry, miss. The coach won't wait on you. You'd best come round the short way.'

Prue followed her around the side of the house towards the yard. But her mind was on the kitten, clasped strongly to her chest. She could not leave it to be drowned! That horrid man might do so, but not she. But how in the world was she to take it with her?

A sudden bright notion jumped into her head. Why should she not bestow it as a gift upon her two charges? All children loved kittens. There could be no difficulty.

They had reached the yard. The stage was

ready, the horses put to, and the guard impatiently beckoning.

'I am coming,' she called. And to the maid, 'Do you think your mistress would mind if I took the kitten?'

'In the coach, miss?'

'I have only a short way to go now. Quickly, tell me if I may take it.'

The chambermaid grinned. 'Suit yourself, miss. I'd like fine to see how you manage with it in the coach.'

But Prue was already at the coach door. Her entry with the kitten was not to go undisputed, however. The guard barred her way.

'Was you meaning to take that there animal inside, miss?'

'Have you any objection?' asked Prue anxiously.

The guard nodded dourly. 'Against regulations, that is, taking livestock inside.'

'But it is only for a little way. I am getting down in three miles. And besides, a kitten is scarcely livestock.'

The man's mouth turned down at the corners, and he shook his head. 'Can't see my way to it, miss.'

'Oh, *pray*.'

But the fellow appeared adamant. In desperation, Prue dived a hand into the pocket of her petticoat, feeling for a coin. She brought out the first one she found. It was a crown piece. Wholly forgetting her straitened circumstances, Prue held it up.

'Will this help?'

A sniff and a toss of his head, and the coin was in the guard's fingers. He bit it scientifically, winked at Prue, and pocketed it.

'All aboard!'

Prue clambered up into the coach as best she could for the wriggling animal tucked under one arm. Fortunately, one of the inside passengers took pity on her and held the kitten while she settled back into her corner. She retrieved it on to her lap, where it mewed for a while, and then curled up and went to sleep under Prue's stroking hand.

It was only then that it came home to Prue what she had done. Five shillings! The poor little creature was not worth a tithe of that. Added to which, she could not be sure of its reception when she came to Rookham Hall.

But this aspect of the matter was less disturbing than the recollection of the spectacle she had made of herself. How angry had been that man. And so sarcastic in his speech. Thank heaven she would never see him again!

At the roadside, Prue juggled with the problem of transporting one mongrel kitten whilst clutching her cloak about her and carrying her portmanteau—an aged item of worn leather that had seen good use and better days—which had been placed by the guard beside her on the ground.

Her acquisition had woken upon her lifting it from her lap when she had to get out of the coach. Its protests were vociferous, and it continued to emit outraged mewls as she tried to comfort it.

'What in the world am I to do? I do wish you will stop crying!'

It then occurred to her that the kitten was very likely hungry. She put a finger to its mouth, and it sniffed and licked, but, finding no sustenance there, resumed its complaints.

'Poor little thing! I am afraid you must wait until we have got to Rookham Hall. And still I do not know how to transport you. I do wish Nell were here!'

But Nell was a world away, and Prue must fend for herself. Clutching the kitten in one hand, she seized up the portmanteau and walked a small way down the lane that led to Little Bookham. The signpost told her it was but a half mile to the village. But even so short a distance presented difficulties in this predicament.

It would not do. She must find a better solution. Halting, she set the portmanteau down again. As she did so, the kitten succeeded in extracting itself from her grasp and leaped to the ground.

Prue made a grab for it, but it eluded her and ran off a little way. She sighed frustratedly.

'Wretch!'

Then she perceived that the kitten had a need more pressing than hunger. How foolish she had been not to think of it! Indeed, it was stupid of her not to have realised that she needed some kind of receptacle to transport the kitten. Only it had all happened so fast that—

Her thoughts died as she was abruptly taken with the cleverest notion. And she had been so ungrateful as to despise the woollen cloak that had formed part of her Seminary uniform! It was excessively old, and beginning to be threadbare. But it had one distinct advantage—capacious pockets.

A few moments later, Prue set out again with a lighter heart, her portmanteau in one hand, while the other cradled a lumpy portion of her cloak that shifted about in vain.

'You will not get out of there very easily, my dear,' Prue informed it triumphantly. 'I only hope you may not be smothered to death!'

When the kitten presently settled, she was half afraid that it might indeed have run out of air. But when she paused to investigate, pulling a fold of the heavy cloth aside, two green eyes peeped up at her from the secure haven of her cloak pocket. Prue was able to resume her journey with a quiet mind.

It did not take long to reach Little Bookham village, which looked to be, indeed, *little*, with a spired church and a clutch of dwellings around a green. Here she was directed by a sleepy yokel to continue along the lane for a quarter of a mile to a turn-off which would lead her to the 'great house'. Prue trusted that this appellation would prove to be the Rookham Hall for which she had asked.

She was tiring by the time she arrived at a pair of wrought-iron gates that let on to a wide avenue of trees, and her arm was aching from having to remain in the same position to support the now-sleeping kitten.

Prue could not see the house. There was no lodge and the gates were open. Her stomach went a trifle hollow and she was conscious of an uncomfortable activity in her pulses as she ventured through the gateway into her new life.

'It may be a little alarming at first,' the Duck had warned, 'but remember that you are a graduate of the Paddington Seminary. Such is our record and reputation that many applications come to us through recommendation. You have been well taught, and you must have pride in your achievements.'

If only her own achievements had been worthy

of the reputation of the Seminary! Well, the Duck would not have sent her out if she had not thought she could fill the post. Prue took heart, taking a firmer hold of her portmanteau and stepping out more boldly.

The house came into sight around the first bend in the drive. Prue's spirits immediately rose. It was a good-sized establishment, but by no means a mansion. The building, of a creamy yellow appearance, was low—two storeys only—and long. There must have been a dozen windows at least, neatly spaced on either side of a central pillared entrance, which was accessed by a short stairway.

The avenue gave on to open lawns that led away, as far as she could see, into banks of trees, bare of leaves for the most part this early in the year. As Prue gained upon the entrance, it became evident that the building was larger than she had at first supposed, stretching away behind. The surroundings were woody rather than cultivated, and a gleam of silver between the trees gave promise of water—perhaps a pond or a small river.

It was a picturesque scene, and there was a pleasant air about it. A far cry from the red-brick world of regimentation that Prue had left behind. She was going to like living here! A tide of gratitude for her good fortune rose within her. If only the girls came to like her, she would have nothing more to wish for.

An elderly butler opened the door. A spare man, he seemed a trifle frail in Prue's eyes. She was instantly smitten with a warm glow of sympathy.

'I am so sorry to have dragged you to the door. Have you not a footman to do it for you?'

A pair of silver eyebrows wrinkled. 'I beg your pardon?'

The hauteur of his tone was not lost on Prue. Recollecting herself, she smiled a trifle nervously.

'I did not mean to say that. Only you seemed so—' She broke off, realising that her intended words might be taken in an infelicitous spirit.

'May I enquire your name?'

'Oh, dear, how silly of me! I am Miss Hursley. The new governess, you know.'

The butler looked her over in a way that made Prue feel distinctly uncomfortable. Then he bowed.

'You are expected.'

He held the door wide, and Prue lifted her portmanteau again and stepped into a spacious hall with a central winding stair that led to an upper gallery. She found herself in surroundings as pleasant as the exterior, with mellow painted walls adorned with two portraits and a landscape. A couple of long tables on to which a plethora of items had been untidily tossed stood on either side of the door.

A candelabrum rubbed elbows with a collection of books, several random papers, and a few ornaments. Near the stair stood a hat-and-coat rack, almost overwhelmed with various items of clothing. The place struck Prue as indefinably masculine.

'Pray come with me, miss. You may leave the portmanteau.'

Hastily, Prue deposited her burden to one side, and followed the butler—who did indeed totter just a little, so she was not so very much at fault!—past the stairway and down a corridor to one side, with a scattering of landscapes on the walls.

A door was flung open, and Prue heard her name announced. She stepped into a large airy apartment, bright with huge windows to one side, and full of long bookcases. From behind a central desk a gentleman emerged. He took a few paces towards Prue, and halted abruptly.

He was tall and rangy, dressed country fashion in plain-coloured clothes. Dark hair fell raggedly to his shoulders about a strong countenance with a jutting nose. He was, as Prue instantly realised, none other than the gentleman of this morning's adventure with the carriage.

* * *

Shock frayed at Prue's senses. Was it a trick of
her mind? Surely it was impossible that coinci-
dence should throw her in the way of her employer
in so unfortunate a fashion? But there was no mistaking those dominating features, or the expression
within them. He knew her for the same foolish
female who had—literally!—run across his path
this morning.

'This is terrible!' she blurted out. 'Are you Mr
Rookham? Yes, of course you are. You must be.'

To Prue's relief, the severity in his face relaxed
a trifle. 'Yes, I'm Rookham. The shock, I dare say,
is mutual.'

A choked giggle escaped Prue, born of embarrassment. 'I could wish the floor would open and
swallow me up!'

'But it won't,' he pointed out. 'There is little you
can do except face up to the difficulty, Miss
Hursley. It is Miss Hursley, is it not?'

Prue nodded eagerly. 'I am Prudence Hursley.'

'Prudence?' The steel eyes raked her. 'A mis-
nomer, if ever I heard one.'

Heat rose into Prue's cheeks, and she burned.
Must he taunt her? She would dearly like to have
repudiated the implication with a good deal of heat.
But Mr Rookham was her employer—that is, if he

did not instantly send her packing! She could think of nothing inoffensive to say in reply.

His lip quivered, and Prue recalled the look. He sounded amused. 'You were not so backward this morning, Miss Hursley. But I perceive your difficulty. You would like to reply in kind, but you find yourself restricted by the peculiar circumstances of our proposed relationship.'

'Well, yes,' agreed Prue, surprised into forgetting the proprieties. 'I should dearly love to retaliate. Though how you observed it has me in a puzzle.'

Mr Rookham regarded her enigmatically. 'I observe something more, Miss Hursley. Your cloak appears to have a life of its own.'

Prue became aware that the kitten, trapped in her cloak pocket, had begun to wriggle about. Abruptly the realisation hit her that her ready excuse for its presence was about to fall upon deaf ears.

She looked up again at Mr Rookham's face, just in time to see his brows snap together.

'Oh, dear God! You've brought the wretched thing with you!'

'I'm afraid I have,' confessed Prue guiltily, probing within the folds of her cloak in an effort to extract the prisoner. 'I had thought to give it to the Misses Chillingham for a gift.'

'Had you, indeed?' came grimly from the irate

Mr Rookham. He shifted back towards his desk. 'I have a good mind to order it drowned this instant!'

'Oh, no! Pray, sir, don't,' begged Prue, clutching to her that portion of her cloak which contained the now vocal kitten. 'I only brought it because the chambermaid told me that the landlady intended to be rid of it in that cruel fashion. I promise it will be no trouble to you.'

'On the contrary. It has already caused me a good deal of trouble. And while you are pleading for its worthless life, you might spare a thought for your own future.'

But Prue was not to be deterred by her own probable misfortune. 'By all means punish me, if you will, for I know I deserve it. Indeed, I had already guessed that you meant to send me back to the Seminary in disgrace. I will bear that, Mr Rookham, but pray, *pray* don't visit your wrath upon this innocent little creature.'

Mr Rookham watched in reluctant fascination as Miss Hursley fumbled in a most ungainly fashion—necessitated, he dared say, by the difficulty of operating in those absurd mittens—to release the animal from its improvised cage. At last she succeeded in producing the object, and held it up, squirming and squeaking, for his inspection.

He perched upon his desk and regarded it with

disfavour. Exasperation warred in his breast with amusement. Miss Hursley was awaiting his response, looking at him with just that disarming expression that had struck him that morning when circumstance had thrown her in his way.

Under a neat round bonnet, black and unadorned except for ribbon ties below the chin, in features unremarkable save for their youth, a pair of soft grey eyes gazed at him in mute appeal. From beneath the bonnet, a stray curl or two peeped out, dusky against a pale forehead.

She was obviously going to be an infernal nuisance. Totally unfitted, if he was any judge, for the task for which he had engaged her. Yet here she stood. A dumpy little thing in a costume more suited to a housewife than a governess, ready to accept her instant dismissal if she might only solicit his mercy for the sake of the mongrel kitten she was now cradling to her bosom. How in Hades could he repudiate her?

He rose. 'Very well, Miss Prudence Hursley. Since you are determined to make a sacrifice of yourself one way or another, you may as well do it here.'

Like a straying moonbeam, her face lit. The oddest sensation came over Rookham, like the daze that accompanied a blow to the head when he had engaged in fisticuffs. He stared at the girl, bemused.

'Do you mean that I may stay?'

With an effort, Rookham wrenched his mind alert. 'Subject to my approval you may.'

'Thank you.' She took a step towards him. 'I will do my best to give satisfaction, and I hope that you will be disposed to approve me in the end.'

'That is debatable,' he said. Her eyes clouded over and he was almost moved to apologise. But her gaze did not falter from his face.

'And the kitten too? May I keep it?'

'As a constant reminder of your folly?'

'I am not like to forget that!' The brief flash of fire in her eyes disappeared as she cradled the animal against her chest. 'But it was not the kitten's fault, sir. And it would have been lost if I had not brought it with me. People are so cruel! Even the guard, you know, would not let me bring it in the coach without a bribe.'

Rookham eyed her with misgiving. 'You bribed the guard? And may I ask how much you gave him for the privilege of transporting that revolting object?'

By the hanging of her head, he saw that his instinct had not misled him. She cuddled the thing closer, and raising her eyes, subjected him once more to that daunting look of contrition.

'You see, I had no time to think. The coach was ready to leave, and the guard so impatient. I had only just decided to bring the poor little thing with me, and so I—'

He cut her short. 'How much?'

'Well, it—it was a whole crown piece.'

She looked so absurdly guilty that Rookham was hard put to it not to laugh. But he was conscious of a slight feeling of compassion. No doubt five shillings was a great deal of money to this scrap of a girl. He must remember to reimburse it.

'Since you have expended so much coin and energy upon the wretched animal, I suppose you had better keep the thing. I should hate to think I had been obliged to put my horses through that nightmare experience for nothing.'

Her face—really, a veritable mirror for her thoughts!—abruptly filled with consternation. Now what?

'You are not going to spring something else on me, I trust.'

She shook her head, the grey eyes filling with concern. 'No, but your horses. I had forgot. I should have asked you before. I do hope they have taken no sort of hurt.'

'Do you imagine you would be standing there unmolested if they had?' He watched in growing amusement as the indignation bubbled up, making her eyes sparkle. He held up a hand. 'No, don't rip up at me. Remember that I am your employer and you cannot afford to anger me.'

It was deliberately provocative, and he knew it. To her credit, she contained her spleen. Her words, however, were unexpected.

'Then it is too bad of you to taunt me, sir, when you know that I cannot with propriety make any attempt to correct you.'

'As we see,' he said drily.

Her face fell visibly. 'I should not have said that, should I?'

Rookham bit back a laugh. 'Have no fear. You have convinced me that perhaps there is steel enough in you to manage your duties.'

She blinked. 'Steel? Oh, dear. Shall I need it?'

Rookham bethought him of the two little minxes who would undoubtedly run rings around this tender-hearted girl.

'You may judge for yourself presently.'

Hardly had the words left his mouth than the door burst open behind Miss Hursley, and his unruly nieces hurtled into the room.

Chapter Two

The cacophony was instant and deafening.

'Uncle Julius, Creggan said she was here.'

'Is this her, Uncle Julius?'

Prue had jumped in shock at their entrance, dislodging the kitten from her grasp. She uttered a cry of warning, but it came too late. Shrieks of delight smote her ears, and she received a whirlwind impression of two bright faces, swinging plaits, and a collection of grasping hands as a streak of motley fur flew round the room.

Seconds later, the kitten had gone to roost under a tall bookcase at one end, and Mr Rookham emerged from the fray with one long plait entwined around each hand.

Under Prue's amazed glance, two identical faces screwed up in protest, and two pairs of hands reached up to grasp at the fingers imprisoning their hair.

'Ouch! Let go, Uncle Julius!'

'You're hurting, Uncle Julius!'

'I shall hurt you more, if you don't be quiet,' threatened Mr Rookham. 'Stand still, the pair of you!'

Thus adjured, the girls froze in attitudes so comical that Prue must have laughed had she not felt so acutely for their discomfort.

'Let it be a lesson to you to wear your caps.'

But to Prue's relief—as great, she must suppose, as that of the girls—Mr Rookham released their plaits, instead laying a restraining hand upon each child's shoulder.

'As you have no doubt guessed, Miss Hursley, these are your charges.'

Two pairs of appraising brown eyes regarded Prue. She blinked. 'You are twins.'

The Misses Chillingham looked scorn upon her.

'"Course we are!'

'Didn't you know?'

'Silence!'

This last from Mr Rookham made Prue bite back the automatic apology that hovered on her lips. After all, how should she have known, if she had not been told? She looked the twins over with growing interest. They stared back at her with a disconcerting lack of self-consciousness in features of angelic innocence.

They were possessed of neat little noses, pert red lips, and dark brown orbs in complexions faintly olive in colour. They were dressed the same, in long-sleeved blue schoolgirl frocks, covered over with aprons, and they looked to be eight or nine years of age.

Prue smiled at them. 'I am so pleased to meet you. How do you do?'

Mr Rookham pushed the one on his right so that she stepped forward a pace. 'This is Charlotte—I think.'

'Uncle Julius, you have it wrong again!' piped up the girl, her tone disparaging.

'I'm Charlotte,' said the other, disengaging herself from his restraining hand. 'In any event, you shouldn't introduce me as Charlotte. No one calls me that.'

'She's Lotty,' said the first, also squirming out of her uncle's hold. 'And I'm Dodo.'

'Dorothy,' explained Mr Rookham. 'And I wish you well of them! If you can find a satisfactory way to tell the difference, pray inform me of it. I am sure the girls will be delighted to show you around, Miss Hursley. Now, for heaven's sake, take them away!'

Feeling a trifle overwhelmed, Prue yet stood her ground. 'Yes, but the kitten, sir. Pray let me coax it out.'

Instant shrieks smote at her ears.

'The kitten!'

'Let's get it!'

Mr Rookham seized the girls, much to Prue's relief.

'No, you don't. You'll only frighten the thing. Let Miss Hursley do it.'

'Oh, yes,' agreed Prue anxiously. She moved to the twins. 'I have only had it with me for a short time, you see, and it is very nervous. Then, if you will help me, I think we must find the poor little thing something to eat. It must be starving by now.'

Two vociferous high-pitched voices reassured her, suggesting an immediate raid upon the kitchen, to which Mr Rookham not unnaturally took exception.

'You may ask Mrs Polmont to speak to Wincle.'

'But Uncle Julius—'

'*We* want to speak to Wincle.'

Leaving them to argue it out, Prue quietly slipped away to the bookcase and knelt down. Sure enough, there was the kitten, cowering away in a far corner.

It took several moments of gentle persuasion, but at last the kitten consented to venture close enough for Prue to be able to recapture it. Only then did she realise that silence pervaded the room, and she rose to find herself alone with Mr Rookham.

'I ejected them,' he explained, gesturing towards the door. 'I doubt if they will be patient for long, so perhaps it will be as well if we postpone any further discussion.'

'Discussion?'

Prue's heart dropped a little. What was to be discussed? She eyed him with no small degree of trepidation.

That flicker at his lips came again. 'Don't look at me as if you suspected I meant to throw you out after all! I had intended to have gone over the circumstances which have led to my hiring you to deal with those dreadful nieces of mine, that is all. But we can reserve all that. Go and see to that wretched animal of yours, and we will talk later.'

Ignoring their uncle's prohibition, the twins had dragged Prue back to the hall and crashed through the green baize door at the back. Her attention on the frightened kitten, Prue had been powerless to prevent this invasion of the domestic quarters. She had entered a feeble protest.

'Did not your uncle say—'

Her new charges had cut her off without apology, pursuing their way down the corridor.

'Uncle said we should talk to Poll Parrot.'

'But she don't like us.'

'And Wincle does! Wincle will do anything we ask.'

If this was an exaggeration, the bulky individual

who presided over the kitchens was at least sympathetic. Keeping tight hold of the squirming kitten, Prue remained by the door. She was fearful of its escaping to run amok among the shiny pots and pans, and the piles of food in preparation down a long wooden table in the middle.

A stout woman with a large red face and a fringed mob cap had been at work on a quantity of pastry. She stood poised with a rolling pin at the ready, and a couple of minions, chopping away to one side, ceased their labours to stare as the twins raced up to the table.

'What are you making, Wincle?' demanded one, diverted from her mission. 'Is it tarts?'

The cook laid down her rolling pin and slapped at the finger which was about to poke at her pastry. 'Get away, do, Miss Dodo! Folks have to eat that, I'll have you know.'

'Wincle, you've got to give us milk for the kitten,' chimed in the other.

'Kitten, Miss Lotty? We don't have no kitten here.'

'Will they be jam?'

'The kitten our new governess brought. See?'

As Lotty pointed—it must be Lotty, for the cook appeared to know one from the other—Prue came under immediate notice from the assembled company of servants. Wincle paused to slap Dodo's hand away from the pastry again, and nodded towards the newcomer.

'Didn't see you there, miss. A kitten, is it?'

'Yes, and you must give us some food for it, Wincle,' persisted Lotty, before Prue could answer.

'And milk,' added Dodo. 'It hasn't eaten for hours, and it's starving.' She eyed the pastry with yearning. 'So am I! And if you are making tarts, Wincle—'

'Greedy-guts!'

'Yes, and I suppose you wouldn't eat any jam tarts, would you, Lotty?'

The cook intervened. 'Oy! Enough of it! That there pastry, Miss Dodo, happens to be for a raised pie for the master's dinner.'

'Well, but you might have some pastry left,' Dodo pointed out, 'and if you *happened* to make some jam tarts—'

'We'll see,' said Wincle. 'Meantime—'

'That means she will make them. Dodo, you're a disgusting pig!'

Incensed, Dodo seized Lotty's plait and pulled it sharply. The other shrieked, and instantly retaliated. Prue watched in dumbstruck horror as the two girls closed with each other. But in seconds they were separated, each held in one floury hand, Wincle's bulk between them, her red face bent towards Dodo.

'Nary a tart will you get from me, young saucebox,

if that's how you're bent on conducting yourself!'
She turned on the other. 'And as for you, Miss Lotty,
I thought you come for that there kitten, not to attack
your sister. I ought to bang your heads together!
Where's that Frenchie when she's needed?'

Both girls instantly stopped glaring at each other,
instead seizing the floury hands that held them.

'Please don't tell Yvette!'

'We'll be good, Wincle, honest!'

'We promise!'

The cook released them. 'Well, see you are, or
it'll be the worse for you both.'

Prue was left wondering who Yvette might be, to
have such an effect upon them. However, she felt
it to be high time that she took a hand, or word of
her uselessness would spread through the household in no time. She pushed forward.

'I do beg your pardon. I should not have let them
come in here, but I have only just made their acquaintance, you see, and—'

'Never you worrit yourself, miss,' said the cook,
pushing the girls aside and bobbing a curtsy. 'It's
Miss Hursley, I take it?'

Prue assented. 'How do you do? I am so sorry to
trouble you, but it was indeed I who brought the
kitten, and I fear it is very hungry indeed.'

Favouring the animal with a croon or two, Wincle

visibly succumbed. 'Ah, the poor little thing. Hungry, are you, mite? Well, if these young imps will be quiet for a moment, we'll see what we can do.'

She might have been only a short time in this house, but it came as no surprise to Prue that the twins wholly ignored the cook's request for their silence. Her concern for the kitten was too acute to allow more than a passing fright at the horrid problem of how she was ever to learn to control them.

The kitten's need for food outweighed its natural fear, and it attacked with gusto a saucer of milk placed under the kitchen table. While it took the first edge off its hunger, Wincle found some broken meats and chopped them into morsels small enough for consumption. She then placed them in a dish and presented it to the twins, bidding them take themselves off to their nursery where they might give the kitten the remainder of its feed.

They had perforce to wait while the kitten finished lapping its milk, which gave Prue an opportunity to air a further need.

'Do you think a box might be found, with a little earth placed in it? I don't know where it should best be situated, but I feel sure it will be safest to have it, if we are to avoid accidents.'

'I know just what you mean, ma'am,' said the cook reassuringly. 'There's no call to look so troubled. I'll see to it. And I'll send up something for the poor mite along o' the meals for the young ladies. If you ask me, you'd best fret more about what that Frenchie will say to it.'

These ominous words caused Prue to wonder uneasily about the identity of the 'Frenchie' as she was led up the stairs by the girls, and along a lengthy corridor. She had looked for her portmanteau in the hall, but it had apparently been spirited away. Prue supposed she must at length be reunited with it, wondering briefly what sort of accommodation had been allocated for her use. The Duck had warned her to expect no undue favours, and to be grateful if she was fortunate enough not to be housed in the attics with the servants.

Since Lotty—or so Prue believed—had charge of the kitten, while Dodo carried the dish of meat, she had leisure to look about her as they went.

The same muted colouring had been washed throughout the house, giving a warm glow to the walls. Portraits and yet more landscapes were interspersed with wall sconces, each fitted with fresh candles, giving evidence that Mr Rookham preferred his house well lit during the night. But presently the way led out into a short vestibule, with corridors leading off both left and right. Straight ahead, the twins took a stairway that turned a corner and led down into a narrower corridor, where there was little light and no visible sign of wall sconces to improve matters when it should get dark.

'This is our part of the house,' announced Lotty, glancing back over her shoulder. 'Uncle Julius gived it over to us *entirely*. So we can do whatever we like here.'

'Yes,' agreed Dodo, adding with a mischievous giggle, 'as long as, he says, we keep out of the rest of the place.'

'Except the gardens.'

'*Some* of the gardens,' amended Dodo. 'You know Uncle Julius won't let us in his precious tillage garden.'

'Treillage, you noodle, not tillage,' corrected Lotty scornfully. 'And that's only because it ain't finished.'

'No, and we ain't allowed in the rose garden neither.'

'But why do you need so many rooms?' interrupted Prue, more to divert them from argument than anything else. For she had lost count of the doors already.

The girls halted and turned. Hefting the kitten into the crook of one arm, Lotty proceeded to count on her fingers.

'One for us to sleep in, and one for Yvette.'

'Then there's Freddy,' added Dodo, 'though he ain't here just now.'

'Who is Freddy?'

'Our brother,' explained Lotty. 'He's older, and Uncle sent him off to school.'

'Only three years older. And we're nearly nine.'

'There's a schoolroom for us, and a chamber for you,' went on Lotty, ignoring her sister's interruption. 'And then there's Mama's room.'

'Only she ain't here.'

'And Mama's maid, and she ain't here neither.'

Remembering that she had been told by the Duck that the girls' mother was not with them, Prue was instantly struck by compassion.

'Where is your mama?'

Lotty took on an air of importance. 'She's gone to London for the Season.'

'She's going to get us a new papa.'

'Be quiet, Dodo!'

Prue regarded her with sympathy. 'Yes, I gathered that your papa has died. I am so sorry.'

'Yes, it's horrid,' agreed Dodo, 'for if he had not died, we would've stayed in Italy.'

Startled, Prue blinked. 'Italy?'

She was disregarded. 'I hate England!' pursued Dodo. 'It's so cold and everyone is miserable.'

'Dodo, that's disgusting!' complained her sister.

'How can you be so selfish, speaking of Papa like that, as if you didn't care that he died?'

'Well, I know, but—'

'Your sister is right,' Prue broke in, mindful of her duty. 'It is not becoming, my dear, to speak in such a way.'

'Pooh!' scoffed Dodo. 'Mama don't mind it. Besides, I did care. But I can't be forever crying about it.'

'Very true.' Prue could sympathise with this point of view, for she had lost both parents. And life, she had discovered early, goes on. 'Nevertheless, it is important to be careful how you express yourself. Others, you know, may be shocked to hear you.'

The brown eyes looked her over. 'You don't look shocked.'

Prue might have responded that she was already too battered by the shocks of the day to feel any more. She refrained, however, merely suggesting that they should proceed to wherever they were taking her.

'We're here,' said Lotty, and threw open the nearest door. 'This is our playroom.'

'Everyone calls it the nursery,' said Dodo, 'but that's silly. We're not babies.'

'No, indeed,' agreed Prue, following them into the room.

It was a large apartment, with two big windows that let on to the back of the house. It was furnished in plain style, with a large table, an aged sofa in old red leather set against one wall, and several chairs with worn leather seats which might better have suited a billiard room. Two long oak chests were set either side of one window, into one of which a female was busy tidying a quantity of items that had been amassed beside it.

The woman straightened up. Seeing the twins, she broke into a flood of French, delivered at high speed and with many exclamatory gestures.

Prue stood mumchance, watching this voluble exhibition, amazed that the girls made no attempt to intervene or explain themselves. The creature was diminutive, but looked to be possessed of a wiry strength. She was dressed in black, with an apron tied around her waist and a crisp, starched cap upon her head which tied in a bow under the chin. Her age was indistinct, but out of features a trifle lined, the only one that made an impression was a pair of snapping black eyes.

The rapid cannonade of French was too difficult for Prue to follow, although she had a reasonable knowledge of the language. But she was astonished to find, when the woman at last ceased speaking, that the twins had clearly been able to understand her.

'*Pardon*, Yvette,' said Lotty fluently, *'mais je désire à vous presenter notre gouvernante, Mademoiselle Hursley.'*

Changing the subject by introducing her new governess? The child was adroit, thought Prue, as she perforce moved forward to make the woman's acquaintance.

'This is Yvette,' offered Dodo. 'She is our nurse.'

The female grunted, and bobbed a curtsy. *'Mademoiselle.'*

'Bonjour. C'est Madame Yvette?'

'Ah, you spik my language,' said the woman in heavily accented English. 'Zat ees good.'

'Yes, but I am afraid you were speaking too fast for me to understand earlier.'

'You, yes-s,' agreed Yvette, glaring at the twins. 'But ze *enfants*, zey understand.' Her eyes came back to Prue, and she gestured into the open chest. 'Sings everywhere! Zey must tidee, no?' Her eyes snapped as she answered herself. 'No! *C'est moi qui peux faire.* I 'ave ze time me, yes-s? I make ze washe, ze iron, ze bedde. I must dresse zem, feede zem. Like bebee zey are.'

Here, a fresh torrent of French broke out, which ceased abruptly as Yvette caught sight of the kitten locked in Lotty's arms. For a moment, she stared in disbelief.

'Uh-oh!' warned Dodo, belatedly concealing the plate of food behind her back.

'Oh, bother!' sighed Lotty.

Prue saw the Frenchwoman draw in her breath, evidently ready to unleash a further spate of complaint. Quickly, she stepped in.

'I'm afraid you must blame me, Yvette. I brought the kitten.'

For a moment, Prue thought she was about to receive the full deluge of the little nurse's wrath. Yvette clearly struggled with herself. Perhaps the impropriety weighed upon her of expressing herself thus freely to the governess, who was her superior in the hierarchy of the house. Prue could not tell, but she was glad to see the woman's lips purse together.

'In zees case, *mam'zelle*, I say nussing. Only I say zat ze *enfants*, zey will clean if ze *petit chat* 'ee make ze messe.' She eyed the twins. *'Vous comprenez?'*

The twins nodded fervently, reassuring her in fluent French.

'*Comme tu dis*, Yvette.'

'Il ne sera pas problème.'

Yvette grunted. *'Je l'espère.'*

'You have no need to concern yourself,' Prue said, adding her mite, 'for the cook has kindly promised to send up a box of earth for the kitten. I am sure there will be no mess.'

Yvette made a derisory noise and held her nose. 'And ze steenk? Zaire weel be no steenk?'

'No, indeed, for I am sure the maids will empty it out frequently.'

The nurse eyed the kitten with suspicion, as if she was waiting for it to disgrace itself there and then. Dodo having laid down the dish of meat, both twins were intent upon watching their new pet consume a hearty meal.

'Alors, c'est folle!'

Having delivered herself of this indictment, Yvette left the room, with all the air of washing her hands of the whole business. Prue was left to the uncomfortable reflection that Mr Rookham had been moved to express himself in much the same terms. Perhaps it had been folly on her part to bring the kitten. Only now that it had been bestowed upon the twins, she doubted that they could be persuaded to give it up.

Bent over the desk which had been provided for her use, with her cloak about her, Prue scratched away at her letter to Nell and Kitty. She had meant faithfully to record all the happenings of her first day, but the hour was already far advanced and the entry into her life of the brown, white and orange kitten had proved so eventful a history that she had only just reached her arrival at Rookham Hall.

She laid down her pen for a moment, and flexed her fingers. Perhaps she should complete the story tomorrow. It was not comfortable to write by the light of a single candle, and the schoolroom was decidedly chilly. She was wrapped in her cloak, with the kitten creating a little splodge of warmth in her lap, but the cold had seeped into her feet and the fingers of her idle left hand.

Concentrating upon her letter, Prue had not noticed that the house was eerily silent. Had everyone gone to bed? Not that she would know. Few members of the household came into this portion of the Hall. The twins had averred that until they arrived, it had been virtually uninhabited, their uncle never having married.

Nothing had been accomplished in the way of education today, for there had been enough to do in becoming acquainted with Dodo and Lotty. She had learned a little of their past, enough to be burningly curious. They appeared to have spent the entirety of their lives abroad, in Italy mostly, and otherwise in Belgium or Austria, so far as Prue could gather. But although they could converse both in French and Italian, as they willingly demonstrated, English was their mother tongue.

But it was not easy to direct discussion with them, and within a short time, Prue had begun to dread the promised meeting with Mr Rookham. Already he doubted her ability to manage her duties. How was she to convince him that she could succeed when her confidence had suffered a severe battering?

Her fond hopes had proved deluded. The Misses Chillingham were far from the little darlings she had envisaged. Had she known, Prue was half inclined to think she must have jumped out of the coach rather than face the horrors in store.

It had been Kitty, she recalled, who had been sceptical.

'How can you know they are darlings? They may be sadly ill disciplined.'

'Like you,' Nell had pointed out. 'And unlike the Duck, I cannot think that Prue will confine them in the attic on bread and water.'

A fate that had frequently overtaken Kitty. Knowing her friend, Prue might have guessed. For Kitty was as wilful as she was pretty, with lush locks of ebony, an engaging smile, and a pair of lustrous brown eyes.

In just the same way, despite their angelic features, the Misses Chillingham were, as Kitty had unknowingly predicted, impossibly uncontrolled. They chattered non-stop, and had a habit of breaking in on one another to introduce subjects unconnected with whatever was going forward at the time. Prue could not tell them apart from their looks, but she was already beginning to recognise each from the style of their conversation.

Lotty seemed to be the more mature, if a trifle patronising in her manner, while Dodo's attention tended to be scattered, and her remarks were the more disconnected. But in the matter of activity, there was nothing to choose between them. Creatures of boundless energy, they were never still. They hopped up and down, raced about, and kept up a constant barrage of small attacks, one upon the other. In short, they were so far from the ideal of ladylike conduct instilled into Prue at the Seminary that the Duck would have thrown up her hands in horror.

How in the world she was to keep them sober enough to sit at lessons, Prue could not imagine. She strongly suspected that the nurse Yvette was the only person with any ability to control the pair. In her presence, Lotty and Dodo were muted, if not precisely quiet. If the nurse was always so ill tempered, it was perhaps not surprising that she could quell them merely with a look.

Not that Yvette contented herself with looks. If she was not attacking them in virulent French, she was muttering under her breath. During dinner, which had been served in the playroom, and which Prue partook of in their company, Yvette had gone about tidying the room, with an eagle eye out for the slightest lapse of table manners. Pouncing like a tiger, she had upbraided one for talking with her mouth full, and the other for leaning her elbows on the table.

Prue had felt sorry for them both, and had redoubled her efforts to make friends. It did not seem to her, however, that the nurse's strictures had any effect upon the twins outside her sphere of influence. The moment Yvette left the room, they had returned to their normal level of exuberance.

That her rule was absolute, however, had been demonstrated when she had come to fetch the twins to bed. Lotty had picked up the kitten, ready to take it with them. Yvette had balked.

'Mais non! Dans le chambre? Jamais!'

And that had been that. Not a squeak of protest from either! Both had looked so disappointed, however, that Prue had assured them she would take care of the kitten through the night. Which had meant that she must remove the box that had been provided for its use to her own chamber.

But that was the least of the matters exercising Prue's mind. Would Mr Rookham not expect the governess to exercise a like control? A forlorn hope. Nell would have had no difficulty. Nor Kitty, she suspected, whose temper had often made her fellow Seminary pupils tremble.

Perhaps she ought to beg Nell for advice. Taking up her pen, Prue dipped it into the ink. But before she could set down a word, the schoolroom door opened with a faint squeak of its hinges.

Startled, Prue looked up to find a tall shadowy form entering, candle in hand. A muted growl from her lap caused her to place a restraining hand upon the kitten's back.

'What are you doing up so late? And why are you sitting in the cold?'

Prue let her breath go. 'Mr Rookham! Oh, dear, you gave me such a fright!'

He made no apology for having done so. He came into the room, pausing by the empty fireplace, the candle held low so that his features remained in shadow.

'You should have asked for a fire to be made up.'

The kitten jumped off her lap, and Prue rose. 'I did not like to. Besides, I am used to the cold.'

'But the twins are not.'

He sounded irritated. Prue made haste to explain.

'We have had no lessons today. For the most part, I have been in their playroom. Getting acquainted, you know.'

The kitten approached his booted feet in a spirit of investigation. Mr Rookham looked down.

'I thought you had given that thing to the girls.'

'I have, but their nurse has forbidden them to take it into their bedchamber.'

He leaned his arm along the plain marbled mantel. 'I am glad to find someone in this house is possessed of common sense.'

Prue picked up the kitten as it returned to the safety of her skirts. 'Poor Folly.'

Mr Rookham's features were only faintly visible, but she saw that quirk at his lips. 'Is that what you've christened it? How very apt.'

'It was what you said,' Prue pointed out. 'And since Dodo and Lotty could not agree, the matter was left to me to decide.'

He straightened. 'Then decide a few other matters, and don't wait to be told! This is not a prison, nor am I a pauper. You must ask for anything you may need, do you understand me?'

Prue nodded dumbly, dismayed by his manner. If he had before been sarcastic, he was now wholly unapproachable.

His gaze fell to the kitten in her arms. 'Ah, yes, I had almost forgot.'

He put a hand into an inner pocket of his coat. It was of a dark stuff, the colour unidentifiable in the half-light. The cravat, worn simply tied, gleamed palely at his throat. He laid something on the mantelshelf.

'You said five shillings, I think.'

Blankly, she gazed at him. 'I beg your pardon?'

'For the kitten.' At the door he turned. 'You had best go to bed. It cannot be good for you to sit about in this cold.'

The door closed behind him, and Prue felt inexplicably forlorn. She shook off the feeling. She was relieved to see the back of him. What a strange man he was! She must hope that she was not to see much of him, to be subjected to such odd moods.

She recalled what he had said, and an abrupt realisation took her unawares. Five shillings? She crossed to the mantel, and felt along the shelf. The item he had left there was soon retrieved. She examined it at her own candle, and found it to be a crown piece.

Touched, and not a little relieved, Prue pocketed the coin. That must be what he had come for. It was kind, after the trouble she had caused him. Prue dismissed a faint feeling of disappointment. There was no reason in the world for her to imagine that Mr Rookham had come for any other purpose.

She picked up her candle and crooned at Folly, cradling him close. The kitten's presence was curiously comforting.

Prue laid down the last of the books that had been placed in the bookshelves at the back of the schoolroom. She had come in early, so that she might see what dispositions had been made, and prepare a lesson for the day.

The twins, neatly dressed and with caps over their hair, had invaded her bedchamber for the purpose of extracting Folly, who had immediately gone to earth under the bed. Prue had been obliged to coax the kitten out herself—having first found it necessary to demand at least three times that the girls held their tongues the while!—and had handed him over, bidding the twins present themselves in the schoolroom at ten o'clock.

She had earlier partaken of breakfast, which had been brought to her on a tray by a friendly maid, who introduced herself as Maggie.

'Mrs Wincle said as I'd best bring it to your bedchamber this first day, miss.' She had set the tray down on a corner commode, and plonked the dressing-stool before it. 'There, that'll do for now. But you'll tell me, I hope, when you decide as where you'd like to have it.'

Prue had been touched by this mark of thoughtfulness, and decided that the cook must also be kindly disposed. The covered platter had contained far more ham than she could possibly eat, together with two poached eggs resting upon fresh-baked bread. Prue had done justice at least to the pot of hot tea, which had been very welcome.

But when she had hurried to the schoolroom at last, her inspection had proved disappointing. There was little here of use in the way of books. She found two collections of poetry that were well above the level of an eight-year old, a book of acrostics, another of maps, and a three-volume novel by Mr Samuel Richardson that would have Dodo and Lotty asleep with boredom within one chapter.

Well, Mr Rookham had said she must ask for anything she needed. She would have to take him up on it. Had no-one thought seriously about what might be needed in a schoolroom? Someone had tried, but the results were inadequate.

There were two desks for the girls, and one facing them for Prue herself, a blackboard behind it. On a table by the wall reposed a large globe of the earth, two slates and a dish of chalk. Beyond that, there was a pile of crisp new paper—of which Prue had partaken last night to begin her journal for Nell and Kitty—with several sharpened quill pens, a blotter, and a bottle of ink from which she had filled the receptacles set into each of the desks. But there was not a text book or primer to be seen.

On the other hand, a fire burned in the grate, dispelling the chilly atmosphere. It felt immeasurably more cheerful than it had last night, and Prue could only suppose that Mr Rookham had given orders for this improvement.

Even as she thought it, the door opened to admit a thin creature of middle years, with pinched features around a beaky nose, and dressed in black bombazine. She gave a prim smile.

'I am Mrs Polmont, the housekeeper, miss.'

Prue recognised the name. Had it been Mr Rookham who had mentioned it? Something about it nagged at her memory.

'The master has requested me to furnish you with anything you might need.'

Prue sighed thankfully. 'That is kind, for I need a great deal! At least, it is not for me, but for the girls.'

The housekeeper cast a frowning glance at the table where lay the various pieces of equipment that had been provided.

'What have we forgotten, ma'am?'

Prue came forward. 'I'm afraid I cannot teach them without books.' She gestured to the book-shelf. 'There is no primer at all, and these volumes are much too advanced.'

'I shall let the master know, ma'am. In the mean-while, would you please come with me for a moment.'

Mystified, Prue followed the woman out of the schoolroom and down the corridor leading away from the Chillingham portion of the house. Climbing the stairway, Mrs Polmont turned to the right and at the next corner, stopped to open a door.

She led the way into a neat apartment, where a south-facing window filtered brightness from a weak sun on to a little sofa. Beside it was an occasional table, and before it a small fireplace, where a bright fire gave out a comfortable warmth. Two straight chairs flanked the fire upon the far side, and set apart by the opposite wall was a lady's secretaire with a straight chair before it.

Prue looked about her in surprise, noting a vase of spring flowers set upon the wooden surround to the window which formed another seat, an oval mirror on the wall and a sporting painting above the narrow mantel. Her eyes came around to find the housekeeper looking at her in the oddest way. Was that the ghost of a smirk upon her lips?

At a loss, Prue searched her mind for a response. 'It—it is a very pretty room, Mrs Polmont.'

The housekeeper inclined her head. 'I have done what I can. The master's orders, ma'am. This is to be your private parlour. There is paper and ink in the bureau, and I have provided you with those books you might enjoy.'

Prue stared at her, amazed. Mr Rookham had ordered this? When he so clearly disapproved of her! What in the world had possessed him? She knew not what to say, and her mind fastened stupidly on the last thing the woman had told her.

'Books?'

The housekeeper moved across to the bureau and pointed out the open bookshelf across the top. Prue had not noticed the volumes that were set within it. Dazed, she followed Mrs Polmont and read one of the titles—*Camilla*. Fanny Burney's story? What a treat! The Duck had never permitted the reading of novels, although Prue had read one or two. Kitty had been noted for getting hold of contraband volumes.

But this was overwhelming. What had she done that Mr Rookham must needs treat her with so much kindness? Only yesterday she had supposed he would despatch her back to the Seminary as fast as he could. And last night he had behaved as if she was an irritant. What was she to make of him?

'I do not know what to say,' she declared truthfully.

The housekeeper eyed her. 'When you do, you'd best say it to the master.'

Prue blinked. 'I beg your pardon?'

'Would it be your wish to have your meals brought to you here, Miss Hursley?'

A faint discomfort entered Prue's breast. She eyed the woman's face and made the discovery that Mrs Polmont had a slight look of a parrot. Memory stirred. Had not the twins made reference to such a name? But the thought faded as a sense of unease built.

In every utterance the housekeeper made, there was a hint of meaning which she could not grasp. Nor had she any notion how to answer this last question.

'Perhaps. Unless the girls would wish me to eat with them as I did yesterday. What do you think?'

Mrs Polmont sniffed delicately. 'It's hardly for me to say, miss.' She paused, and once again Prue was made uncomfortable by the look in the woman's eyes. 'Time enough to decide. It's possible the master has an opinion.'

Without knowing why, Prue felt a compulsion to repudiate this suggestion. More to dispel her own unformed fears than anything else, she made a hasty decision.

'I will eat luncheon with the girls, and take breakfast and dinner in here, if that is not too much trouble.'

Mrs Polmont smiled thinly. 'No trouble, ma'am. Would there be anything else for the present?'

'No, I thank you.'

Prue moved quickly to the door and walked out of the room, aware that the housekeeper followed her. About to walk off down the corridor to return to the schoolroom, she abruptly recollected her immediate problem. She turned quickly.

'Mrs Polmont.'

The woman was heading in the opposite direction, but she halted, turning. 'Miss?'

'Do you know whether Mr Rookham has any children's books in his library? At least I could start them on a simple story.'

'Why do you not have a look, Miss Hursley? I am sure the master will not object.'

Prue experienced a sudden hollow at her chest. Have a look? Yes, and encounter Mr Rookham himself! What with last night and now the little parlour, she should not know what to say to him.

'I—I should not wish to disturb him,' she said, improvising. 'Later will do.'

She was about to turn away again, when the housekeeper's voice checked her.

'You won't disturb him, miss. The master is out riding and has not yet breakfasted. It will be a good hour or more before he settles to his estate work.'

There were books, books, and more books. But nothing, it would seem, that was remotely useful on an immediate basis. Driven partly by consciousness of swiftly passing time, and partly by the fear of being discovered here by the master of the house, Prue knew her search had been cursory.

At sight of the eight huge bookshelves that lined the walls of the library, she had almost run away again. But Mrs Polmont had been standing in the doorway, and Prue could not make the ignominious exit for which she longed. Instead, she had assembled her courage and walked deliberately into the middle of the room, looking about in a manner that she had hoped appeared resolute.

The housekeeper had stood poised a moment longer, and then thankfully retired, closing the door behind her. Prue had discovered that her knees were shaking, and fairly staggered to a seat by one of the long windows. From here, she had taken in the daunting prospect ahead of her.

The library was a long room, dominated by the big oaken desk—placed to take advantage of the heat from the fire—which was apparently Mr Rookham's working headquarters. Prue remembered that at least, but her arrival yesterday had been so taken up with the dreadful recognition of the master of the house, that she had not taken in much more.

Now she noted that the desk was awash with stacks of piled papers, and an overlarge blotter formed the only open space upon its surface.

A series of windows let in light, with scrolled

seats before them. But all across one end and down the long wall opposite, interrupted only by the fireplace and a single door, stood the massive bookshelves, loaded down with the biggest collection of volumes Prue had ever seen. A far cry from the library tended by Mr Duxford at Paddington.

On the walls either side of the main door hung charts and pencilled drawings, which looked to encompass a form of design work. They were far from neatly placed, one having been piled on another and tacked to a boarded surface against the wall, so that they overlapped everywhere like an undefined mosaic. Prue had wondered briefly at them. But catching sight of the time on a case clock over the mantel, she had jumped hastily to her feet and darted across to inspect the first of the bookshelves.

But her search had been in vain. There was plenty of Latin and Greek, but she had abandoned any hope of discovering anything for children in simple English.

Just as she was about to give up altogether, she discovered a bank of books in foreign languages. She reached thankfully to pull one out for examination. But a rapid review of the Italian it contained proved it to be far beyond her grasp of that tongue. Those in French might be more within her capability, but she was uneasily aware that the twins must outstrip her in that language. But still nothing for children! Impatient, Prue exclaimed aloud.

'Oh, this is too bad! You would think that with such a multitude of books, there would be something I could use!'

A voice spoke from the door near the fireplace, making her leap with shock. 'I must apologise for the deficiencies of my library.'

Chapter Three

Her pulses crazily fluttering, Prue burst into intemperate speech. 'Must you do that? I do wish you would not creep up on me in this tiresome fashion, Mr Rookham!'

He gave an ironic little bow. 'Once again, my apologies. I have been watching you for several moments. You were so absorbed, I hesitated to interrupt you.'

But Prue had recollected herself. 'I b-beg your pardon, sir. I should not have—I mean, I had no intention…' She faded out, horribly conscious.

'You had the intention of finding a book, I gather.'

'For teaching.' She made a desperate effort to steady her breath. 'Your housekeeper said I might come in here. She told me you were out riding, or I would not have…'

But Mr Rookham did not appear to be annoyed.

He strolled over to where she was standing, his eyes travelling along the shelves.

'What precisely were you looking for?'

Distinctly disturbed by his presence, Prue shifted a little away. She hardly knew what she replied.

'Something for children. Anything, as long as it is simple. But I can find only these volumes in French and Italian, and they are too advanced to be of the least use.'

'Something simple, eh? In English?'

He was searching as he spoke, and Prue backed off the more, her eyes on the ragged cut of his dark hair. She answered him at random, taking in, as if for the first time, the loose-limbed figure and the casual set of his clothes. If he had been riding, he had certainly changed, for his simply tied cravat was clearly fresh, and he had on a frock coat the colour of wine, with a waistcoat of lighter hue beneath and buckskin breeches moulded to a pair of long thighs.

He looked round at her, and Prue hastily cast her eyes in another direction.

'Tell me what it is you need.'

'An English primer,' said Prue automatically, moving to the nearest window and plonking down upon the seat. It did not occur to her that she ought not to sit uninvited in her employer's presence. She was only glad of the support beneath her that made it no longer necessary to remain upon legs suddenly become unruly. She made herself look up.

Mr Rookham was standing before the bookshelf, facing her now, in an attitude of ease, one hand resting on his hip. He was not at all good-looking, decided Prue. How would he be, with such distinctive features? That jutting nose, for one thing. But the lean strong countenance was compelling.

'Is that all?'

'All?' she reiterated stupidly.

'An English primer, you said.'

'Oh, yes—how silly!' She made an attempt to pull herself together. 'I cannot teach them without it, you see. But I thought that if I could find a simple children's story, I might have begun with that. But I suppose the French will have to do.'

To her surprise, that quirky look appeared at his mouth. 'A waste of time. Dodo and Lotty speak and write both French and Italian with fluency. It is their English that is poor.'

Prue nodded, feeling a little less flustered. 'Yes, I heard them conversing with their nurse in French, and they gave me a sample of their Italian.'

He laughed. 'I trust it did not shock you. In my experience, they delight in cant phrases in that

language. Probably because Yvette does not understand it and cannot correct them.'

From which Prue deduced that he was himself
fluent in Italian. She reassured him. 'If they had
used coarse language, sir, I would not have understood it. But why do you complain of their English?
Indeed, I was surprised to hear they had been
abroad, for they are well spoken and fluent.'

'You think so?'

She regarded him uneasily. 'Do not you?'

'No, I do not! They are impertinent minxes, and
the style of their conversation is most improper,' he
said crushingly.

'Oh.' Blankly said.

His brows rose, and Prue felt more was required
of her. 'Well, I did feel perhaps their grammar…'

'Grammar? Only wait until you see how they write
English, and you may complain of their grammar.'

Daunted, Prue sighed. 'Oh, dear.'

'You may well sigh. They cannot spell either,
nor write without blots. You would do well to concentrate your efforts upon these things, if you
manage to teach them nothing else.'

Indignant, Prue forgot herself. 'Well, and so I
would if there was anything I might use to do so!'

Mr Rookham eyed her with a slight feeling of
satisfaction. That had pierced her armour. She was

certainly on the retreat today. But the spurt of defiance was of short duration. With mixed feelings, he saw contrition enter her face.

'I beg your pardon, sir. But you did say I should ask for anything I might need.'

'Pray don't apologise, Miss Hursley. I dare say I deserved to be taken to task.'

'But I did not mean—'

He threw up a hand. 'Don't let us fall into so foolish a dispute. We would be better employed if I embarked upon the matters I meant to discuss with you yesterday.'

A look of alarm entered her face, and he frowned. 'What is the matter? What have I said to frighten you?'

'Nothing at all. I am not frightened, I assure you, sir.'

She was a poor liar. And she was shy of him again, averting her eyes. His own fault, no doubt. He could not fathom why he had spoken to her in that fashion last night. He was inclined to think he'd had too much brandy. He recalled feeling outraged—why, he could not tell—to find her sitting alone in that freezing room with but a candle and her abominable kitten for company.

If she must sit up at night, let her at least do so in a warm room! He trusted Polmont had carried out his instructions. Perhaps his housekeeper had not yet shown her the parlour?

She was looking at him in a manner that reminded him irresistibly of a skittish colt, as if she could not decide whether she ought to run away, but was nevertheless intrigued enough to remain.

'I merely wished to explain the circumstances that have led to your being employed here.' Casually, he strolled down to the next window, and looked out. 'My sister is a widow. She married an impecunious fellow who fancied himself a poet. Chillingham's mother was Italian, and he inherited her artistic temperament. Or so he thought.'

'Are the twins artistic too?'

Rookham looked round, shrugging. 'Possibly. I wouldn't know. They arrived here a little before Christmas. They have been living abroad, you must know, travelling a good deal.'

'Yes, they said they had been in Brussels and Austria as well as Italy.'

'Among other places. Chillingham eked out a living teaching English wherever they went. Trixie—my sister—tells me that for the most part she undertook the children's education herself. But there were governesses or tutors—French or Italian for the most part—whenever they could afford it.'

He glanced round again, and found upon Miss Hursley's features the most profound expression of compassion.

'Poor things,' she uttered in distressed tones. 'How dreadfully hard it must have been for them.'

Yes, he might have known she would react that way! 'Spare your tears, Miss Hursley. Trixie assures me that she has thoroughly enjoyed her life. And you can see that the twins are none the worse for wear. Nor is my nephew.'

'Ah, yes. Freddy, is it not?'

'The twins told you? Freddy is eleven. I have packed him off to Eton. But I promised Trixie I would find a governess for the girls, so that they might be readied for a future in the English style.'

Miss Hursley nodded in a sage fashion that sat oddly with her air of innocence. 'I begin to see. The girls told me, sir, that their mother intended to remarry.'

'Oh, yes.' He knew he sounded cynical, but he was unable to help it. 'Not, you understand, that she has anyone particular in mind. But she assures me that she will find a suitable candidate.'

Miss Hursley blinked. 'Oh.'

'Is that all you can find to say?'

He was aware that he was snapping, and noted the wariness in the governess's eyes. He knew an impulse to retract, apologise. But before he could formulate the words, she was offering an answer.

'To tell the truth, sir, the twins did suggest some such scheme, but I took it with a pinch of salt. Children are apt to misunderstand the activities of their elders.' Uncertainty entered the grey eyes, and she became hesitant. 'I must say that it seems a little…'

Irritation flared, and he supplied her with the missing word. 'Mercenary?'

'Oh, no, I—'

He cut her short. 'Don't let us quibble, Miss Hursley. It is mercenary. And quite unnecessary. I am well able to provide both for my sister and her children.'

'Oh.'

Rookham turned abruptly, and took a hasty turn about the library. What had he expected from the girl? He did not know why he was telling her all this. Why the matter should trouble him, he did not know. If the truth were told, the last thing he had wanted was to be saddled with a set of youngsters! The life he led suited him very well, and he had no wish for change. Yet a sense of duty—and perhaps a nod to his deceased mother's probable wishes?—made him baulk at Trixie's insistence on managing her life for herself. He had sent

Chillingham money enough through the years, as Trixie well knew. But this, she had averred, was different.

'Nothing will induce me, my dear Julius, to throw myself and my offspring upon your mercy. I could not endure to be such a charge on you. Besides, I value my independence, my darling brother.'

In vain had he said that such a marriage as she contemplated would curtail that very spirit of independence.

'No, Julius, for I shall not allow any husband to ride roughshod over me. But I need a household of my own. Let me alone to take care of my future. But while I am about it, if you will keep my girls for me, I will be eternally grateful.'

As he recalled the path he had chosen for the furtherance of his nieces' future, it dawned on him that the result of his endeavours was staring at him in a manner both perplexed and—if he was any judge—fearful.

He threw up a hand. 'Forgive my abstraction. Where was I?'

'Your sister, sir?'

'Ah, yes. She has gone to London, which is why I have engaged you. But since I do not know what the outcome will be, I felt obliged to give you warning that the position might be temporary. I cannot answer for my sister's requirements when she resumes charge over her daughters.'

Miss Hursley jumped up, a light of eagerness in her face. 'But perhaps if I were to prove able, sir, she might consider keeping me?'

He was obliged to bite back a laugh. 'Anything is possible.'

Those grey eyes searched his. 'But if, as you say, their schooling has been a trifle haphazard before now…'

'She will not object to someone who chases kittens across the path of an oncoming carriage?'

The eyes took fire, but Rookham saw her resolutely tighten her lips together. She was clearly determined not to rise to the fly. He relented.

'No, that was unfair. But if you are desirous of making yourself indispensable, perhaps you had best make a start.'

She visibly relaxed again. 'I suppose I had. I will ask the girls to write, I think, and then I may judge what is needed to improve their English.'

'An excellent notion, Miss Hursley. As for the books, give me a list, and I will send to Leatherhead for whatever you need.'

Prue thanked him and made for the door. He called out to check her. 'By the by, Miss Hursley. Do you care for your parlour?'

She turned to him, her features transformed. And the light in them quite took his breath away.

'I don't know why you should have been so kind, sir, when I have done everything possible not to deserve it. I have never had a bedchamber of my own, let alone a parlour! I don't know how to thank you.'

For a moment she stood poised, as if waiting for him to speak. Rookham could not utter a word. The light slowly died out of her face, and she walked quickly out of the library.

Through the window of the schoolroom, Prue contemplated the persistent drizzle outside. Small chance that the twins would be able to redeem their oft-repeated promise to show her around the gardens. It was a pity, for she was sure that the opportunity to expend their restless energy outdoors would help to focus their wayward concentration.

The past few days had not been easy. It was Wednesday, and it seemed impossible Prue had only arrived one week ago today. It felt already like a lifetime, for she was required to have the twins at lessons for several hours, morning and afternoon, with the exception of Saturday afternoon and Sunday. Not that this rigorous regime would have been a hardship, if only the girls had been attentive!

Far from it. If one was not fidgeting about the

room while Prue tried to help the other with her reading, both were complaining about the necessity to work upon their English. They did all they could to deflect her, from teasing Folly into interrupting the proceedings to dropping their books on purpose so as to lose the place.

For want of any other success, Prue at least could congratulate herself on managing most of the time to tell them apart. Not for any discernible difference in their features, but from an indefinable separation in the way they moved and spoke. She could tell it was Dodo who spent more time wondering what was to be on the menu for dinner than minding her book, and that the one who argued with every rule of grammar was Lotty. When they were still or silent—which was rare—she would have had no idea which was which except for the fact that each had appropriated a desk to herself. And resented any intrusion by the other!

Guiltily aware that, after some dozen lessons, she had accomplished little in the way of improving their English—despite the help of the books she had requested which had been brought from Leatherhead within two days—Prue had racked her brains in vain for a method which might catch their interest in the subject.

Then by chance last night, the twins had come

into her parlour, seeking Folly for his meal, and found her engaged upon her almost daily letter to her two friends at the Seminary. Lotty had caught sight of her own name on the sheet, and instantly demanded to be told why Prue was writing about her. The explanation had provoked both girls into stating that if Miss Hursley was to set down stories about her charges, they ought to retaliate by writing about their governess.

Fired with this notion, Prue had set paper down in front of each this morning and challenged them to do exactly that. Two pairs of brown eyes had eyed her with suspicion.

'What, write about you?'

'Why not?'

'But what should we write?'

'You could say what you thought of me when we met. I have set down what I thought of you, and you did say you wanted to give your own account of me.'

Lotty and Dodo had looked at each other, and then turned their gazes back upon Prue.

'But won't you be cross if we say things about you?'

'Not if it is the truth. I only hope it may not be too horrid!'

Both girls giggled. But they looked dubious.

Inspired, Prue reached out to remove the paper she had set before them, sighing.

'Well, I had not realised you were so faint-hearted.'

Lotty bridled. 'Faint-hearted? Us?'

'Pooh!' scoffed Dodo. 'We ain't even afraid of Yvette.'

Prue might have disputed this statement, for the evidence suggested otherwise. However, she did not refer to it, but only laid aside the papers and moved to the pile of books.

'We will read instead.'

But both Lotty and Dodo jumped up and seized the papers, declaring that they would write about her.

'If you don't like it, it's your fault,' Lotty averred.

'But you can't read it 'til we've finished,' warned Dodo.

Half an hour later, they were still writing. Prue was left with nothing to do, except watch the laborious scratching of their pens, and wonder with misgiving what they might be writing of her. Every so often they would leave off writing to confer in whispers and giggles, which was not encouraging.

Rising from her seat, Prue had shifted to the window, absently stroking Folly who had ensconced himself on the ledge. She suppressed her doubts, feeling that she deserved credit for having successfully induced them to write at all. The spelling was bound to be atrocious, the grammar poor and the handwriting untidy. But that could all be mended.

Mr Rookham's opinion of their skill in written English had been borne out, she reflected. Which thought immediately reminded her of the disquieting fact that she had seen her employer only once since that uncomfortable occasion in the library the morning after her arrival, and that on a visit to the village church on Sunday when no private conversation was possible.

Not that Prue had expected to see him. Why would the master of the house be interested in the day-to-day activities of a mere governess? He had done more than enough for her comfort, and that must content her. Prue tried hard to be contented. Only she could not rid herself of a ridiculous delusion that her first encounter with Mr Rookham had created a bond between them. It was nonsensical, and she did not know where she had come by such a notion.

It was just that whenever she thought of him—and that she should do so was not extraordinary, she reflected, for he was her employer and uncle to the twins—it was with a sense of familiarity which must be singularly misplaced. But why had he been so thoughtful? Providing her with a parlour, an unheard-of luxury for a governess. Yet when she had thanked him, he had just stared at her!

She had wasted far too much time in worrying over what she had said. Had she been too confiding? It was not her place to be giving him snippets of her history. But warmth crept into her bosom when she remembered how he had consented to let her remain, when he must have thought her a witless nincompoop. It made it the more imperative that she prove her worth.

'Finished.'

Prue turned. 'Excellent. May I see?'

Lotty held out her paper, but Dodo leaned over from her own desk and grabbed her arm. 'Not yet! Wait for me.'

'Hurry up then, lazy bones.'

'I'm nearly done.'

There was such a light of mischief in Lotty's eyes as caused a resurgence of Prue's earlier foreboding. What had she let herself in for? Well, she could hardly object now. Steeling herself, she waited for Dodo to complete her final sentence. A faint tattoo rose up in her breast nevertheless as she finally took possession of both sheets of paper.

Aware that the girls were sniggering, Prue returned to her desk and, with deliberation, laid the papers down before her.

At first glance, she took in the many blots and crossings-out, and the distinct lack of grace about the letters. Dodo's was perhaps a trifle the neater, but it was clear the content had little to offer as Prue cast her eyes down the sheet.

Dodo's initial focus was on Prue's appearance. Her grey gown and the black bonnet received the disparagement of 'dowdy', with which Prue could not but agree. There followed an effusion on Folly, including the raid upon the kitchen which concentrated not on finding food for the kitten, but on the pastry making and Dodo's subsequent enjoyment of the jam tarts, which had, sure enough, made their appearance at dinner that evening. To Prue's relief, she had been relegated after that to a mention only in connection with Folly's activities.

There was but one item at which Prue might have taken offence. Instead she was immediately stricken with guilt.

'If only bad Yvette did not stop us having Folly in our bedchamber, he would like us more than Miss Hursley which he don't nohow.'

She had so hoped the twins did not mind it that Folly had steadfastly attached himself to his rescuer. While he happily ate and played with the girls, it was into Prue's lap that he jumped for a snooze. Indeed, Folly had made her parlour his headquarters so that she had been obliged to transfer his box to that room. He followed her to the schoolroom, and scratched on her bedchamber door at night, and Prue had not the heart to refuse to admit him.

But it was not Folly's choice that caused Prue to feel remorseful. She was distressingly aware of desiring this companionship, and knew that the kitten had become a substitute for the loss that she continued to feel keenly. She had not known just how much she would miss Nell and Kitty. Folly was the only balm to a nagging loneliness.

It was best, perhaps, that she made no comment upon the inclusion of this little spurt of Dodo's jealousy. She looked up from the sheet and smiled at the child.

'Well done, Dodo.'

Lotty frowned. 'You read hers first? But I finished before her!'

'Well, I am going to read yours now,' said Prue.

'That's not fair.'

Dodo immediately broke into crowing triumph, which led automatically to a squabble. Feeling unequal to the task of pacifying the twins, Prue ignored them and turned her eyes to the top of Lotty's sheet of writing.

This was a different proposition altogether. Was it malice that caused the girl to apostrophise her preceptress as a 'dowdy little brown mouse'? It was not, as Dodo's comment had been, a reference to her attire only. Lotty's description was entirely devoted to the deficiencies of Prue's qualifications as a governess.

'I don't think she could be a guvnes. She don't look like one. She look like a dowd. She don't look like she dance or nuthing. She bring a kitten which Yvette don't like cos stink and mess. She don't get cross or shout. She don't teech nothing not yet. Mabe Uncel Joleos won't keep her.'

Prue tried to tell herself that this effusion was intended to annoy rather than to hurt. Lotty could not know how nearly she paralleled Prue's own assessment of herself nor how close to the bone she came with that remark about her uncle's intentions.

Without meaning to, she glanced across at the child, and found Lotty regarding her with challenge in her eyes. Was she expecting an explosion? Well, let her be disappointed.

Without a word, Prue rose from the desk and began to write the misspelt words from both sheets upon the blackboard. As she did so, she wondered what Lotty intended by this. There could be no doubt that the impertinence had been deliberate. Was it to test Prue? Did she suppose that a just revenge would be enacted?

If Nell were here, what would she do? Oh, but

Nell would not have induced such a horrid indictment from her pupils. By now she would have established herself as an authority in their eyes. No child would dare write such unkind stuff of Nell!

Completing the words, Prue turned to the girls. She was a trifle cheered to see a perplexed frown upon Lotty's face. Dodo was merely waiting.

Taking another couple of sheets of clean paper from the stack, Prue laid them down in front of the girls.

'These are the correct spellings. You will write each one out ten times. As neat as you can, if you please.'

Dodo groaned, but a flash of respect showed for a moment in Lotty's eyes. But she caught Prue looking at her, and lifted her chin as she dipped her pen in the inkwell. Prue retired to the window again.

Without thinking, she picked up Folly, who woke with a faint mewl. Prue cradled him to her chest. At once a loud purring began to issue from the kitten's throat as he settled comfortingly into her embrace.

Discontented, Julius Rookham pushed away his plate and shoved his chair back from the table. Why he should find it tedious to dine in solitary state, he had no notion. Had it not ever been his habit? Certainly since he had abandoned the effort to cut a figure in society.

His interest in town life had been timely, but

ephemeral. Urged by his widowed mother to apply himself to the task of finding a wife, at the age of nineteen Julius betook himself to London, following the time-honoured method. Willing, if a trifle unenthusiastic, he remembered casting himself into the accepted modes of conduct that passed among the dedicated fashionables of his class for entertainment.

Gaming and incessant parties had palled quickly, as had the simpering sighs of those females his fond parent had thought fitting to push in his way. He had returned with relief to Little Bookham, unbetrothed, but having acquired a mistress among those females of dubious virtue who made up the *demi-monde*.

Thereafter, while he had dutifully accompanied his determined mama upon the annual excursion in which his sister was currently engaged, Julius had made no real effort to marry himself off. The sudden and unexpected demise of his mother when he was three and twenty had furnished him with an adequate excuse to remain for the future upon his estates.

The loss of his inamorata had been inconvenient, if not distressing, but he could scarcely have expected her—as she had engagingly informed him—to retire from a glittering career in the capital to bury herself in the wilds of the country. Julius could not but acknowledge the justice of her decision.

'It ain't that I don't care for you, my lovekin,' she had informed him, fluttering a haresfoot over her elaborate maquillage as she gazed at her exquisitely designed countenance in the mirror. 'Only I can't and I won't eke my days out in a cottage, obliged to depend upon a visit from you once or twice a week for company.'

She had swirled back to the bed in a swish of taffeta, and leaned over him for a kiss. 'What you need, lovekin, is to find yourself a nice little milkmaid as won't pine her heart out for a night at the play, and will be contented with a few prettifying gewgaws.' She had winked. 'You'll be a deal better off, for she won't cost you near as much as I do.'

Lily had been nothing if not expensive. Julius had not availed himself of her advice, however, for at home he was not plagued with the ennui that attacked him in London. Able to pursue his abiding interest uninterrupted, he had allowed the years to roll on without notice. Apart from an occasional foray to town on business, or to the races, Julius had remained upon his estates, reasonably contented.

His sister's descent upon him had been, if not unwelcome, a slight source of irritation. But since little could be done in winter, with the ground hardened by frost and the old wood dying on the trees, the necessity to put his attention on the needs of Trixie and her offspring had not interfered unduly.

But with his sister's removal to London, and the arrival of the governess he had hired, Julius had anticipated a speedy return to his labours with the onset of spring.

Yet here he was, near mid-March, and for some inscrutable reason found himself delaying the work that must be put in now if he was to be beforehand with his plans for the summer. A stupid sort of lassitude overtook him whenever he picked over the designs that had occupied each waking hour up until his household had been augmented.

And tonight, as he had partaken in a desultory way of the dishes sent in—God send Wincle did not take offence!—he had been overtaken with a sense of dissatisfaction at the lack of company at his board.

He reached out for the port and poured himself a liberal glassful. Perhaps he was missing Trixie. But that was nonsense, for she had been only a recent addition at the table, and briefly too. Besides, without her presence, it had again become unnecessary to dress for dinner, which suited his easy habits. Perhaps he should invite his agent to dine with him again? It was a while since the last occasion he had extended that courtesy to Rawcliff.

Next week, perhaps? Too late for this, for it was already Friday.

But the prospect of Rawcliff's company did nothing to alleviate his growing sense of discontent.

Julius took a moody swig of wine. This was nonsense. He had been idle too long, that was all. On Monday he would call Hessle in and make an inspection of the treillage, which must be finished before April.

Cheered a little by his decision, he lifted his glass to his lips and tilted his head back.

A piercing scream blasted his ears, causing him to choke upon the liquid in his throat.

For a few inaccessible moments, he was fully occupied in spluttering and coughing, utterly unable to make the slightest move towards investigation or discovery. Out of the corner of his eye, he noticed the footman, left in the room by Creggan, who had presumably retired to prepare the parlour for his reception.

Gesturing helplessly over his own shoulder, Julius made a desperate effort to make his urgent need understood. Through the hideous sensation of rupture at his chest he took in vaguely that Jacob looked shocked. Impatiently, he gestured again.

A moment later, the flat of a heavy hand descended two or three times against his back, and the choking subsided. With admirable presence of mind, the fellow seized his master's discarded glass and filled it from the water pitcher.

Julius took it gratefully and drank deep. Laying it down, he found himself once more able to speak, if with a trifle of hoarseness to his voice.

'Remind me to increase your wages!'

Jacob grinned. 'Thank you, sir. Are you fit now, sir?'

'Thanks to you, yes. But what was that infernal screeching?'

The footman shrugged, looking concerned. 'I couldn't rightly say, sir. Sounded like it come from the east side. Mebbe one of the young ladies, sir?'

'What, the twins? No, the pitch was not high enough.' As he spoke, he was making for the door. 'But it was certainly from that direction.'

In the hall, Julius found Creggan already halfway up the stairs. The butler, carrying a double candelabrum, was accompanied by his groom, armed with a broomstick.

'What in Hades do you think you are doing, Beith?'

The servants halted, turning. The groom brandished his weapon with relish. 'Might be marauders, guv'nor.'

'Female ones, I presume.' Julius headed for the stairs. 'Take it away, you fool! I will investigate.'

Shaking off the footman, who offered to accompany him, Julius took the candelabrum from his butler and swiftly made his way towards that side of the house he had given over to the use of his sister's family. As he got to the stairway and began to negotiate the narrower passage, a sound of frantic hissing reached his ears.

He quickened his steps, passing down the corridor beyond the rooms occupied by his nieces, drawn by the growing sound of half-whispered pleadings.

'Out, I say! Shoo! Shoo!'

Light spread from an open doorway ahead. A few strides, and Julius stopped short on the threshold.

Within the room, he beheld Miss Hursley, clad in a grey dressing-gown as unprepossessing as the garments he had previously seen her wear, and engaged in a losing battle to rid her bedchamber of a pair of fat and recalcitrant frogs.

The augmented light distracted Prue. Looking up, she perceived her employer standing in the doorway. Her heart sank and she spoke without thinking.

'Oh, dear. *Must* you discover me in so ridiculous a situation, Mr Rookham?'

Julius strolled into the room. Doubtless immobilised by the sudden access of additional light— for the bedchamber was scantily illuminated by a single candle by the bed and another on the mantel—the frogs sat blinking in the middle of the wooden floor. From the four-poster beyond, where the figured blue wool curtains hung untidily open as if they had been wrenched aside, the kitten was watching with apparent interest, adding its mite with a disapproving hiss. Julius looked down at the culprits.

'I suppose I need not ask how it comes about that you have been invaded by these revolting amphibians?'

Prue sighed. 'You have guessed it, I dare say.'

'It rather leaps to the eye, does it not?'

His features were thrown into partial shadow by the candles he held, but she saw the quiver at his lips, and a little of her dismay abated. It gave way to an unaccountable flurry at her bosom, and it was with slight breathlessness that she answered him.

'It is rather obvious, perhaps.'

Mr Rookham eyed the invaders. 'Of course, had I not come upon you attempting to persuade them to remove themselves, I might well have thought otherwise.'

Prue blinked. 'I don't understand you, sir.'

His brows rose. 'Don't you? Do you tell me that your predilection for rescuing beasts in distress does not extend to frogs? My dear Miss Hursley, how unkind. Merely because the creatures are ugly is no reason for you to leave them to a cruel fate.'

Torn between indignation and laughter, Prue let out a gurgle. 'I confess I do not like them. But if they will only remove from here, I have no quarrel with them at all. Besides, they are not the ones in distress!'

'Ah, then I gather it was you who emitted that shriek of terror?'

Recalling it, Prue's cheeks grew warm. 'Did I disturb you, sir? I am so sorry.'

'Disturb me?' Mr Rookham stirred one of the frogs gently with the toe of his boot, but it did not budge. 'Why, no, Miss Hursley. Had it not been for the prompt action of my footman, I should at this moment be as undisturbed and motionless as this frog.'

'Mr Rookham, what in the world are you talking about?'

He looked up from contemplation of the frog. 'Your scream, Miss Hursley. I happened to be in the act of drinking wine just at that moment, and I nearly choked to death.'

A wave of consciousness swept over Prue. She gazed at him aghast. 'Oh, Mr Rookham, no! Oh, dear.'

'Yes, I believe my reaction was a trifle more violent than that,' he said in a musing tone. 'Which was why, I imagine, it did not immediately occur to me that the annoyance must have emanated from you. Had I stopped to think about it, however, I have no doubt that—'

'Oh, you are being deliberately provocative!' interrupted Prue with a good deal of heat. 'I wish you will not be tiresomely teasing, sir, and help me instead.'

He gave an exaggerated start. 'Help you? When you have done your best to send me to an early grave?'

'Mr Rookham, pray stop! I don't believe you choked at all. You are saying it merely to put me at a disadvantage.'

Julius regarded her with satisfaction. He had succeeded in thoroughly ruffling her feathers. Yet if he were to speak in a way that made her believe him, he was sure she would be altogether distressed. He smiled.

'Shall I rescue you, damsel in distress?'

A huge sigh erupted out of her. 'Would you, indeed? I own I should much prefer not to deal with them myself.'

Julius moved to the dresser and laid down the candelabrum. As he did so, one of the frogs made a sudden spring.

'Take care!' cried Prue, backing away as it landed again not a foot from Mr Rookham's boot.

From the bed, Folly arched his back and emitted a growling protest, hissing distractedly and galvanising the second frog. It took a leap in Prue's direction. She gave a gasp and withdrew circumspectly to the head of the bed.

Julius stepped into the fray. 'Open the window!'

Prue hastened to obey, pulling the heavy drapes aside and throwing up the sash window. She heard movement behind her and, by the time she turned, saw that Mr Rookham had grabbed one frog in either hand, seizing them in scientific fashion behind the head. At a mewl from Folly, she glanced to the bed and found the kitten now prancing on the pillow, as if he knew that entertainment of a high order was about to be provided.

Prue stood aside to let Mr Rookham by, shifting back to the bed. In mingled triumph and dismay, she watched as he unceremoniously flung the frogs out into the night.

As he pulled the window shut, relief flooded her, not unmixed with guilt. An involuntary sigh escaped her and she sank on to the bed, automatically reaching out a hand to Folly, who danced over and butted at her fingers.

'Well, Folly seems to feel it a victory, but I confess I am sorry for them, poor little things.'

Mr Rookham turned. 'I might have known it!

Unless you are referring not to the amphibians, but to my erring nieces?'

'Oh, no,' said Prue, gathering up the kitten and cuddling him. 'I was just thinking how uncomfortable it must be for the frogs upon landing.'

'On the contrary. They have extremely strong hind legs, and will have taken flight when they found themselves in the air. You had better spare your sympathies for Dodo and Lotty!'

'Oh, no, no. I shall not speak of it to them at all.'

'You may not, but I shall,' said Julius grimly. 'Though I am inclined to do more spanking than speaking!'

Horrified, Prue jumped up in haste, the kitten leaping from her hold. Folly bounced on to the floor and ran to sniff at the place where the frogs had been. Prue barely noticed.

'Pray do not say so! I am persuaded you cannot mean it.'

'I most assuredly do,' he averred, making for the door.

Prue sprang forward to bar his way. 'Mr Rookham, I beg you won't do anything of the kind! It is merely a prank.'

'A prank that frightened you into screaming.'

'Yes, but that was only because I came upon the creatures unexpectedly when I drew back the curtains of the bed. Once I realised what they were, I knew at once how they must have come there and—'

'Only an idiot would not have known!' interrupted Julius without ceremony. 'And since neither twin emerged from their bedchamber on hearing you scream, there can be no doubt of their guilt. They could not have slept through that!'

'No, indeed, for they are only just down the corridor,' agreed Prue, suddenly frowning. 'The only wonder is that Yvette did not hear me.'

Julius gave a grim laugh. 'No wonder there. My sister tells me that Yvette sleeps like one dead. Nothing wakes her. Well for my nieces, I may say.'

Prue gazed at him, a horrid thought assailing her. 'Why? I know she is strict, but surely she would not—' She stopped, seeing the answer in Mr Rookham's face. 'She beats them? How dreadful!'

A trifle of impatience showed in his face, and he shifted away towards the dresser where he had laid down his candles.

'My dear girl, how in Hades do you suppose those two imps are to be controlled? Or do you imagine my sister is so cold-hearted as to allow her daughters to be treated with cruelty?'

Prue had moved with him, too upset to consider how she spoke. 'How can I say, sir, when I do not know your sister?'

'You may take it from me, then.'

She gazed at him in defiance. 'May I? Barely a moment ago, you threatened to spank them!'

'It was no mere threat, I assure you. And I don't mind telling you it would give me a good deal of pleasure!'

Prue did not know whether she was more angry or distressed. She had thought him so kind a man. Now here he was, talking casually of a beating as if it was a thing of no moment. And to speak of enjoyment in it!

Amusement crept into Mr Rookham's features. 'I see that I have become a monster in your eyes, Miss Hursley.'

She dropped her gaze from his, for she could not deny it. She moved away a little. Suppressing the instinct that urged her to rail at him, she tried for a neutral note. But her throat was constricted.

'I cannot approve of—of the infliction of p-pain, sir, even in p-punishment.'

'Then I fear you are destined to be ridden over roughshod for the duration of your stay here.'

His tone was cool and impersonal, and Prue felt suddenly distanced. She could not look at him.

'Then it must be so. If that means I have proved myself to be unsuitable for the position, then let that be so as well.'

Chapter Four

There was a short silence. Miss Hursley's movement away from him had left her in shadow, but Julius eyed her profile with dawning respect and an odd sensation in his chest, a swell of emotion he could not name. Without thought, he moved closer. Reaching out long fingers, he tilted her chin, forcing her to look at him. The grey eyes were unexpectedly bleak.

'What a tender-hearted creature you are, Prudence.'

He did not know that he had used her name. Nor was there thought behind his further words.

'You are a rare specimen, my dear girl. But you have it wrong. Do you think you have entered a den of unkindness?'

He released her, noting the change in her expression, as of a lift of hope. His lips twitched.

'Use your eyes, Miss Hursley. Do the twins

behave as if they had been ill treated? A more exuberant pair of monkeys I have yet to meet. It is only the threat of Yvette's hairbrush that keeps them in check.'

Prue blinked. 'Hairbrush?'

'Yes, I believe she had kept it for years, purely for the purpose of serving as a useful deterrent. Trixie informed me that a few judicious applications at the start of Yvette's rule were sufficient to ensure obedience. It is rare that she finds herself obliged actually to use it.'

Once more, Prue found herself overcome by indignation. 'But you said—'

'Yes, I did say that she would beat them, and she would,' averred Julius impatiently. 'If that is what it takes to stop them from playing tricks upon their new governess.'

Prue drew herself up. 'Then I beg you will refrain from informing her, sir. If I cannot succeed by my own methods, I had rather fail. Besides, such a proceeding could only serve to undermine my authority.'

'Yes, if you had any.'

The grey eyes took fire but, not much to his surprise, she said nothing. He watched her stalk to the door, and turn, frigidly polite.

'I thank you for your assistance, sir, and I will bid you a very good night.'

He grinned. 'Dismissing me, Prudence? And with such a convincing air of authority. I am suitably chastened, and hasten to obey.'

Receiving only a dagger look, he picked up his candelabrum and went to the door, where he paused, regarding her mutinous features with an air of bland indifference.

'One thing more, Miss Hursley.'

'Sir?'

'The next time you feel inclined to create such a commotion, pray save it until after the dinner hour. I do so hate to waste good port.'

Consternation spread across her features. 'Did you really choke?'

'But I told you I did.'

'I thought you were teasing me. How dreadful! Oh, dear, are you sure you are all right?'

'As you perceive.'

'Mr Rookham, I am truly sorry!'

'Don't be, since it was not your fault.'

But a glow of satisfaction entered his breast. Had he not known how penitent she would become? Only her expression was already altering to anxiety.

'You won't say anything to the girls, will you?'

'And undermine your authority? I should not dare!'

With which, he left the room quickly before she

could retaliate. The door snapped shut behind him, and he could have sworn he heard a muted squeal of frustration.

The gardens were far more extensive than Prue had supposed when she had arrived at Rookham Hall. Accompanying the two girls upon an exploratory ramble, she was delighted to be taken first towards the water she had glimpsed through the trees. It proved to be an extensive pond, inhabited by various fauna, including frogs.

She had said no word of her adventures upon the previous evening, preferring to pretend that nothing untoward had occurred. The twins had probed, with an airiness that was singularly unconvincing.

'Did you sleep well, Miss Hursley?' asked Lotty with a smirk.

Dodo smothered a giggle. Prue glanced briefly at her, and then back to her sister.

'Very well, I thank you, Lotty. Did you?'

Lotty looked her in the eye. 'I was woken by something.'

Prue assumed a sympathetic mien. 'What a shame. Did you manage to get back to sleep?'

A trifle nonplussed, the child nodded. Dodo's brown orbs went from Prue to her sister, and back again. She choked off another snigger. Prue turned to her.

'Are you quite well, Dodo?'

Dodo gave a gasp, coloured up, and shrugged. "Course.'

'Good.'

Prue rose, crossing to the window. 'It is a fine day. Perhaps we might go out, since it is Saturday, and you can show me the gardens. We shall do our spelling as we go.'

She turned in time to catch the look exchanged between the twins, and silently congratulated herself on the success of her tactics. If nothing else, she had puzzled them. They could not refer to the frogs without confessing their knowledge of the event, and so they were cheated of crowing over her.

As they came out of the Hall through a side door, the twins exclaimed at seeing their uncle about to set off somewhere in his phaeton.

'He is going for a drive!'

'Shall we ask him to take us?'

Prue seized them both. 'You will do no such thing. In the first place, Mr Rookham is likely on business of his own. And in the second, we have our lesson to do.'

'Oh, bother!'

As Prue attempted to silence their vociferous protests, the groom was seen to let go of the horses' heads, and leap up behind as the phaeton took off, rapidly gathering speed. Prue watched it out of sight around the bend in the drive, momentarily lost in a memory of that first horrid meeting.

'Uncle Julius drives ever so fast.'

'He's faster than anything!'

'Don't you think so, Miss Hursley?'

Prue came to herself with a start. Fast! What would they say if she was to reveal that their uncle's speedy progress had been responsible for Folly's sojourn at Rookham Hall?

'I think we should get on with our walk,' she said firmly.

But as they started off down the open lawns that led through clumps of trees, Lotty nearly succeeded in robbing Prue of her poise.

'When I was awake last night, Miss Hursley, I thought I heard Uncle Julius talking in our part of the house.'

Prue's heart skipped a beat. But she must not hesitate! 'Did you, Lotty?'

'I heard him too,' piped up Dodo, encouraged by her sister's effrontery.

'Dear me. Perhaps you both dreamed it.'

It was lame, and Prue knew it—even without Lotty's look of scorn. But the memory of her encounter with Mr Rookham was anything but comfortable. Horribly aware of having spoken much too freely, she was still more troubled by the warmth that overtook her at the remembrance of his untoward familiarity. At the moment of his touching her—she could almost feel still the pressure of his fingers upon her chin!—she had been too upset to realise what he was doing.

But when he had left her—with so teasing a remark that she had been moved almost to slamming the door!—she had been overtaken with a dreadful sense of having behaved with impropriety. As for Mr Rookham, what had possessed him to conduct himself towards the governess in that disrespectful fashion? And twice he had called her Prudence!

At the memory of his smile, of his gentleness, Prue had found herself trembling so much that she had gathered up Folly, cradling him to her bosom for comfort. Taking a not unnatural exception to being squeezed so tightly, the kitten had squirmed to be free. But when Prue had clambered into bed, leaving the candle alight beside her, Folly had been willing enough to play at cat and mouse, pouncing on Prue's foot as she moved it here and there underneath the covers.

She had participated absently, lying upon her pillows in a state of suppressed agitation, as in her mind she had gone over every detail of what had occurred during Mr Rookham's untoward visit. Folly had long tired of the game and curled himself up in a doze by the time Prue had become sufficiently calm again to blow out her candle and contemplate sleep herself.

It had not been until this morning, when the twins presented themselves in the schoolroom with the light of anticipation in their faces, that Prue had recalled that her fracas with the frogs had been the cause of her employer's descent upon her.

'This way, Miss Hursley!'

Coming to herself, she discovered that the twins had run on ahead, and the gleam of water had widened into a pond so large that it was almost a small lake.

'This is pretty indeed!'

The pond was set in a half-surround of trees, their leaves just now in bud, with a profusion of reedy shoots, and purple iris peeping here and there. Within the pond lay vast flat leaves of water lilies, and the busy sound of insects crept through the still air, together with an intermittent croak.

'Look, Miss Hursley! Frogs!'

Prue bit her lips upon the exclamation that rose to them. She looked where Lotty was pointing, and observed one of the slimy green creatures on the bank, half in, half out of the water. It was slimmer than those which had been placed in her bed, but there could be no doubt that this pond was where the girls had found its sturdier brethren.

Dodo was at her side, smirking. 'Don't you like frogs, Miss Hursley?'

Prue swallowed down a rise of resentment. She must not allow their taunts to affect her. She summoned a calm tone.

'I am not fond of them, Dodo.'

'Then you would not care for a pet frog,' stated Lotty, smiling with odious superiority.

'I prefer Folly, I admit.'

The kitten had been left behind, for fear of his becoming lost in this alien garden. He had been introduced to the outside world only for short periods in the twins' charge.

'Oh, well, Folly prefers you, too,' said Dodo sulkily.

Prue thought it better to ignore this. The twins appeared determined to force her into a reaction. Prue was equally determined they would not succeed. She took refuge in education.

'How do you spell frog, Dodo?'

Prue almost laughed out at the disappointment that spread across the child's face. But she was able to spell the word. Looking about her, Prue subjected the two of them to a barrage of spellings, using the everyday objects that surrounded them.

Drawing away from the pond, she requested them to lead her elsewhere so that she might find new words.

'We'll take you to the gardens,' said Lotty.

'I thought these were the gardens.'

'Pooh!' scoffed Dodo. 'This is nothing. Uncle Julius has about fifty gardens.'

'What a fibber you are, Dodo! 'Course he hasn't.'

'Well, he has lots and lots.'

Lotty turned to Prue as she led the way through two clumps of trees. 'Did you know that Uncle Julius is mad on gardens?'

'Is he? How is that?'

It was as well, Prue felt, that Lotty had looked away again, for she was convinced her consciousness at this further mention of him must be evident in her cheeks. How she managed to speak with such apparent unconcern she would never know.

It was Dodo who answered. 'No reason. He just likes gardens. Mama says gardens are his pashing.'

'His what?'

'She means passion,' explained Lotty. 'Dodo, you iggorant noodle, you don't know any words!'

'It is ignorant with an "n", not iggorant,' Prue pointed out. 'And I do wish you will not scoff at your sister.'

At which, Dodo at once began crowing in

delight, while Lotty pouted. It was therefore Dodo who gave the first explanation as they arrived at a bank of laburnum tunnelling through into the picturesque world of Mr Rookham's gardens.

Prue became rapidly bewildered as she was led down walkways, and up wide stone steps. Around walls of hedge they went, down a wide grass area flanked by a stone wall.

'This is the bowling green.'

Up another set of stairs, and she found herself confronted by a barrier of trelliswork that stretched in two directions.

'We can't go in there,' announced Lotty, whose sulk had not lasted much beyond the tunnel. 'That's going to be the treillage garden, Uncle Julius says, and we're not allowed in because it's full of wood and nails.'

'And we might get cut, he says,' added Dodo. 'But you can peek through because there's no flowers yet either.'

Prue declined to peek, having a lively apprehension of her employer's likely remarks should he chance to discover she had done so. The rose garden was also skirted, being another forbidden area. But the twins fell in delight upon a closed-in terrace that featured an old covered well upon a paved centre, and a few wild rose bushes scattered about. The trees and shrubs of the enclosure gave the garden an air of wildness, and a great oak in one corner completed the picture.

The effect was altogether pleasing, and while Dodo and Lotty created echoes down the well, Prue wandered about, finding that the place lent her a feeling of tranquillity.

Of which, she reflected, she was much in need. For she found herself taken up by the hint of romanticism hidden in Mr Rookham's character. Surely the man who had so strong a feeling for gardens as to cause the creation of such beauty must possess an unusual degree of sentiment? A thought which Prue found distinctly disturbing to her peace of mind. It would be better, perhaps, if she did not learn too much more of her employer.

No further attempt was made by the twins to draw Prue on the subject of frogs. But their assaults upon her defences were not at an end.

Twice during the following week, Prue found a scattering of ink spots on the paper in the bureau that had been placed for her use in her little parlour. On the next Monday evening, she almost jumped out of her skin upon lifting the cover of one of the dishes sent up for her consumption at dinner. For beneath it was a plateful of worms.

Prue could only be glad that she had not screamed. It was a truly disgusting trick to play, and she was certain that not all her pleadings would have saved the twins from Mr Rookham's just revenge.

She was about to ring the bell, having slammed the cover back down and risen hurriedly from the table, when she recollected that to call one of the servants could only mean discovery for the girls. They could not, she believed, have effected this prank with the assistance of Mrs Wincle in the kitchens. Nor indeed any of the servants.

No, they must have secreted the plate and cover from one of their own supper dishes, and hidden it among her own. It had become her habit to sit in the schoolroom preparing work for the morrow before making her way to the parlour in time for dinner. Since the girls ate some time before she did, they must have had ample opportunity to sneak into her parlour.

They had probably planned it yesterday; after the usual morning visit to church, they had spent the day out of Prue's sight.

Picking up the plate of worms, and firmly holding the silver cover over it, Prue took a leaf out of Mr Rookham's book and moved to the window. The worms were emptied into the bushes below.

Cautiously, Prue tried the other two covers, and found her meal intact beneath them. The episode had nevertheless destroyed her appetite, and she was able to swallow little of the food. A circumstance which brought Mrs Polmont to her room within a short time after the tray had been removed.

'Wincle wishes to know if the meal was not to your taste, Miss Hursley.'

Prue hoped desperately that she did not colour up. 'Oh, dear. Pray tell her it was nothing to do with her cooking, Mrs Polmont.' Impelled, she invented an excuse. 'I am feeling a trifle out of sorts, that is all.'

Which, when all was said and done, was not far from the truth. The sight of the worms had made her distinctly queasy.

The housekeeper peered at her, too closely for Prue's comfort. Her voice was respectful, if not warm.

'Is there anything I can get you, ma'am? A dose of salts, perhaps?'

'No, no, I shall be perfectly well after a good night's sleep, I am persuaded.'

Mrs Polmont appeared doubtful and the parrot look became pronounced. She sniffed. 'If you say so, Miss Hursley. However, I'd not wish the master to think I'd done nothing to aid you.'

'For heaven's sake, don't tell him!' cried Prue, alarmed.

She then wished that she had held her tongue, for

the housekeeper regarded her narrowly. 'I understand as you had a disturbance a few nights back?'

'Last week. It—it was nothing. I thought I
saw…I mean, it was dark and—'

'You've no call to explain it to me, ma'am. If the
master is satisfied, it's not for me to cavil.'

With which, she bid Prue goodnight and left the
room. Her manner made Prue decidedly uneasy. Was
there a hint in it? She could only be glad that she had
seen nothing of Mr Rookham these few days, except
for yesterday's visit to church in the village. And
since her position demanded that she remain dis-
creetly in the background, there had been no
exchange between them beyond the commonplace.

She had watched him greeting various persons—neighbours and tenants, so the twins had
informed her the first time she had accompanied
them. The girls had frisked about him, for it
seemed to Prue that several of Mr Rookham's
acquaintances had a kindly word for 'Miss
Charlotte' and 'Miss Dorothy'. It was no part of
her duty to involve herself in these gatherings,
and her employer was under no obligation to
present her to anyone. Except the parish priest,
and he had done that upon the first Sunday. Well,
it was only what Mrs Duxford had led her to
expect. She was nobody, and if Mr Rookham on

occasion treated her as if she indeed had an identity, it would be idle to expect any such recognition in public.

Prue would not allow herself to acknowledge the slightest disappointment. Instead, she concentrated her mind upon the unspoken struggle with her charges.

The following morning, she worked the girls hard, making them first read aloud from one of the improving stories she had caused to be purchased, and then write at her dictation paragraphs from the book in their best copperplate. Every error had to be written over, and she allowed them no let up right through until Yvette came in to get them for luncheon.

'Zey are late,' complained the Frenchwoman.

'Oh, dear, are they?' said Prue innocently. 'They were working so industriously that I forgot the time. Well done, girls. You may go now.'

The twins scampered out as fast as they could.

But the battle was not yet won. Prue found herself waiting, over the next few days, for some other manifestation. She suspected that the twins were testing her, pushing her to see how far they might go before she acknowledged their attacks. Whether they supposed she would lose her temper, or simply punish them, she did not know. But their tactics were neither original nor unexpected.

The Duck, wise in the ways of the young, had prepared her students well. 'Naughty children will always make a point of discovering your limits. Set them early, and you will gain the mastery. But never, *never* allow them to see that they have succeeding in gaining the upper hand, or they will inevitably end by ruling the roost.'

By now, Prue thought unhappily, Nell would have unfailingly stopped the twins in their tracks. While she had succeeded in baffling them by refusing to acknowledge the assaults, Prue had no notion how she was going to set limits upon them. But one thing she was determined upon. She would neither lay a hand upon them herself, nor give them up for another to do so.

In the event, the crunch took her unawares.

Thursday morning had been difficult. Prue had set the twins a translation from the French, hoping that a little work in a language that gave them no trouble might help to ease the difficulties of English.

Her hope proved misplaced. The girls began easily enough, quickly making sense of the simple French sentences. But their attitude changed swiftly when they discovered that they were required to adjust their translations to correct grammar and write them down in a neat fist.

Between Lotty's sulks and Dodo's complaints, Prue had a trying time. She persevered, hampered by Lotty's bid to pretend to stupidity in translation in a vain attempt to postpone writing. Dodo merely tried to change the subject, asking frequently whether it was not time for luncheon.

Prue could not but be relieved when the hands of the clock, having crawled their way around the hours, at last informed her that this purgatory was at an end.

'Very well, that will be all for this morning.'

Lotty waited by the door while her sister collected Folly from the window sill. It had become their habit to take him out for a little before luncheon was served.

'Are you coming to eat with us, Miss Hursley?'

Prue glanced at Lotty, instantly on her guard. Since she invariably did take luncheon with the girls, why the question? Had they again planned something horrid for her plate? And in their presence, so that she had no opportunity to dissemble! What in the world was she to do if they should play a trick upon her in full view of Yvette? She affected puzzlement.

'Why should I not, Lotty?'

'No reason. I just wondered.'

Dodo, having attached the kitten to her chest, passed her sister to step through the door. 'Come on, slow coach!'

The door shut behind them, leaving Prue prey to a lively apprehension. She tidied the books and slates away with automatic haste, her mind alive with conjecture.

What did those terrors intend to spring upon her this time? They would surely not dare to do anything obvious which their nurse might notice. It could not be as bad as the worms, she decided in relief. Then it must be something that would appear accidental.

One or two caterpillars hidden among the vegetables, perhaps? A spider or beetle released upon the table? Well, she must bear it with fortitude. Nevertheless, she shuddered with disgust at the thought.

As she made her way to her bedchamber to wash her hands and tidy her person, Prue resolved to keep a wary eye upon the details of whatever food was presented to her. She opened the door to the playroom with caution, and sighed in relief when she discovered that only Yvette was present.

'Ou sont les enfants?' demanded the Frenchwoman instantly.

'Are they late? Perhaps they are still outside.'

'Wiz zees *petit chat*, I sink, zat *mademoiselle* 'ave give to zem.'

Prue bore the accusing gleam in the woman's eyes without comment, for she was becoming inured to the unforgiving nature of the nurse. Yvette would never cease to blame her for introducing the kitten into the household.

She went to take her seat at the table where the covers were already laid and the dishes set out. Which was promising, for if the girls were still out, they could not have had time to interfere with the contents. Unless they had intercepted the footman as he carried up the meal? She eyed the silver covers with a rise of trepidation in her breast.

As she pulled out her chair, there came the galloping of feet in the corridor outside. Yvette was heard to mutter in protest, and then the door burst open and the twins flew into the room, hurtling over to the table, both pretty faces overlaid with distress.

'Miss Hursley, we can't find Folly!'

'He escaped into the bushes!'

'We looked and looked, and—'

'He ain't nowhere to be seen!'

Her apprehensions were forgotten as a riffle of alarm swept through Prue's veins. Without realising what she did, she seized hold of one twin's shoulder, unaware which one of the girls it was.

'Where? Where did you lose him?'

'In the gardens, but—'

'Where in the gardens? Come and show me!'

As she swept towards the door, grabbing up the other child on the way, Prue heard only vaguely the rattle of French that broke out behind her. She had no time now to deal with Yvette. She must wait, as also must their luncheon. Finding the lost kitten was of far more importance than food.

Together, the three of them hastened towards the east stairs which led down to the convenient side door. Contrary to Prue's expectation, the girls did not halt in the immediate vicinity where there were bushes enough in which Folly might have hidden. Instead, with Dodo clutching her hand and dragging her along, she perforce followed where Lotty led them.

'Where in the world did you take him?' she asked, panting a little. 'Why could you not keep near to the house?'

'Folly wanted to see the other gardens,' explained Dodo brightly, rushing Prue along a path that ran down the side of the wide lawns.

'That is nonsensical. Come now, the truth, if you please!'

Lotty paused on one foot at the edge of a set of steps. 'Why shouldn't Folly explore?'

Breathless, Prue halted and put a hand to her midriff. 'Precisely because of what has happened. He is too little to be let loose in the wilds of such a big set of gardens.'

The child hunched a pettish shoulder. 'He has to learn some time.'

Feeling unequal to engage in argument, Prue merely urged her to hurry along to where they had last seen the kitten.

'Yes, do come on,' agreed Dodo, 'for I am beginning to be hungry.'

In a moment or two, the faint sound of a distant mew came to Prue's ears. She stopped abruptly.

'Listen!'

There was a silence, and then the plaintive cry came again, causing a stabbing at Prue's heart.

'Oh, poor little Folly! Where are you, my precious?'

Out of the corner of her eye, Prue caught a venomous look upon Dodo's face. But at that moment, there was no room in her either for sympathy or regret. The kitten's plight took her whole attention.

'Which way?' she uttered distractedly. 'Oh, dear, I wish he might call again.'

A little to her surprise, Lotty started off once more. 'It was this way!'

With unerring speed, the child led the way down a green alley and a further set of stairs. Sure enough, the sound of Folly's complaints grew stronger, and puzzlement was added to the anxiety lurching through Prue's bosom. Was there not a slightly hollow sound to the cry? It echoed, the closer they approached.

In a moment, Prue found herself in the wild garden that she had so much admired, with a well at its centre. For an instant, she stood poised at its entrance, looking about her. Only half aware that the girls were standing either side of her, eyeing her in a searching manner, Prue listened for the kitten's mew. She called out to him.

'*Folly*! Folly, where are you?'

As if he heard her, the kitten's cries started up again. The echo was evident. Memory stirred, and Prue's eyes turned towards the well. Dread hammered in her chest, and her feet moved without volition. Reaching the well, she gripped the surrounding wall with both hands and peered over the edge.

It took a moment or two for her eyes to adjust to the darkness below, and the continuing sounds of Folly's distress caught at her heartstrings. At last she discerned within the murk the gleam of his little green eyes at some distance down the well.

'Folly! Oh, poor mite!'

She shifted back, looking wildly round for a means by which she might succour the kitten. How was she to do? A long stick? Or could they find a ladder? She must think of something, and fast! Before the poor thing should drown. The wonder was that he was still alive!

Only then was it borne in upon Prue that a heavy chain hung down the centre of the well, suspended from a beam in the wooden cover above it. She stared at it, abruptly hit by confusion.

'If there is a chain, then where is the bucket?' she wondered aloud.

Leaning forward again, she stared down the well-hole. Grasping the chain with one hand, she moved it slightly. A protest erupted from the kitten below, and Prue saw movement. Incredibly, Folly had fallen into the bucket!

Wasting no time in speculation at the marvel, she searched for the means by which the bucket was to be lifted and found a handle. With the intention of giving an instant instruction, she glanced about for the twins.

Unaccountably, they had retired to the entrance to the gardens, where they stood watching her.

'Help me, one of you!'

Neither moved. They seemed to be rooted to the spot, their features inscrutable. Uttering an impatient exclamation, Prue shifted quickly around the well and grasped the handle. It turned easily enough. Unaware that she held her breath, Prue kept her eyes glued upon the opening to the well, watching for the bucket's arrival.

Folly's unabated complaints grew louder as he neared the surface, and Prue's heart twisted. It felt an age that she turned and turned upon the handle, but at last the wooden bucket hove into sight. It was then borne in upon Prue that she could not let go of the handle to lift the kitten out, for it would instantly hurtle back down. She looked over to where the two girls stood aloof.

'Come and hold this!'

Once more, neither moved. Prue stared at the identical faces. Abruptly, she noted in them an odd mixture of eager anticipation and fear. In a sudden flash of recognition, the whole hideous proceeding fell into place in her mind.

This was no accident. Folly had not fallen into the well. He had been placed there—and left for Prue to find!

Shock froze her for an instant of disbelief, to be swiftly succeeded by a sensation of intense horror. It must have showed in her face, for their expressions altered and they glanced at each other, question in each countenance.

Folly mewed, and Prue brushed aside her distress for the moment. But her voice sharpened.

'One of you come and hold this handle. *Now*!'

Galvanised, both twins leaped forward. Waiting only until one of them had taken her place, Prue reached out and seized the bucket, bringing it carefully to rest on the edge of the well. From the periphery of her vision, she saw two small hands reach out.

Blind fury took Prue, and she slapped them violently away. 'Don't dare touch him!'

Seconds later, the kitten was safe, cradled close to her bosom. Prue crooned at him, and he shifted about in her embrace, clawing at her and purring madly.

Only then did the enormity of what had been done to the kitten truly come home to Prue. She had no need to make enquiries, nor had she to look far for the reason. There could be no doubt that the twins had deliberately put the animal through this horrifying ordeal only to cut at their governess.

Prue's gaze came up, and found them staring at her, eyes wide in their pretty little faces. So innocent! So sweetly angelic. Yet they had done everything in their power to alienate their governess. Even unto this!

Bitter hurt rose up to choke her, and her erstwhile resolve crumbled, loosening her tongue. Her throat ached, and her words came out in little above a whisper.

'How could you do this? How could you use poor Folly so?' Tears blinded her, blurring their faces, but she could not stop. 'It is one thing to engage in m-mischief. The frogs—the worms—those I might endure. But *this*—' Sobs choked her, and she could barely get out the words. 'To visit your tricks upon a poor defenceless c-creature, to put him through so horrid an experience—and only to t-tease me! How could you be so unfeeling, so downright *cruel*?'

Her voice failed, and she was unable to prevent the tears that chased one another down her cheeks, or to stifle the rising sobs, although she tried to spare the kitten, cradling him gently, and doing her best to prevent the movement at her chest from disturbing his ease.

So intent was Prue on this task that she had no room to spare for the distraught looks upon the faces of the twins. Vaguely she took in that her outburst had shocked them, but she was past caring. Unknowingly, she uttered words that completed their discomfiture.

'Pray go away, the two of you. I cannot bear to look upon you at this present!'

Then she turned from them, and walked away into the garden's wilderness, her distress augmented by a corroding sense of failure.

Julius Rookham eyed his nieces with a good deal of misgiving. It must be a matter of moment to induce them to disturb him at his luncheon. But having barged their way in, brushing past Creggan— who was properly scandalised, by the expression of hauteur upon his features—they were now standing before him, both shamefaced and mute.

'What have you done now?' Julius asked in a resigned tone.

The last time he had been subjected to this sort of thing, a confession had at last emerged of the girls having trodden down one of his beds of re-planted seedlings.

He pushed his chair back from the table and threw aside his napkin. 'Out with it! I have no desire to wait here all day. What is it?'

One of them—was it Lotty?—raised solemn eyes to his face. 'It's Miss Hursley.'

A sharp sensation jabbed at his stomach. 'What has happened? Speak out, girl!'

'She's crying and crying and *crying*,' volunteered the other twin, suddenly throwing up her head. 'She won't stop!'

Julius stared at her, conscious both of bewilderment and dismay. 'Why is she crying? Where is she?'

The first twin lifted her chin with a touch of defiance. Instantly, Julius realised it was Lotty.

'We made her cry.'

'That does not altogether surprise me,' he said drily. 'What have you been doing?'

Dodo spoke up again, faintly whining. 'It was Lotty's notion, not mine.'

Her sister dug her in the ribs. 'You helped, you sneak!'

Julius nipped this in the bud. 'That will do. I don't wish to listen to you squabbling. Explain yourselves at once!'

'Well, it was Folly, you see,' came grudgingly from Dodo. 'Lotty put him down the well in the bucket.'

'We *both* put him down the well,' corrected her sister.

'And then we fetched Miss Hursley to find him there,' added Dodo. 'And then she cried and cried.'

'But Folly was perfickly fine,' Lotty averred. 'Only Miss Hursley said it was cruel.'

A vision of Prudence's face crept into Julius's mind from that first day, when she had begged him for the kitten's life. He could well imagine how this petty act of unkindness might have struck her.

Without bothering to enquire into their reasons, Julius rose abruptly.

'You wait here, both of you.'

But as he made for the door, and swept through into the hall, he found the twins at his heels. Turning on them, he threw out a hand.

'I said, stay here!'

'But we want to come,' protested one.

'After all, we made her cry,' said the other importantly.

'Which is why you will remain out of Miss Hursley's sight. But you will certainly be seeing me again, and in the not too distant future. An interview that you may be sure will be excessively unpleasant—and very likely painful! Now go to the nursery until I send for you.'

He did not wait to see the effect upon them of this ominous threat, but headed directly for the front door.

It did not take him many minutes to reach the garden he had dubbed his Wilderness. But by the time he got there, he was so incensed with his nieces that his mind dwelled with some degree of vengeance upon them. What their motive had been in this he was unable to fathom. But it was a trick which cast into the shade the episode of the frogs in Miss Hursley's bedchamber.

He spied the governess the instant he entered the

garden. She was sitting on the ground, her back resting against the oak on the far side. Julius paused briefly, beset by a confusing sensation of warmth that overlaid his anger.

She did not stir as he started towards her, and Julius trod softly, not wishing to startle her. Within a few feet of where she sat, he halted, abruptly becoming aware that she was asleep. So too was the kitten, a curled ball of patchwork lying in her lap.

Julius felt something give in his chest as his eyes went back to her face. Upon the girl's cheeks were traces of her tears.

Chapter Five

Julius regarded the picture for a few moments, beset by the oddest desire to gather Miss Hursley up into his arms for the purpose of administering precisely the comfort that she had evidently given to the kitten.

Folly woke first, lifting his head to blink green eyes upon the intruder. Rising, he stretched and yawned, and then sat upon his haunches, contemplating the master of the house with splendid indifference.

His movement disturbed Prue, and she opened her eyes. The sight of Mr Rookham startled her into sitting bolt upright. A protesting mewl from her lap alerted her to Folly, and sudden remembrance. The girls! She had sent them away.

Julius threw out a hand. 'Don't be alarmed. The twins told me what happened, and I came to see that you were none the worse for their mischief.'

'Oh,' Prue uttered lamely. 'They told you?'

He smiled. 'I think your distress frightened them a little. I cannot think they would have confessed otherwise.'

A sigh escaped Prue. 'I am afraid I did not spare them, but it was a horrid thing to do.'

'I quite agree. Nor should you have spared them.'

The kitten jumped from her lap and Julius came up to her, holding out a hand. 'Let me help you up. You will take cold if you remain there. The ground is a trifle damp.'

Prue allowed him to pull her to her feet, conscious of the warmth of his hand and the strength of his grip, which made her retreat a little the instant he released her.

'Thank you, sir.'

That enigmatic expression had settled upon his strong features. 'Now tell me, what possessed my nieces to put your protégé through this ordeal?'

Prue looked away. Evidently the twins had refrained from informing him. She would prefer not to explain it, for fear that it might involve her in revealing the whole catalogue of their activities. Mr Rookham appeared to read her mind.

'Come, Miss Hursley. You had much better tell me the whole, or you are unlikely to procure the slightest relief for them—as I anticipate you will wish to do.'

She glanced quickly at him, consternation in her face. 'You are going to punish them?'

'Don't you think they deserve it?'

Prue wrung her hands. 'I don't know! Had you asked me just when I discovered poor Folly at the bottom of the well, and had recognised their hand in the act, perhaps I should have answered yes.'

'But now that you have calmed down, your common sense has deserted you,' he offered grimly.

'That is unfair.' She regarded him with challenge in her eyes. 'Is it lack of common sense to dislike to see pain inflicted? If I had agreed to it on the spot, it would have been revenge—and that cannot be right.'

Julius frustratedly shook his head. 'Can't you see a difference between revenge and a just chastisement? How are they to learn?'

He was treated to that look of hers, half a plea and half something else that he could not identify. But its effect was instantaneous. His resolve melted even as she spoke.

'I do not know, Mr Rookham. But I had as lief they had not an instance of a painful interlude at your hands which they are able to set at my door!'

Julius was moved to give her a rueful smile. 'I am loath to admit it, but there is something in that. Judging by their demeanour when they came looking for me, I suspect they may already have learned a lesson.'

But Prue was beset by a resurgence of that hideous sense of failure. She watched Folly pounce on an insect that had dared to move in his sight. A sigh escaped her, and she spoke her thought aloud.

'It is all of a piece. I am a poor creature in their eyes, and they can only think the less of me for this episode. Nell—or even Kitty, I dare say—would never have succumbed to tears in the presence of their charges.'

'Since I don't know either Nell or Kitty, I cannot comment,' came from Mr Rookham.

Prue started, her eyes flying to his face. 'Oh, dear. I had forgotten you were there, Mr Rookham! Nell and Kitty are my very dearest friends. From the Seminary, you know.'

'Ah, I see. And you would have me believe that either one of them would have handled the situation better than yourself?'

'Oh, without doubt. You had better have asked for Nell in the first place—her name is Helen Faraday, but we always call her Nell. Indeed, I suspect she would have been suggested, only that she had been put up for another post and the gentleman had written the very day your engagement was given to me that he thought her too young. Besides, she was the best of us, and no one could expect her to take up a temporary position.'

That giveaway quiver at his lips came. 'Unlike you.'

'No,' agreed Prue seriously. 'For one could scarcely blame anyone for taking me only on trial. Or Kitty, if it came to that, but not for the same reasons. Though I feel sure Kitty would have refused you.'

Mr Rookham looked amused. 'Should I feel insulted?'

Prue unsuccessfully smothered a gurgle. 'By no means! You see, Kitty—Katherine Merrick, that is—is a sad case, for she has impossible ambitions. You needed to have been a lord before she would consider coming here.'

'I see. And why is Kitty so high in the instep?'

Upon the point of blurting out the unfortunate nature of her friend's dubious background, Prue caught herself up, and hurriedly waived the matter aside.

'That is neither here nor there. But you may be sure she would have managed better than I have.' She drew a breath. 'I am afraid you were right at the start, sir. I am totally unfitted for this position.'

Mr Rookham regarded her with one of his enigmatic expressions. 'Did I say that?'

'No, but you thought it. I am certain that your opinion of me marched with Lotty's. And the melancholy truth is that I cannot blame either of you.'

Julius could not refrain from laughter. An indignant look was cast upon him, and he threw up a hand. 'If you will speak so absurdly, what do you expect? Whatever I may have thought of you at the outset, do give me credit for being able to recognise your good qualities. As for Lotty, what makes you suppose she holds a poor opinion of you?'

Prue quickly looked away, embarrassed. She could not tell him how she had foolishly invited that opinion—in written form, too! He would undoubtedly laugh at her again. She evaded the question.

'She has made it obvious.'

'And does Dodo also hold this opinion?'

'Oh, no. She has not Lotty's perception. But Dodo is unfortunately a little jealous of Folly's preference for my company. I have tried to ignore it—as I have done all their attempts to rattle me, but—'

Julius interrupted her without ceremony. 'All? How many attempts have there been? I witnessed the episode of the frogs, of course, but there have been other instances?'

Regretting her words, Prue tried to retract. 'It was nothing much, I assure you. At least, nothing that could succeed in unsettling me.'

'Until they hit upon this method.'

His voice was flat and unemotional, but Prue was not deceived. She gazed up at him in a good deal of dismay.

'I did not mean to tell you any of this. It was not my intention to complain of the girls. It is far more my fault than theirs, Mr Rookham!'

At this, a little of his rising anger veered irrationally towards the girl herself. 'Indeed? Did you encourage them in any way?'

'It is of no use to speak in that sarcastic way, sir, for you know it to be the truth.'

'I know nothing of the kind!'

'You do, Mr Rookham, for you said it yourself.'

'Don't be so absurd!'

'You did,' insisted Prue. 'That night when you helped to rid me of those horrid frogs, you said that I had no authority over the girls, and you were right.'

Julius threw up his eyes. 'For God's sake, girl, I was teasing you!'

'Well, whether you meant to tease or not, it is perfectly true. I have no authority over them, and it is therefore unfair to punish them when I have failed to curb them. I should have put a stop to it immediately.'

'Then why didn't you?' he demanded wrathfully.

Prue flung frustrated hands in the air. 'Because I

am quite useless, Mr Rookham! Have I not been telling you so?'

Julius regarded her in silence. What was he to do with the wench? Were there no limits to which she would go to save those wretched children from their just desserts? He felt the anger dissipating, and shook his head.

'You are impossible, Prudence, do you know that? And don't dare to agree with me!'

To his intense delight, a smile dawned, lighting her face. Without thinking, he reached out and brushed her cheek with one finger. The expression in her eyes altered, and Julius drew back. He made his tone deliberately impersonal.

'I don't suppose you had luncheon in all this fracas? The girls disturbed mine.'

'No—we were just about to take it, when they came rushing in to say that Folly had become lost.'

She sounded breathless. Julius glanced at her, but she was not looking at him.

'You had best come to the dining parlour and partake of something there. Meanwhile, I shall see the girls in the library. They should have eaten by this time, but I don't want you to see them again until I have spoken with them.'

Prue kept her eyes firmly lowered, but the flurry of her pulses quickened. And not entirely due to what he had said. She tried to keep her attention on his words rather than on that brief but tender gesture at her cheek.

Spoken to the girls, he had said. Did that mean that her pleas had succeeded? He had made no promises, and she dared not re-introduce the subject. She had made enough of a fool of herself for one morning. The wonder was that Mr Rookham did not immediately send her packing!

She collected Folly, and followed her employer out of the gardens, prey to the most unruly sensations at her bosom.

The twins were unusually subdued as they stood side by side before their uncle's desk, where he perched, regarding them with unrelieved severity. Julius wondered how much of their demeanour was owed to fear of what he might do, and how much to the dismay that had brought them to him in the first place.

They had obeyed his summons to the library, but accompanied by their nurse, who had been brandishing a hairbrush. From her voluble remarks, Julius had gathered that the twins had not only given her an account of their activities, but had begged off punishment by telling her that their uncle had already promised to deal it out.

Julius had cut the woman short, expressing himself in rusty French. 'Thank you, Yvette. You may safely leave the matter in my hands.'

The nurse had curtsied to him, and cast a glare upon her two erring charges, before taking herself off. Julius noted that his nieces were visibly relieved. It was evident that their fear of the fierce little Frenchwoman surpassed their apprehension of the unknown. For their uncle had never before been called upon to correct them. Perhaps they hoped that he would not carry out his threat.

He had a good mind to disabuse them instantly, but with the image of those pleading grey eyes in the back of his mind, he contented himself with looking them over in silence until they began to fidget.

'Stand still!'

They froze at once, and two pairs of apprehensive brown eyes peeped up at him. Julius folded his arms.

'Would you agree that what I should do is take a stick to you both?' Both sets of eyes widened, and two dark heads were vigorously shaken. 'Can either of you tell me why not?'

They looked at each other. Then back to his face.

'Because it would hurt?' ventured one of them.

'Dodo, you stupid!' uttered the other. 'It's meant to hurt.'

'Quite right, Lotty, it is,' agreed Julius, relieved of

the necessity to enquire which twin was which. 'And since you hurt Folly, not to mention Miss Hursley, don't you think you deserve to be hurt back?'

'But we never hurt her!' protested Dodo. 'And Folly didn't get hurt neither. He was perfickly all right.'

'Oh, was he? How would you like it if someone were to put you in a great big box on a rope, and drop you down the side of a mountain?'

Dodo made a face. 'But it was a well, Uncle Julius, not a mountain.'

'Noodle! He means it was like a mountain to Folly.'

'Oh.'

Julius looked at Lotty. 'So you at least understand that it hurt the kitten?'

Lotty lifted her chin. 'Maybe.'

He narrowed his eyes, his tone icy. 'I beg your pardon?'

The child flushed and hung her head. Dodo, noted Julius, merely looked puzzled. Prudence had judged aright. Dodo had not her sister's intellect. He addressed himself to Lotty.

'Let's try again. Do you understand that the kitten was hurt by what you did?'

It was a struggle, he guessed, but Lotty looked up at last, her gaze direct. 'Yes.'

'Thank you. And do you further understand that you hurt Miss Hursley even more?'

There was defiance in the brown gaze, but it wavered a little. Julius waited, glancing once at Dodo, whose puzzled eyes went from her sister to her uncle and back again. When it came, the admission was sudden, and irate.

'I never meant to make her cry! Why did she cry so? I thought she would just be cross and shout at us. She's just a dowd and not like a governess at all. Why don't she just shout at us? Yvette shouts at us all the time.'

'Yes, and we don't mind it,' agreed Dodo, adding her mite. 'Lotty said if only Miss Hursley would shout at us, we wouldn't do nothing bad no more.'

Julius got up abruptly from the desk, causing the girls to start back. He ignored them, walking hastily away to one of the windows and staring out. He saw nothing of the woody trees that lined the route to the stables and the domestic quarters set at a distance behind the house. In his inner eye, all he could see was the expressive features of Miss Prudence Hursley.

Oh, she had her phases! He had seen her indignant, with even a spark of anger in those tender eyes. She was frequently forward, wholly outside her role, expressing herself in terms totally unsuited in a governess to her employer. But in a million years, she would never resemble the nurse Yvette!

Without thought, he turned upon the girls, unaware of the hasty manner of his speech, of the biting tone with which he berated them.

'You don't know how lucky you are! Here is a woman blessed with the tenderest of natures, the kindest of temperaments. And you can think of nothing better to do than to goad her into losing her temper! Well, I tell you now, she will not do it.'

He became aware of the two faces, staring at him with blank incomprehension. He crossed hastily back to stand before the desk, unable to help the rapidity with which the words left his tongue.

'Would you wish to know why you have not yet been beaten for these pranks? I would have spanked you for the frogs, but that Miss Hursley begged for mercy for you. Your governess herself, who was the subject of your tricks. Nor could she bear the thought that I might punish you for today's disgraceful behaviour. You called her a dowd, Lotty. In appearance perhaps she is. But she is quite other than that in her heart, and you two impertinent, unfeeling little devils have not the wit to see it!'

Whether his words went home, Julius could not tell, but the harsh manner of his utterance was beginning to have an effect. Both sets of dark orbs were luminous with unshed tears. He did not relent.

'I hope you are both thoroughly ashamed of

yourselves. You should be. A more heartless pair I trust I may never meet!'

He clamped down upon his churning emotions, for both twins were swallowing on hiccuping sobs and Dodo was knuckling her eyes. Lotty, he was glad to see, looked thoroughly shamefaced, but she was making a valiant effort to sniff away her tears.

'Don't think you are to get off with a mere scold,' he told them more moderately. 'You are confined to your bedchamber for the remainder of the day, where you had best think how you are going to make your peace with Miss Hursley.'

Lotty bit her lip, and sniffed dolefully.

'And one more thing,' decided Julius. 'I will instruct Mrs Wincle to provide you with no sweet-meats or treats for a full week.'

Dodo's sobs redoubled at this, but Lotty merely dropped her eyes, as if this was of less account than the inevitably embarrassing meeting with her governess.

Feeling that he had made up in some measure for the upset Prudence had endured, Julius dismissed them. Although the interview had not gone according to plan, he believed that on the whole it had been effective—perhaps more so than if he had administered a beating. But then he had not bargained for the intensity of feeling that had attacked him on realising what Lotty had been trying to do to the innocent and unsuspecting Miss Prudence Hursley.

The dining parlour was a roomy apartment, sparsely furnished, with walls almost bare of decoration bar a couple of paintings and one large mirror. There was not that atmosphere of stuffy formality which Prue had been led to expect.

There had been great emphasis upon table manners at the Seminary, in preparation for those few occasions when the governess might be required to dine with the family. As their female charges approached maturity, it would be natural, the Duck said, for them to be allowed into the adult world. Their governess would naturally keep them company, for no young lady could be relieved of such care until she had emerged from the schoolroom to be presented at Court.

At Rookham Hall, the table was not overlong—or if it was, the leaves must have been removed, Prue thought—and there were but two dressers to one side where dishes might be placed. Mr Rookham had obliged her to sit to one side of his own place at the head of the table, where she was immediately served with a selection of cold meats and pickled cabbage.

During her employer's absence, she had been far

too worried to partake of much of the food, but had cut up a portion of meat and served it to Folly under the table. She had braved the butler's disapproving look rather than be parted from the kitten. After all, it was Mr Rookham who insisted upon her sitting at his board, and he had said nothing about removing Folly.

By the time he returned, Prue's plate had been removed and she was disposing of a couple of Wincle's excellent jam tarts.

'Well, that's that,' said Julius, seating himself at the head of the table, and signing to the butler to pour him wine. He tutted at Prue's expression.

'You need not look so troubled, you goose! I merely gave them a scold, and sent them back to their bedchamber for the rest of the day.'

A huge sigh escaped her, and her features lit. 'Thank you, sir. I am very much relieved.'

There came that giveaway tremor at his lips, but he spoke with decision. 'But this really is their last chance. One more trick like that, and they will certainly feel my hand!'

Prue eyed him dubiously. 'Did you tell them so?'

He grinned as he lifted the glass. 'I forgot, as it chances. But that is easily remedied.'

She watched him sip his wine, and made a silent resolve to prevent the twins from committing any further mischief of a like nature. Pushing back her chair, she made to rise.

Julius reached out and grasped her wrist. 'Don't go yet!'

His grip was warm, and a hollow opened up unexpectedly in Prue's insides. She eyed the strong features, unaware that she leaned a little away from him. A frown came into his eyes, and he released her abruptly.

'I beg your pardon. Of course you may leave, if that is your wish.'

Prue did not wish it at all, but she could hardly say so. She rose, and hovered. The enigmatic look was back on his face, and she knew not what to say to him. An absurd sensation of guilt rose up—as if she had hurt him! She sat down again abruptly, unable to think of a single word to say.

There was a short silence. Julius watched her downcast face, and cursed himself. He had made her ill at ease, when his whole desire had been the opposite. He signed to Creggan.

'Will you take a sweetmeat?'

Looking up, Prue found the butler presenting to her a platter containing an array of dainties. Feeling she had something for which to make up, she selected a sugared almond and a squared piece of marchpane.

Nibbling, she dared to face Mr Rookham once

more, and found him taking up a couple of glazed orange pieces.

Catching her gaze, Julius smiled. 'I wish you will tell me more about these friends of yours. The paragon Nell, and—who was it?—the girl with the high-and-mighty notions.'

Prue was obliged to laugh. 'Poor Kitty. It is not her fault, for she has a mysterious background. Nell would tease her, but the melancholy truth is that none of us can claim half as interesting a story.'

'You have now thoroughly intrigued me,' declared Julius. 'You will have to reveal all forthwith.'

Amused, he watched her throw a hand to her mouth, those expressive eyes peeping over it in consternation.

'Oh, dear, I should not have said anything.'

'Too late, Miss Hursley.'

She grimaced. 'But it is the most shocking tale— at least the way Kitty told it.'

'You will find me utterly unshockable. Come, I insist upon knowing all.'

Prue sighed, popping the almond into her mouth and brushing a powdering of sugar off her fingers. 'Well, everyone knew the story that was given out. Kitty was born from a misalliance made by her father—Mr Merrick that was—with a country girl. Both, it is said, had perished in an accident.'

'Unfortunate,' commented Julius. 'But do you say there is doubt about this history?'

'So Kitty claims. To be fair, it is perfectly true that her memories do not bear it out. Or they seem not to do so, shocking though it is to give credence to her notions.'

'Ah. I perceive there is some disgraceful secret involved.'

Prue saw his mouth twitch. 'You may tease, sir, but it is outrageous—if it is true. Kitty believes she was instead the outcome of an unfortunate liaison between a high-born gentleman and an equally high-born married lady.'

Her employer evidently found this funny.

'You might well laugh, Mr Rookham,' she said severely, 'but the outcome is not at all amusing. You see, Kitty fancies herself of much higher worth than a governess. Despite Nell's strongest encouragements, she has refused to prepare herself properly for the future which must be hers.'

Julius found her air of anxious concern both endearing and amusing. 'Whereas you and this Nell have been diligent in so doing, I take it?'

'Well, I tried, and Nell is exemplary. She was diligent, if you like, for she believed her future to be inevitable. For though she kept it close, she claims there is nothing unusual to her background, any more than my own.'

Curious, Julius regarded her with interest. 'Which is?'

'Oh, the veriest nothing. My father was a parson, and my mother was the doctor's daughter in the village. They were both carried off by an outbreak of scarlet fever when I was little more than six or seven.'

An unexpected pang smote Julius. He felt an overwhelming urge to compensate her. Only he had no way of doing so, beyond a word of sympathy. He could give her that at least.

'How unfortunate! I am so sorry, Prudence.'

She coloured, shaking her head. 'Pray don't disturb yourself, Mr Rookham. I was very lucky, for although my grandfather the doctor had already died, the priest who came in my papa's stead was kind enough to take me in. Later he arranged for me to go to the Seminary so that I might have the means whereby to make my way in the world.'

Julius could not help himself, the harsh note pronounced. 'And you call yourself lucky?'

She nodded vigorously. 'Indeed I do, sir. I might have ended in the workhouse, you know, for although there were people to care for me before Mr Wilby came, they could not have supported me for long.'

A burning feeling of resentment flourished on her behalf in Julius's bosom, but he forced himself to speak as normally as possible.

'Undoubtedly a worse fate.'

Puzzlement overspread her features, and he knew he had been less than successful at hiding the intensity of his feelings. Hell and damnation, how misplaced they were! What had it to do with him?

'Pray do not feel sorry for me, Mr Rookham, for I am far from sorry for myself. Indeed, I have been quite happy at the Seminary, for I had Nell to guide me, and Kitty to amuse me with her fanciful imagination.'

A sudden gurgle of laughter escaped her, and Julius was conscious of warmth cascading into his chest. It was all he could do to enquire into the cause.

'What is so funny?'

'I was thinking of Kitty, though why I should laugh, I'm sure I don't know. She made me as mad as fire!' Prue was unaware of her own motion as she leaned confidingly towards him. 'You see, Kitty would only try at the particular subjects which she considered appropriate to the life of a titled lady. She is near fluent in French and Italian, she can dance like a fairy, and she plays the pianoforte quite magically.'

'Useful accomplishments for a governess, surely?'

'Yes, but not without the rest. In all other respects, she pretended to be as inept as I am. Had she made the attempt, I am sure Kitty could have managed to sew well and read the globes far better than I.'

Her indignation drew a laugh from Julius. Unthinkingly, he reached out and laid his hand over her unquiet ones.

'You should not speak of yourself so disparagingly, Prudence. You have gifts of your own that are worth more than any mechanical skill.'

Prue felt her pulse go out of kilter. She knew her fingers trembled and hoped he did not notice. She tried to answer him out of lips grown stiff and unwieldy.

'Th-thank you, Mr R-Rookham. It is kind of you, though I cannot imagine what m-makes you say such a thing.'

The look in his eyes made her melt inside. 'Therein lies much of your charm.'

She knew not what to say. The pressure of his fingers lifted from her own, and she breathed more freely. Seeking distraction, she reached absently towards the platter of sweetmeats. Recollecting her manners before she could take one, she snatched her hand back again, and stood up abruptly.

'I have taken up far too much of your time, sir.'

A slight frown came into his eyes, and the strong chin lifted, making his nose jut out the more. 'So you wish to go, after all? Yes, very well.'

Dismayed by his sudden curtness, Prue pushed back her chair and shifted out from her place at the table. She had to force herself to look at him.

'Thank you, sir, for helping me with the twins.'

Mr Rookham shrugged. 'I have done nothing out of the ordinary. But you must let me know if you have any further trouble.'

The tone was a dismissal. Prue's heart sank. She dropped a quick curtsy, and went to the door, where she belatedly recalled the kitten.

'Oh, dear. Where is Folly?'

Mr Rookham immediately swept a glance about the room, and then lifted the tablecloth to look beneath it. The butler intervened, moving to the other end of the table.

'The animal, sir, is in this chair.'

'Been keeping an eye on it, eh, Creggan? Well, I don't blame you. Let Miss Hursley fetch it, or we shall be chasing it all over the room!'

Prue was already bustling to the indicated chair. She scooped up the kitten and hastily left the parlour, feeling once again baffled by Mr Rookham and his odd changes of temperament.

She retreated to the schoolroom, where she prepared a lesson for the morrow, and thence to her parlour to write an account of the day's events to her two friends. Talking of them to Mr Rookham had somehow brought them closer.

Taking out Nell's last letter, she read over it again. Her friend had applied for two more positions, neither of which—as she reluctantly confessed—had the attraction of that one she had missed.

Prue sighed. It seemed extraordinarily unfair that Prue was herself settled before the best of the Duck's pupils. She wished that wretched fellow with his strange request had not thought poor Nell too young.

Even Kitty had envied that position! A widowed lord, looking for a governess for his daughter. And living in a lonely castle tucked away in a forest. Indeed, Lord Jarrow had made no secret of the fact that it was an isolated place and his child an untamed creature who would need careful handling.

Who could be better suited for such a post than Miss Helen Faraday? The Duck had said so, and all the girls had agreed. Except Kitty. What an incurable romantic she was! Though it was true that one could more easily picture her in a gothic castle, as she insisted, than dear sensible Nell. And then Lord Jarrow had rejected Nell on the score of her youth and inexperience. Prue had been desperately disappointed for her, more so than Nell herself.

'Had he only met you, Nell, I am sure he must have seen at once how sensible and clever you are.'

Nell, typically, had refused to be cast down.

'After all, it is just as the Duck has always warned. You know well that is why she does not attempt to send any of us out before we are old enough. Besides, I can well understand that Lord Jarrow might look for a governess of mature years. A female of two and twenty must seem to him ridiculously young for his needs.'

But in her letter, Nell admitted that she did not like the other posts she was trying for half as well. Prue settled down to writing her commiserations, guiltily aware that she had been less than truthful in her turn even to this most trusted confidante. Only how was she to explain in a letter the unorthodox nature of Mr Rookham's dealings with her?

If she could, she would not. For although Nell and Kitty wrote separately to her, she knew that her own letters back were shared. She might have turned to Nell for advice—who better to give it? But to have Kitty's imagination go to work upon the matter could only make a mountain where none existed!

Mr Rookham was her employer, and that was the end of it. There could be nothing more. There *was* nothing more. If he had asked her to remain at luncheon, what might she read into that? She had been distressed, and perhaps he wished to put her at ease. If he had called her once or twice by her Christian name, what could it mean but that he was kindly disposed towards her? And merely because he had touched her, closed his fingers over her hand so that a flurry had disturbed the natural rhythm of her heartbeat, she need think nothing of it beyond the fact that Mr Rookham was a gentle sort of man.

It was harder to dismiss that other touch—oh, so lightly had his finger caressed her cheek! And he had spoken of her *charm*. There had been that in his eyes that Prue must count herself a fool to take notice of. It could mean nothing.

If Prue was to suppose he meant other than kindness, then she would be obliged to think the worse of Mr Rookham. And that she could not bear. For her education at the Duck's hands had been thorough. No aspect of what might be expected had been omitted, including dire warnings of errant conduct that might conceivably occur in the gentleman of a household which any of the girls could inhabit.

Prue could not endure to discover that Mr Rookham was of that brotherhood who took advantage of a young female in her position. The Duck's words had been severe.

'Do not be deceived into thinking that your class affords you protection. There are those unscrupulous enough to attempt to inveigle a young lady into an unforgivable liaison. If you should find yourself tempted—and you may well be, make no mistake!—you must remind yourself that only ruin and disaster can ensue. You had better leave altogether than allow yourself to be compromised.'

The Duck had not scrupled to outline the exact nature of the ruin and disaster that must inevitably follow a female's fall from grace. All the girls had guessed that the homily had been particularly addressed to Kitty, whose ambitions—so Nell had averred in the privacy of their common bedchamber—laid her open to such attacks. It had not occurred to Prue, under no illusions about her personal attractions, that she might become the object of undue attentions.

True, Mr Rookham was unmarried, and the Duck—under no illusions about the sanctity of marriage!—had warned that the majority of gentlemen who behaved in that unscrupulous way were husbands. But her preceptress had not led her charges to suppose that a bachelor might be any less so.

'Do not imagine that an unmarried man will respect your status any more than another. Nor should you anticipate that having ruined you, he might right you in the eyes of the world. That is the stuff of novels, my dears, and has no bearing on real life. Gentlemen do not commonly seek a wife from among the ranks of those females obliged to earn their living.'

Which had effectively put paid to Kitty's impossible dream. But Prue had not anticipated that any of these precepts could apply to her situation. Not that she could accuse Mr Rookham of attempting to compromise her. Only there had been those few little intimacies, and she could not help recalling the odd looks she had received from Mrs Polmont when that female had shown her the little parlour set aside for her use.

On the other hand, Mr Rookham had entered Prue's bedchamber and made no attempt whatsoever upon her virtue. Nor had he shown himself to be in the least little bit attracted to her person. Which was a distinct relief, decided Prue, ignoring a sinking at her chest. No, he was merely kind, and appeared—inexplicably—to find her amusing.

Guiltily aware of having behaved towards Mr Rookham with no small degree of licence, Prue was moved to congratulate the good fortune that had made him a perfect gentleman. Or perhaps, she decided, coming down to earth again, she ought rather to thank her own lack of attributes. After all, it was unlikely that any gentleman—certainly not

Mr Rookham!—would look twice at a dowdy brown mouse.

Reminded of Lotty's remark, she instantly chided herself for expending her thoughts upon her employer, when she ought rather to be thinking of his nieces. Uneasily she wondered how they would behave towards her in the schoolroom on the morrow. And how should she conduct herself towards them?

Prue slept indifferently, and partook of breakfast in her parlour, perforce feeding Folly too since the twins did not come in as usual to collect him. In a little trepidation, she made her way to the schoolroom.

On opening the door, she discovered that the girls were already seated at their desks. They had their backs to her, but she saw their heads turn briefly, although they did not venture to catch her eye, nor to speak. As she arrived at her own desk, they both stood politely.

'Good morning, Miss Hursley.'

It was chorused, and subdued. Slightly taken aback, Prue eyed them, wondering whether or not to refer to yesterday's fracas. Four dark orbs stared back at her, and at her continued silence, perplexity entered them.

'Oh, pray sit down,' she begged, taking her own seat.

They did so, gazing at her with growing interest. Prue struggled against a desire to run from the room. What should she say? Instinct told her to behave as if nothing had happened, but that would be cowardly. Besides, it was because she had steadfastly refused to refer to their naughtiness that they had been driven to try her too far.

No, she must make a stand. She tried to smile.

'I think perhaps we should start again, don't you?'

They looked at each other, and then back to Prue. Solemnly, both nodded.

'I am afraid I am not very good at this. You see, I am learning just as much as you are. This is only my first post, and I did so want to do well at it.'

'Your *first*?' Dodo burst out.

'But you are not *our* first,' said Lotty.

'No, for we have had so many governesses that we cannot count them all.'

'And they got cross with us, and shouted.'

'Why don't you shout, Miss Hursley?'

Prue shifted uncomfortably, but it did not occur to her to prevaricate. 'I have a great dislike of people shouting at me, and I would not care to make others uncomfortable by that means. Especially children.'

The twins appeared nonplussed by this explanation. They stared at her as they might a freak in a sideshow.

'You look at me as if you thought me mad. What is so odd about it? People are different. You must not expect everyone to be the same.'

'But don't you care that we put frogs in your bed?' demanded Dodo.

'And the worms!' Lotty sounded positively agitated. 'I made sure you would have said something after the worms.'

'But then you would have won,' Prue defended herself. 'I did not wish you to know that you had affected me.'

'Wasn't you scared?'

'Wasn't you disgusted?'

Prue shuddered. 'I was both scared and disgusted. And though I was a trifle sorry for the frogs—for your uncle threw them out of the window, you must know—I had no compunction in getting rid of the worms.'

Both girls fell into laughter at the fate that had overtaken the frogs. But after a moment or two, they became silent again, and Dodo nudged her sister. There was a whispered colloquy, and Dodo jerked her head as at a secret signal. Lotty cleared her throat.

'Dodo wants to know if you will still let us play with Folly.'

Prue felt a lurch at her chest as she caught a look of real contrition in Dodo's face. She clasped her fingers tightly together on top of the desk.

'I refuse to believe that either of you would have done as you did had you thought more about Folly, and less about me.' There was a tremble at Dodo's lip. Prue smiled at her. 'My dear child, you have no need to be jealous because Folly chooses to come to me. You see, he thinks of me as his mother. But you are his friend.'

Dodo began to cry. 'But I w-wasn't his f-friend, or I wouldn't have p-put him down the w-well.'

'But you will never hurt him again, I am persuaded.'

The girl shook her head, sniffing.

'It was my fault,' said Lotty suddenly. 'I thought of it, Miss Hursley. Dodo would never have done it if I hadn't said.'

Prue sighed. 'I know, Lotty.'

Lotty frowned. 'You never said so!'

'No. But it was you who wrote about my shortcomings. Dodo was far more interested in Folly than she was in me. So it had to be your brain behind the mischief.'

'Well, it was,' admitted Lotty, a trifle sulkily.

Prue's tone gentled. 'You have a very good brain, Lotty. I am sure you could put it to better use.'

Lotty said nothing, but her eyes grew luminous,

and Prue suddenly saw that she had won after all. Jumping up, she came around the desk and impulsively held out her arms.

There was a brief pause. And the next moment, two unhappy faces were buried in her shoulders, damping her gown with their tears.

Clutching a jar and an improvised net on a stick, Prue stepped gingerly on to the first of a series of protrusions of uneven stone that led across one end of the pond to an apparent island beyond. The girls, having tripped across the improvised causeway without a tremor, were already busily engaged in hunting the shallows for tadpoles.

It was not an occupation that appealed to Prue, but she felt herself honour bound to engage in it. A week of exemplary behaviour on the part of the twins had resulted in her declaring a holiday to reward them. Besides, it was the first day of April, and it would be well to avert any pranks. Fully and happily occupied, her charges would be less likely to be thinking of mischief.

'What would you care to do? You may choose anything you wish, provided it is not an activity of which your uncle may disapprove.'

Unable to believe their good fortune, for several moments the girls had been unable to think of anything they might like to do. To encourage them, Prue had offered to teach them how to make buttercup and daisy chains, for the onset of spring had yielded a crop of these wildflowers. Both Lotty and Dodo had rejected the suggestion with scorn, preferring pursuits of a more enterprising nature. Tadpoles had won the day.

The twins had raided the kitchen quarters in search of suitable jars, and ransacked the chest in their playroom for butterfly nets. Since they had only two, it became necessary to construct one for Prue's use.

'Do not concern yourselves over me,' had pleaded Prue, by no means anxious to join in. 'I will content myself with watching you.'

But this would not do at all for the twins. Miss Prue—by which new appellation they had taken to addressing her, Lotty having spotted the pet name at the top of a rare letter from Kitty—must not be deprived of the pleasure of collecting tadpoles! Netting had been begged from Mrs Polmont, wire and a stick from one of the gardeners. A few judicious, if inexpert, stitches had transformed these items into a collecting net of dubious efficiency, which the twins had proudly presented to their governess.

Prue wobbled precariously, uneasily eyeing the

shallow waters below. If only the girls had not objected, she would infinitely have preferred to remain on this side of the pond. But there was, so Dodo averred, a greater profusion of tadpoles over the way where they were to be seen dipping their nets.

She glanced at them briefly, and discovered them to be deeply engaged. Perhaps they might not notice if she were to make a quiet retreat. Turning a little, she looked back to the shore behind. Her heart sank, for it seemed almost as large a step to negotiate to get back as it did to go forward to the next stone.

The twins proved not to be too fully occupied to notice her hesitation.

'Come on, Miss Prue!'

'It's easiest to do it quickly. Jump!'

Jump? Prue eyed the target ahead. The twins were bobbing about on the other side.

'There's a flat bit right there, see?'

'Jump on to the flat bit!'

Prue gathered her courage and launched herself forward. She landed, and struggled for balance. But encouragement from the far bank steadied her. The next jump was not as hard, and she gained a little in confidence. It was tricky, but she found that the jar and net in either hand gave her ballast and helped her to balance as she negotiated the stone pathway. Triumphant, she landed on the island, a little breathless, but unharmed.

'There, that was not so bad,' she uttered on a laugh.

'S'easy!' averred Dodo.

'Look how many tadpoles I've got already,' said Lotty, holding up her jar where a number of the black squiggly creatures were swimming around.

Prue eyed them with disfavour. 'What are you going to do with them?'

'Keep them and watch them grow into frogs.'

Uneasily wondering where the girls intended to keep the tadpoles, Prue refrained from enquiry. She felt sure she would dislike the answer.

'You have to get some, Miss Prue.'

Prue suppressed a sigh. 'Very well.'

Following the twins to the edge of the water, she leaned over at their direction to look into the hollows. Prue had to peer closely, but at last she was able to make out that a great splodge of darkness in the murky deep, which she had taken for vegetation, was in reality a veritable army of black darting dots beneath the water.

She started back in faint alarm, and her boots slid in the marshy bank beneath her feet. Alarm turned to panic as she tried to regain her balance. Both jar and net went flying, the ground gave below her, and her knees caved in.

Next instant, she was plummeting down and found herself immersed in two feet of water, with black dots scattering in every direction.

Chapter Six

Unable to take in what had happened, Prue remained in a daze for several seconds while the moisture soaked into her garments and crawled icily on to her skin. She became aware of muffled shrieks, and discovered that Lotty and Dodo had succumbed to riotous hilarity.

The creeping cold pushed Prue into action. Plunging both arms into the depths, she heaved herself up under the suddenly hefty weight of her sodden petticoats. The effort to get upon her feet left few dry patches upon the grey Seminary uniform. Prue had never felt so wet in her life.

Aided by the combined strength of the still giggling twins, Prue dragged herself back on to the bank. The chill in the air whipped through her drenched jacket, and she realised that her most pressing need was to return to the house and change her clothes. At which point, she remembered that she was on the wrong side of the pond.

'Now what am I to do?'

She paid no attention to the vociferous advice of the two girls. For no consideration would she attempt to cross upon the stones again in this condition. Her clothes felt as if they weighed twice as heavily as normal, and she would undoubtedly fall in again. She looked about with a feeling of growing desperation.

'Is there no way to get round by land?'

"Course not, it's an island.'

'You could go in a boat, if we had one.'

'If we had one,' Prue repeated flatly.

'Only we don't.'

'No, we don't,' Prue agreed.

A shiver took her as the cold seeped into the damp, and she knew she must act at once. She looked across the water. 'Is it any deeper in the middle?'

The immediate conflicting responses of the twins made it clear that they did not know.

'After all,' she told herself, 'if I am to fall in again, I may as well wade through and avoid that discomfort.'

She decided to brave it, and stepped out gamely into the water, swishing through with difficulty, the twins shrieking instructions and encouragement.

'Careful, Miss Prue!'

'You can do it!'

'Go faster, Miss Prue!'

Go faster? She could not even hold up her petticoats! The wet had penetrated through all the layers beneath, making them too cumbersome to lift.

Ignoring the girlish squeals, she concentrated all her attention upon keeping her feet, hoping that the water would not rise higher than her knees. As she struggled against the pressure of the water, she felt her spirits drooping as heavily as her clothing. It seemed she could do nothing right.

But, miraculously, the bottom of the pond deepened only slightly, and at last she found herself within range of the opposite bank. Relieved, she pulled a trifle faster—and almost went over! Her heart in her mouth, she checked again and thrust through the last few feet, almost falling upon the bank as she reached it.

There was less mud on this side and it was a relatively easy matter to drag herself up. Panting a little, Prue remained only to instruct the twins not to linger, and then began the long trek homeward, walking as quickly as her condition would allow, and dripping puddles as she went.

Halfway across the lawns she spied two figures standing before the house, engaged in discussion.

One was a fellow in the homely garb of a workman. The other, to Prue's immediate consternation, was Mr Rookham.

Prue paused briefly, and a tattoo built up in her veins. Must he be there just as this moment? She had not seen hide nor hair of her employer since the day of Folly's misadventure. Yet he manifested himself precisely when she would most wish to have avoided meeting him. Was it not just like Mr Rookham to make so inopportune an arrival?

Well, there was nothing to be done about it. She was both cold and distressingly damp, and she had to get to the house as speedily as possible. She must brave his inevitable amusement.

Holding her head high, she struggled on, more than ever aware of her dripping garments. Her pulses skittered as she saw Mr Rookham turn, and knew that he had spotted her. He paused, staring for a moment as if he was unsure whether his eyes deceived him. To Prue's dismay, he began to stroll towards her, leaving the workman standing.

Prue's legs ceased to move, seemingly of their own volition. Mr Rookham approached steadily. In a few strides, he was within several feet of her. Prue saw his expression change, and he slowed, his gaze raking her person from head to foot. He stopped directly in her path, and that quirk appeared at his mouth.

'Dare I ask, I wonder?'

Prue had endured much without complaint, but there was a limit. 'Is it not obvious? I fell into the pond! And before you find a way to amuse yourself at my expense, sir, pray take notice that I am far from enjoying the circumstance.'

His smile was sympathetic. 'What happened? Have you been attempting one of your heroic rescues?'

'No, I have not,' stated Prue crossly. 'If you must have it, I was attempting to catch tadpoles with the twins. Only as usual, my ineptitude caused me to make a complete fool of myself. Now you may laugh if you choose!'

'I don't choose, so you may stop ripping up at me!' But the amused quiver came again. 'Only do tell me. What precise educational activity were you engaged in? It is not usual to trouble the heads of girls with science.'

Prue positively glared at him. 'It was not educational. I had given the girls a holiday, to reward them for being good all week. Only they chose to catch tadpoles, so—'

'So you felt yourself obliged to join them. I see. Well, if you take my advice, you will in future remain upon the sidelines and let them do the catching.'

'Thank you,' said Prue with awful politeness. 'I am in dire need of such advice.'

Julius laughed. 'My dear Miss Hursley, that remark is almost worthy of my own attempts at sarcasm.' He threw up a hand as the governess opened her mouth to retort. 'Don't waste your breath! You would be better employed in changing your clothes than bandying words with me.'

He was rewarded, to his secret triumph, with a fulminating look, but Miss Hursley chose retreat. He watched her almost stamping her way up towards the side door of the house, and congratulated himself on having raised her spirits.

She had looked altogether woebegone at the moment he had encountered her—a state of affairs he had discovered to be unsettling. Indeed, almost every encounter with the girl had a deleterious effect upon him, he decided, as he started back to where Hessle awaited him.

But as he resumed his discourse with the head gardener, his mind dwelled obstinately upon the picture of the governess in her dilapidated state. He could not deny that he had been amused—the more so when she attacked him!—but a feeling of guilt crept over him. She must have been cold to the bone. He should not have kept her talking.

He hoped to God she would take care to warm up thoroughly. Had she enough sense of herself to do what was needful? Julius doubted it. Had he not caught her that first night writing in the cold of the schoolroom?

Abruptly concerned, he cut in upon Hessle's long-winded explanation of his scheme for the treillage garden.

'Never mind that now! I have something I must do at once. We will talk of it later.'

Ignoring the fellow's astonished look, he broke quickly away and went into the house, banging straight through the green baize door, and shouting for his housekeeper. She emerged from her sitting-room, looking astonished. Julius ignored this, and waved away several other servants who came popping out of the kitchen quarters.

'Polmont, I need you!'

He exited back into the hall, and turned there, finding his housekeeper immediately at his back.

'What is amiss, sir?'

'Miss Hursley has had the misfortune to fall into the pond,' he disclosed without preamble. 'She has gone up to change, but I desire that you will arrange for her to have a bath. Make sure she warms herself thoroughly, and that she puts on clean, dry clothes. Have you understood me?'

He received her customary nod, and a prim curtsy. 'Certainly, Mr Rookham.'

'Well, don't stand there! Go up to her at once

and tell her to prepare for it, and then set about it immediately.'

The housekeeper set off up the stairs, but Julius suddenly bethought him of Prudence's ill temper, and called her back.

'Just a moment!'

She paused. 'Sir?'

'If Miss Hursley should object or make any difficulties, inform her, if you please, that these are my orders. And send Yvette down to keep an eye on the girls in her stead.'

He watched Polmont hurry away, feeling that he had done much to atone both for his laughter and his earlier neglect. But he could not help a sneaking amusement at the thought of Miss Hursley's probable reaction. She would be astonished, he dared say, and possibly as cross as crabs. Only she would not advertise it to her employer!

She was far too conscious of her position to attack him without immediate provocation. It was only when she was face to face with him that he was able to break through that pervasive humility. It was infinitely pleasurable to startle her out of it. He should not do it, but the temptation was irresistible. And it had led him, to his annoyance, to cross the boundary of correct propriety.

A circumstance of which Miss Hursley herself

was become all too wary. He knew it, and had kept out of her way on purpose. For in her presence he was conscious of so vivid a sense of kinship that he found himself too ready to forget the gap that lay between them. And the instant he did or said anything that might be construed as a form of intimacy, Miss Hursley showed herself to be 'Prudence' indeed.

He heard footsteps above him, together with a telltale muttering. Looking up, he perceived the little Frenchwoman tripping down the stairs. She had wrapped herself in a voluminous black woollen cloak against the vagaries of the English weather.

'Ah, Yvette, good. Miss Hursley is temporarily indisposed. I desire you to go and ensure that the twins don't follow her example.'

'Bah! Zey do not fall, *ces enfants*,' announced Yvette in a grumbling way. 'Ze *gouvernante*, she 'ave ze mind in ze sky. *Qu'elle est folle!*'

Julius let this pass, and merely adjured her to hurry out to her charges, himself making his way back to his library.

But the nurse's disparaging remarks irked him. Could she not see beyond the physical? Yes, Prudence was unhandy and inept. She knew it herself! Had she not said so? Yet to Julius, she had qualities of greater worth than mere physical prowess. Why should she be judged only on her appearance and an unfortunate lack of coordination of hand and eye? Not to say head and eye on occasion, recalling the girl's original contretemps with his carriage in Leatherhead.

Although his nieces had apparently moderated their ideas of their governess. Did she not say that they had been good all week? A miracle! Then Miss Hursley was more successful than she knew. He must remember to congratulate her.

The warmth of the water was soothing, and all trace of that sensation of damping cold had left Prue's body. The bedchamber felt like a hothouse, what with the roaring fire before which had been set the tin bath she was currently occupying. The maidservant, who had hovered with another of the big jugs, ready to add more hot water, had left the room in response to an instruction from the housekeeper relayed by one of her colleagues.

Left alone, Prue gave herself up to the wonderfully new sensation of being pampered, allowing thoughts to drift dreamily through her mind.

It was odd how wetness could feel this good in her changed circumstances. Only a short time ago she had experienced excessive discomfort from the saturated garments clinging to her legs. It had been difficult to remove them. Indeed, she was inclined to believe that she might yet have been struggling to extricate herself had it not been for Mrs Polmont's timely arrival.

The housekeeper had knocked just when Prue had managed to drag off her jacket and was fighting with the strings of her grey petticoats, which had become tangled into an impossible knot. Prue had been fired with hope of rescue.

'Pray, who is there?'

'Mrs Polmont, ma'am.'

Relieved, Prue had instantly desired her to enter, and begged for her help. For several moments, the housekeeper had been fully occupied in wrestling with the recalcitrant knot. Once the petticoat was freed, she had begun assisting Prue to remove it.

'I can manage now, I thank you.'

At which, Mrs Polmont had dropped her bombshell, stunning Prue into amazed silence.

'I am here to help you, Miss Hursley. It is at the master's orders.' She had crossed to the bell-pull and tugged it vigorously. 'I will set the maids to prepare your bath.'

Prue had blinked. A bath? At Mr Rookham's orders? And she had lost her temper with him! Her conscience smote her, warring with a glowing sensation of warmth in her bosom. How kind and thoughtful was this man—and towards a mere governess!

In a daze, she had allowed the housekeeper to assist her to remove her clothing, and had towelled herself dry and wrapped up in her dressing-gown while Mrs Polmont had conferred with the maid who came in answer to the bell.

Presently there had come a procession of young females bearing a tin bath, a screen, and a succession of jugs. The girl Maggie had presented her with a glass of warm milk, which she had drunk, watching with pleasurable anticipation the steam beginning to rise from the bath.

Too grateful to make the slightest objection, Prue had allowed herself to be bustled into the tub of deliciously hot water, wondering uneasily whether she was asleep and dreaming.

Such luxury as this had never come in her way. Bath day at the Seminary had been a mad scramble among some fifteen other girls, each determined to secure a favourable share of the limited supply of hot water. It had been quite as humid, crowded into the little round bath-house in a chattering profusion of girlish giggles and shrieking demands for the soap. But to lie at her ease in this fashion, to be waited upon hand and foot, must be outside the realms of reality.

The doorlatch clicked, and Prue looked round to see that Mrs Polmont had re-entered the room. She approached the bath, and stood looking down at Prue, the parrot look pronounced.

'Your clothes have been taken to the wash-house, Miss Hursley. They will be cleaned and dried. I trust you have other warm garments to wear? If not, you have only to mention the matter and I will find you something.'

'Oh, dear,' uttered Prue faintly. 'I had not thought of that. I am so used to that particular costume, you see.'

'So I had supposed. Only I do not wish the master's wrath to fall upon my head, if he should discover that you had been improperly clad for the weather.'

The blanketing comfort of Prue's semi-dreaming state began to dissipate. There was a note in the woman's voice that struck a distinctly unpleasant chord. And threw Prue's tongue into action.

'But it has nothing to do with Mr Rookham!'

The woman's face became pinched. 'Has it not? It seemed to me that the master was finely agitated over your welfare.'

Prue stared up at her, mute. A slow pulsing started up below her breast, and the heat was abruptly uncomfortable. There was a look of superciliousness in the housekeeper's face, which added immeasurably to her unease.

'Mr Rookham is—is very kind,' Prue ventured, trying for a calm note. 'I am indebted to him for this unlooked-for mark of thoughtfulness.'

'Is it unlooked for, indeed?'

Prue's enjoyment was shattered. She dropped her eyes. 'Is there a towel, Mrs Polmont? If you would be good enough to pass it to me, I may get out of the bath.'

A thin smile crimped the woman's mouth, but she did as she was bid, collecting a large towel that had been thrown over the screen, which readily enveloped Prue as she stood up to receive it. With a gratifying sense of triumph, she found herself able to look the housekeeper directly in the eyes.

'Thank you, Mrs Polmont. You may retire, for I can manage for myself now.'

'As you wish, ma'am. But the gown? Shall I find something suitable for you to wear?'

'No, I thank you,' returned Prue with dignity. 'I am sure I have a gown that will serve the purpose.'

The parrot look pinched the creature's face. 'If I read the master aright, ma'am, I take leave to doubt that you possess any gown suitable to his purpose.'

With which, Mrs Polmont dropped a curtsy that seemed to Prue smugly ironic, and withdrew. Still as a statue, the towel clutched about her, Prue waited until she heard the door open and close. Then she let her breath go and buried her face in the warm towel, her heart pattering against her ribs.

There could be no mistaking that dreadful creature's meaning. But she was wrong. She must be wrong! If Prue was to believe in the implication, she had only one recourse. To flee from Rookham Hall as fast as her legs would carry her.

Wholly unaware of what she did, she stepped out of the bath and began automatically to rub herself down with the towel. Her mind was all chaos, her pulsebeat awry.

She would not believe it of him! Was Mrs Polmont jealous that she should suppose her employer to be angling to make Prue his *mistress*?

The word burned in her head. For that was what the spiteful female had meant her to understand. Merely because he had arranged for her to have a bath? But he had only laughed at her when he met her in the gardens! There had been nothing amatory in his demeanour. How could there be? She must have looked a shocking wreck.

No, it was ridiculous. She knew Mr Rookham for a man of simple kindness. Had he not kept her here at the outset, when all common sense must have dictated that he should send her packing?

A horrid doubt assailed her. Why had he not dismissed her? She recalled his entry into the schoolroom that first night. He had behaved in an inexplicable fashion towards her—gruff and not at all 'kind'. And then there had been the business of the parlour. Mrs Polmont's suspicions must have been aroused then, for had she not smirked in that knowing way? Were there grounds for it?

Prue wondered uneasily if she was being stupidly naïve. It was not the first time Mr Rookham had behaved towards her with undue particularity. Why had she not questioned this business of making her take a bath? Well, because she had been touched by it. And she had been so very cold and uncomfortable that her wits had gone begging.

She felt hot all at once, and realised that she was standing so close to the fire that her naked skin was roasting. Prue glanced down at the lines of her own figure. The familiar lumps, with which she had lived without complaint these many years, were all at once ugly. Tears started to her eyes, but a species of rage rose up in her breast.

How nonsensical was the housekeeper's notion. As if Mr Rookham—or indeed any gentleman in his senses!—could regard her as an object of desire. Had she not always been dumpy? Had it not forever been a case of chalk and cheese between herself and her two dearest friends? Not that Prue had minded. How could she be jealous of her darling Nell? Though Nell, who had height as well as those honey-coloured locks and pretty green eyes, could not hold a candle to Kitty. But then Kitty had been the toast of the Seminary.

To be sure, there were others who were plain and ordinary. But Prue knew herself to be among those with the least claim to beauty. She dabbed the towel to her eyes and sniffed down the idiotic tears. What reason had she to weep? She was not at risk. How could she possibly have caught Mr Rookham's amorous interest? A man whose eye could envision the beauty of the gardens of Rookham Hall? It was absurd!

A conviction that might have sunk her into gloom had she not been distracted by the entry of Maggie, who had been attending her in the bath.

'If you are done, miss, I'm to fetch the bath away and everything.' The maid blinked at her. 'Goodness, miss, ain't you dressed yet? Here, let me help you, or you'll not be in time for luncheon. Them twins are to come in with that Frenchie, so it won't be long now.'

Glad of the opportunity to take her mind off her disturbing thoughts, Prue gave her attention to dressing. Maggie, a friendly soul, chattered on as she hunted in the press for Prue's clothing.

'Now let's see if you've a clean shift, miss. Do you stay by the fire, we don't want you taking cold again. This one?'

Prue approved the plain cotton undergarment. 'Yes, that will do, thank you. And you will find my second pair of stays in the same drawer.'

'Here they are.' The maid bustled towards her. 'Now, do you lift your arms, miss.'

Prue felt insensibly comforted as Maggie dropped the shift over her head, twitched it into place, and set about tying her stay laces. There were no malicious words to upset her here! Impulsively, Prue put a question.

'Do you think it strange that Mr Rookham should insist upon the governess having a bath?'

The maid laughed. 'It ain't for me to say, miss, but since you ask, I can't say as I do.'

A tiny spark of hope sprung up in Prue's bosom. 'What makes you say that?'

'Just let me tie this lace first. Tight enough? There, then. I've fetched out an underpetticoat, miss. Only which gown was you meaning to wear?'

Prue went to the press and brought out the blue linsey-woolsey gown that Nell had helped her to make. It was of plain cut, and—unhampered by the dictates of fashion—had its waist set into the proper place instead of under the bosom. The bodice was modest, made high to the throat, and it had long sleeves, fitted, but not tightly à la mode.

'If I'm to have my say, miss,' resumed Maggie as she proceeded to tie the underpetticoat on, 'it's typical of the master.'

'Is it?' Prue was eager now. 'Has he done anything of the sort before?'

The maid picked up the gown and began to gather it ready to throw over Prue's head. 'Well, something like, miss. I remember when Wincle cut her hand bad on one of they big knives, the master come into the kitchen to find out what all the commotion were about. And I'm blowed if he didn't set to and stop the blood hisself! Then he had the doctor sent for, and Wincle were put to bed and give brandy for the shock. All at the master's orders.'

Prue was glad to disappear inside the gown just at that moment as the maid flung it over her head. For, curiously, this history had not the effect upon her that she had anticipated. By its evidence, she was to recognise that Mr Rookham's thought for her welfare—and had she not supposed it herself?—had its origin in a simple care of his fellow man. A supposition that made her chest feel as if a lead weight had descended upon it.

Chiding herself for stupidity, she forced herself to listen to Maggie, who was prattling away as she helped Prue to dip her arms into the sleeves and then began to work on the buttons all down the front.

'When that Mrs Chillingham arrived, the master didn't turn a hair. He give over this whole wing to them straight. And he turned round and put the boy to school. Then he fetched you to the girls an' all. There, that's the front done.' She gave the gown a tug or two to straighten it. 'No, miss, what I say is, you couldn't find a gennelman as is more generous than the master, not if you was to hunt across the country.'

A judgement that surely put paid to the ridiculous idea harboured by Mrs Polmont. Prue was sorely tempted to try the maid with that one. But Maggie—who was busy buttoning Prue's cuffs— would surely suppose her to be hankering for Mr Rookham's attentions. Which, she abruptly realised with a spurt of indignation, must be just what the housekeeper meant!

What had she done to deserve that suspicion? Nothing at all! But here Prue's conscience intervened. Had she not allowed herself licence in Mr Rookham's company? She spoke to him with a freedom that was hardly allowable in a governess. Admittedly, Mr Rookham encouraged it. But that did not excuse her own conduct. It might well have led a lesser man to think that she would welcome his advances.

Yet these interchanges had been in private. Upon what evidence did Mrs Polmont base her suspicions then? Unless she had overheard their conversations? It made Prue's skin crawl to think that she could have been spied upon. Was the creature prone to listening at doors? In a house such as this, it would be easy enough to prowl unseen.

Well, Mrs Polmont would have no further cause to make such ugly suppositions, determined Prue, taking a hairbrush to her hair as Maggie set about gathering the debris from the bath.

There was nothing for it but to avoid encounters with Mr Rookham. Fortunately, he did not seek her out—manifest proof of his complete uninterest! But there had been those accidental meetings when his familiarity had led her into a like ease.

It would not do. Should she meet him for the future, she would assume a mien wholly submissive. Then he would not be tempted to make game of her, and lead her into a fatal tendency to bandy words with him.

And should any sneaking wretch be disposed to try to glean an item detrimental to her reputation, they would be wasting their time!

Resolved, she thanked the maid and left her to clearing up. Heading for the playroom, she entered all unsuspecting upon the ribald taunts of Lotty and

Dodo. She had forgotten whence had arisen the need for her bath. Since there was no malice in the twins' teasing, Prue forbore to scold, instead successfully turning their attention by pointing out that Folly required their services for his share of luncheon.

She wished she had so ready a turn for her own attention, which remained obstinately upon an intrusive image of their uncle's strong features.

From an upstairs window above the front portico, Julius watched the game of battledore and shuttle-cock taking place out in the April sunshine. Every so often, a streak of orange and brown shot across the improvised court, causing the younger combatants to shriek imprecations at it, for the elder's attention was inevitably drawn from the game.

Unable to drag himself away, Julius had remained throughout two bouts in which Miss Hursley was soundly beaten by each of the twins. What held him there was the thrust of enthusiasm with which the governess struggled to keep up. Several times he saw her stop and lean over, holding one hand to her side where her breath evidently laboured.

His nieces—drat the little beasts!—gave no thought to the discomfort of their preceptress. All they could think of was to crow at her in triumph, berating 'Miss Prue' for being slow. Readily could he have banged their heads together!

He could have stopped it, merely by opening the window and leaning out with a word of command. He was loath to enquire too closely into his reasons for refraining. Miss Hursley could take care of herself. The more fool her if she allowed the brats to run rings round her in this fashion. It was all of a piece!

Unaccountably irritated, he turned away from the window, and resumed his progress down the stairs and thence to the library. His plans were behind, and he must complete the design for the furtherance of the Rockery, where he was planning to extend the layout to include a central maze.

But to his annoyance, as he set himself to the work, his pencil doodled idly and his mind dwelt irresistibly on the excessively distracting conduct of Miss Prudence Hursley.

What had she against him? Since that ridiculous episode of the disastrous tadpole collecting expedition a little more than a week ago, he had scarcely exchanged two words with the wench. Why? Because she was studiously avoiding him! That certainty could no longer be ignored.

Not that he had sought her company. What had he to do with the governess? But prior to the tadpole event, upon those few occasions when he had encountered her, there had been an agreeable exchange of badinage. At least, he had amused himself with goading her into retort. And Miss Hursley had obliged him by succumbing. So readily indeed that her present demeanour was frustrating beyond endurance!

There had been that occasion the other day, when he had come upon her seated in the sunshine in one of the cosy nooks in the gardens, reading to the twins. Their attention seemed to be divided between her voice and a desultory game with Folly, where he chased after a berry on a twig dragged playfully across the ground.

Julius had listened in astonishment as he realised that Miss Hursley had selected the gruesome story of 'Blue Beard' from an edition of Perrault's *Histories, or Tales of Past Times*. Was this one of the books she had chosen to be brought from Leatherhead?

Julius had interrupted the session, requesting to know why, if she must read them fairy tales instead of some improving work, she should have chosen one particularly revolting?

'What a tale with which to frighten the ears of innocent girls!'

Miss Hursley had reddened, as if she thought

him to be seriously displeased. Before he could investigate this further, the twins had broken in.

'But we like it, Uncle Julius!'

'Yes, it's 'citing,' said the other, capturing the kitten who was attacking the stationary berry. 'Not like that stupid *Sleeping Beauty*.'

'No, or *Cinderella*. They're noodles.'

'*Red Riding Hood* was good, only I think the wolf should have swallowed her up!'

Julius eyed them with disfavour. 'What a disgusting pair you are! Miss Hursley, I withdraw my remarks. I perceive that you are less at fault than I had supposed.'

But the governess had remained apparently chastened. Barely glancing at him, she had answered, in so submissive a fashion that he had hardly recognised her.

'If it is your wish, sir, I will read them no more such fairy stories.'

He had not taken in the gist of the protests that erupted from the throats of his indignant nieces, for he had been staring at Miss Hursley in perplexity. Julius had found himself responding in a depressingly stiff fashion, which in no way expressed the disappointment that he felt.

'If it is what Lotty and Dodo enjoy, far be it from me to cavil. Do just as you see fit, if you please.'

With which, he had turned on his heel and retired, baffled, and subject to an unpalatable annoyance. He could find no reason for her altered attitude towards him, but it had preyed upon his mind so that he had paid a visit to the schoolroom at a time when he might reasonably expect to find the governess working by herself. His nieces, whose natural vivacity had not long been buried by his displeasure, had told him in one of their expansive moments that Miss Hursley was to be found there before dinner.

She had been seated at her desk, but had jumped up at his entrance, shifting quickly away to the window. Julius had paused by the door, feeling an unreasoning hurt. He knew he had spoken curtly.

'What is the matter?'

Miss Hursley had given him an odd little smile, and turned away to stroke the kitten. A ploy to avoid him, he was persuaded. She had sounded— yes, bleak.

'Nothing is the matter, sir.'

'Are you sure?'

'Yes, quite.'

And there the subject had closed for a moment. She had volunteered nothing more, and he had not known what to say. Constraint had yawned between them. He had been in the throes of making up his mind to tackle her more directly, but she had suddenly cleared her throat.

'Would you care to see an item of the girls' work, sir?'

A bright voice, but metallic in quality. False. So patently false! Why? *Why* was she behaving like this?

But he had been unable to form the words to demand an explanation, and the next moment, Miss Hursley had picked up two articles and moved to present them for his inspection, Folly frolicking at her feet.

Julius had taken them mechanically, staring blankly at a pair of ill-sewn hearts made out of red felt, and stuffed.

'Pin cushions,' she had told him helpfully.

He had given a short laugh. 'Heart-shaped? How in Hades did you persuade them to work upon so sentimental a project?'

A faint shadow of her former manner had emerged in a swift little smile that briefly lit her face. 'I told them they were blood red because they had been cut out of murdered victims.'

'Good God, Prudence! You are as unprincipled as my nieces!'

She had looked at him with the air of a startled fawn. Then she had snatched back the hearts and restored them to their place upon the table to one side. Catching up the kitten, she had dropped a curtsy, her tone lowered.

'If you will forgive me, sir, I must not be late for dinner.'

Julius had stepped aside and allowed her to leave the room, attacked by an acute sense of outrage.

Thereafter, he had seen her only at a distance now and then. Except at church on Sunday. But he had made it a rule to maintain protocol on such occasions—for her sake. To bring Miss Hursley into public attention could only serve to make her the subject of local gossip.

But it was too bad that he could not bear to approach her in his own home, risking another rebuff. She had rebuffed him! What ailed her to be treating him to this tactic of distancing?

For the life of him, he could not accuse himself of having said or done anything to anger or distress her. On the contrary, had he not shown himself to be sympathetic to her difficulties—even interested? Was there not a natural empathy between them? He had thought so at least, and it had seemed as if Miss Hursley shared his belief.

To his chagrin, he felt aggrieved by her altered attitude. The more so because it was clear that the twins had taken her to their hearts. They might treat her to derision when she attempted to emulate their prowess at various games, but there had been no repeat of those efforts deliberately to tease her into reaction.

A guilty pang smote him. Had he not done exactly that? Was it perhaps his habit of teasing her into retort that had finally driven her to repudiate him? No, he would not believe that. For despite her cross remarks, she had been amused on occasion. Or had he entirely mistaken her? Perhaps she had not derived enjoyment in the encounters.

However it was, the absence of that hitherto friendly badinage gnawed at him. He began to wish that his sister might fulfil her intent of finding herself a husband. It was unlikely that she would approve Miss Hursley, for it was debatable whether his nieces were learning anything useful. Fairy stories and pin cushions were unlikely to equip them as accomplished brides in the admittedly distant future.

But whether Trixie intended to keep the wench or not, Julius at least would be free of her pervasive presence in his house. It was distinctly odd how a person could imprint their personality upon every part of a place, despite being physically confined to one area.

Sighing, Julius pulled his papers towards him and made another attempt to concentrate his attention upon the work in hand. He had just managed to absorb himself in the task, when a sudden battering on the door was succeeded by the entry into the room of Miss Prudence Hursley herself, out of breath and looking decidedly anxious.

'Pray help me, Mr Rookham! I have lost them!'

It had not been with unmixed emotions that Prue had sought out her employer. She was all too aware of having alienated him with that new reticence she had shown towards him. It had been necessary to remind herself that her object had been to distance him. Only she had not bargained for the distress it would occasion in her own breast.

But the twins having disappeared without trace, her natural instinct had been to rush to Mr Rookham for aid. Having entered the house by the side door, and deposited Folly in her parlour, she had sped along the corridor, her agitation overlaid with apprehension—and a curious feeling of relief. She could not blame herself for this meeting!

Mr Rookham jumped up immediately upon her entrance, his nose jutting out strongly, a frown upon his brow.

'Don't be absurd!' he barked. 'You cannot have lost them. I dare say they are hiding from you.'

Prue hesitated in the middle of the room, eyeing

him with wary dismay. His manner was altogether unfriendly.

'Perhaps they may be,' she ventured, 'but still I cannot find them.'

'I thought you were playing at battledore and shuttlecock. How have they evaded you?'

There was no diminution of the severity of his expression, and Prue's pulse began to beat in an uneven tattoo. She wondered vaguely how he had known that, and did not realise that she entwined her fingers together as she spoke.

'They tired of the game, for I was no match for either of them. And then they chose to play at hide-and-go-seek and—'

'Ah! I said they were hiding from you, did I not?'

'Yes, but they were not—not from me,' uttered Prue desperately. 'They were hiding from each other. Or so I thought. I kept my eye all the time upon the one who was searching, and they answered me when I called. Then I heard a cry— and then silence. I called and called, but there was no reply. What am I to think but that some misadventure has befallen them?'

Julius set his teeth. She was wearing that vulnerable look, and he was not going to let himself be touched by it! Nevertheless, he could not ignore such an appeal.

'Very well, we will go and look for them,' he said, crossing past her to the door. 'But I will lay you ten to one that they are merely playing one of their tricks.'

He opened the door, and gestured for her to precede him. He felt her constraint as much as his own as they went in silence to the front door and out into the gardens. He halted.

'Which way?'

'They were near your treillage garden,' Prue answered, starting off in that direction.

'Oh, were they?' came grimly from Mr Rookham.

'Pray don't scold them for it,' begged Prue, turning her head briefly. 'They did not go inside.'

'Well for them!'

Prue said nothing, feeling all the weight of his displeasure to be directed at herself rather than his nieces. There was no mistaking his mood, for his tone was as gruff and ill-tempered as he had shown himself that far-off day when she had first arrived at Rookham Hall. Instinct led her to keep her tongue, for she felt him to be dangerous.

With Julius in the lead, they started out through the laburnum tunnel and, by devious ways unknown to Prue, arrived at the treillage garden.

'Nothing here,' he said, having made a circuit around the trelliswork. He checked at the entrance. 'One moment.'

Prue watched him go inside, and heard immediately the deep notes of men talking. In a moment, Mr Rookham came out again, accompanied by two gardeners.

'Strike out towards the forest, Pudsey. And you, Garth, go and fetch Hessle from the rose garden, and the two of you cover the west side. I will take the upper portion here, including the Wilderness.'

The men nodded, and went off in separate directions. Julius watched them go, and then turned back to Miss Hursley.

'That should do it. Among the five of us, we should discover the little minxes soon enough.'

A measure of relief lessened a little of Prue's agitation. 'Ought we to call, do you think?'

'We will only alert them, if they are determined to hide.'

'But they won't hide from you, sir,' Prue pointed out.

Julius looked at her. He had not meant to say anything, but it slipped out before he could control the words.

'Unlike you?'

She flinched, looking away. 'Where should we go next?'

Her evasion touched him on the raw. 'Don't turn the subject! At least have the grace to answer me.'

Prue's lip trembled, and her heart felt as if it skipped several beats. She did not dare raise her eyes to his face.

'I cannot answer you.'

There was a pause. The silence seemed to pulse between them. Julius willed himself to hold back the tide of protest battering at his tongue. He turned back into the path.

'This way.'

The hammering in Prue's breast subsided a trifle, and she followed him towards a rise of curved stone steps, flanked by a fall of herbiage over the containing walls. At the top, the scene opened into a wide plain where a central portion was an ungainly mix of turned earth and rubble.

Julius saw the direction of her gaze, and felt impelled to explain it. 'There will be a maze here. I call it the Rockery, which is what it used to be.'

He pointed to where the edges of the garden rose in a graduated slope, dotted with coloured rocks where the greenery was interwoven. Here and there a few buds had opened, showing promise of a variety of colour.

Prue glanced at it but briefly. 'Yes, the girls told me that gardening is your passion.'

'I must show you a few of my designs some time.'

She looked back to find the steel eyes upon her. Involuntarily, she smiled. 'I should like that.'

Light flashed in his gaze, and Prue abruptly recollected herself—and their mission. She turned quickly away, and her eyes swept an arc about the garden. There was nowhere to hide.

'They are not here.'

'Obviously. We are only passing through.'

He headed off again, his pace quickening. Prue followed, stricken to silence again by the coldness of his tone. She began to wish she had not enlisted his aid. Only she had not known that he would show himself to be disturbed by her withdrawal. She could not prevent a stupid sort of elation from rising in her breast.

The way led them along a winding wall, traced with a climbing plant, and thence into a place she recognised the instant she saw the well. Here, indeed, were trees and shrubs enough to conceal a pair of determined children.

But Mr Rookham did not immediately set about a hunt among the various potential hiding places. He moved slowly to the well, and leaned upon the wall, looking down into its depths. Wondering if he supposed the children might have fallen in, Prue ran up to the edge, and peered in also.

'Surely they are too big to have got down there?'

Julius straightened abruptly. 'Can't you forget those wretched girls for a moment?'

The grey eyes widened. 'But that is why we are here.'

'I know it.'

His glance locked with hers, and there was a breathless pause. All thought of his nieces went right out of his head. Without volition, he spoke the thought in his mind.

'What has happened, Prudence? What have I done?'

Chapter Seven

The words were softly uttered, and Prue's will died. She could not bear to hurt him further. And Mr Rookham was hurt!

'Nothing, upon my honour! It is not you, sir, but I who am to blame.'

Julius heard the words, but it was the husky note in her voice that acted upon him. The well was between them, but he reached out and caught at her hand. His demand was urgent.

'What is it then, that you have done? Tell me, for I am at a loss to understand.'

She tried to pull her fingers out of his hold. The grip tightened. 'Pray let me go, sir.'

'Only if you promise not to run away from me.'

Prue shook her head. 'I will not run.'

Still he did not release her. 'And you'll explain?'

'I will try.'

He let her go, and she seized the fingers in her other hand, feeling them tingle. Her heartbeat was uneven, her mouth dry. But she had promised, and she had to speak out.

'Well?'

Prue flicked a glance at him, daunted once more by the renewed curtness in that one word. She sank down upon the edge of the well so that she need no longer face him.

'You see, I have forgotten my position, sir.'

Julius felt an instant stab of conscience. If she had forgotten her position, then so had he. Was it that which had made her so shy of him? He shot the words at her.

'You are not the only one. But what of it? Why should you not enjoy a little friendly conversation? Why should not I?'

She would not look at him. He noted the faint flush in her cheeks. Her voice was pitched low.

'I am a governess, sir. It is not fitting that I encroach upon my position. It can give rise to—to—'

To his own dismay, anger flooded him. He tried to speak without showing it, and signally failed.

'To what? Give rise to what?'

Prue's eyes shot up, and her tone strengthened. 'To misconceptions, Mr Rookham!'

'Upon your part, I suppose. Or is it mine?' He

flung away. 'I see what you are at! I knew it. I have known it all along.'

His gaze turned back upon her, and Prue blenched at the fierce look of him. Just like a hawk! With that jutting nose and those steely eyes. All gentleness was gone.

'I am too familiar, am I not, Miss Hursley? I wonder what I am after? Could it be that I am scheming to ensnare you? Are you now the object of my lusts?'

Colour flew into her cheeks, and she rose hastily from her perch. He took it that she meant to fly from him, and strode quickly over to seize her arm.

'No, you don't, my good girl! I will not suffer you to remove from here until I have your answer.'

'Let go of me!'

The tone was vibrant, for Prue was quite as furious as he. But he did not release her. He towered over her, as dangerous as he had been at the first moment of their meeting when she had run in front of his carriage.

'Is it what you think? Is it?'

Prue threw it at him, wholly defensive. 'Yes, if you must know! Only I would never have spoken of it in terms so disgracefully indelicate.'

Julius fairly flung her from him. 'I thank you for your intelligent reading of my character, but I beg to inform you that I am not yet reduced to such straits!'

Prue crumbled inside, and did not know how her eyes were instantly stricken. But Julius saw it, and the entirety of his fury collapsed. He threw out a hand, gripped by remorse.

'I didn't mean that! I was angry—outraged—I didn't know what I was saying.'

Her lip quivered, and that haunting little smile appeared. 'You need not apologise, sir. You have mirrored my own thoughts.'

He knew not what to say. She was unbearably hurt, and he had no means to undo the harm. He struggled to put his thoughts into words.

'Miss Hursley, this has been all a mistake. You must know how much enjoyment I have had in your company—brief as those moments have been. If I led you to suppose I am one of that brotherhood who take advantage of females in your situation, I cannot sufficiently regret it. I never meant to do so. I only—devil take it, what have I done?'

He took a turn about the well with hasty steps. Glancing at her, he saw with relief that the piteous look of those eyes had been replaced by her usual expression. Or nearly so. Was there yet a dimness there? How could he atone?

'Come, Miss Hursley, you must admit at least that you have felt a degree of pleasure in our little conversations.'

'Too much so,' she agreed, subdued.

Prue had gone numb now, and she could feel a dissatisfaction in her employer, in his restlessness. She must mend matters.

'I told you at the outset, Mr Rookham, that it was my own fault. I know that you only meant to be kind—and sometimes to tease. But it is not seemly in me to be seen to be at so much ease with my employer.'

Julius frowned in quick suspicion. 'Then it was not your notion? Who else, pray, could have put it into your mind?'

'No one, upon my honour,' protested Prue, vigorously shaking her head. The last thing she wanted was to draw Mrs Polmont's further enmity and spite by giving her up to her employer. In Mr Rookham's present mood, he would undoubtedly complain of it to her—and make matters worse.

'You see, we were warned at the Seminary,' she told him urgently, in a bid to divert his attention. 'And it was instilled into us that it was our own conduct that would determine whether we should be subjected to—to unwanted attentions.'

'I see.'

Julius found himself pacing again. It had not been the girl's fault. She was very young. How should she be able to see the difference between an amatory advance and mere friendliness? A rush of compassion seized him, and he turned back to her.

'Prudence, don't be so hard on yourself. You are condemned to a life of drudgery—here or elsewhere. Are you not to be permitted a modicum of enjoyment?'

Prue answered him with difficulty. 'If I allow myself such licence, sir, perhaps I will feel the more deprived at the lack of it—when I move on.'

Silence fell again, and Julius found the words echoing strangely in his head. *When I move on.* As she must, one day soon. Either with his sister, or to another post. He did not know that he smiled at her.

'Life is short. You should snatch its rare moments of pleasure where you can.'

Prue wanted to weep, but she did not know why. She found Mr Rookham was holding out his hand to her.

'Cry friends, Prudence. You are quite safe from me, I promise you.'

As if she did not know it! Prue gave him her hand, and as the warmth of his fingers closed over hers, she was sure she must succumb to the crushing weight at her chest.

But a sudden flurry of noise in the offing proved blessedly distracting. And productive of a surge of guilt. She had forgotten the twins, but here they were. She snatched her hand out of his.

'We found a nest of spiders, Uncle Julius!'

'There were millions and millions of them!'

'You should have seen them, Miss Prue, they ran all over everywhere.'

'And we couldn't catch them, for they were so fast—'

'They were mostly babies, and we wanted to bring one to show you, but—'

Prue shuddered, and was thankful to be spared further details by the intervention of Mr Rookham.

'Will you hold your tongues, your horrible little brats?'

'But, Uncle Julius—'

'Enough! I don't think Miss Prue cares to hear about spiders.' He turned to his head gardener, who was flanked by the other two men, one of whom must have been instrumental in the recovery of the twins. 'You'd best smoke them out, Hessle.'

A flood of protest greeted this suggestion, and the fellow nodded in a surly fashion. 'Ain't no call for you to go fretting, little missies. Leave 'em alone, and they'll soon be back in the nest. Only you don't want to go for catching spiders, for there are them as are poison.'

Predictably, the girls threw scorn upon this suggestion, and Prue felt it incumbent upon her to remove them from the scene. Saying that she would find some information about spiders so that they could see for themselves that the gardener spoke nothing but the truth, she shepherded them away towards the exit.

She could not resist glancing back as she stepped on to the path. To her acute disappointment, she saw that Mr Rookham was far too heavily involved in discussion with the three men to be interested in witnessing her departure.

The oppression of Prue's spirits continued throughout the remainder of the day. By the time she sat to prepare her lessons for the morrow, the suspicion of a headache began to nag at her. At last Dodo came in to the schoolroom to fetch Folly for his meal, and Prue thankfully left her work and made her way to her little parlour for dinner.

She found Mrs Polmont awaiting her. The light was fading outside, and the woman's face was partially in shadow despite the glow from the candelabrum that was always placed upon the mantel at this time. Yet Prue could feel the woman's malice.

'Oh, dear,' she muttered fretfully, 'am I late?'

The housekeeper moved forward, stepping into

the light. Her features were pinched, and her eyes glittered.

'There will be no dinner here tonight, Miss Hursley.'

Prue stared at her. 'I beg your pardon?'

'The master requests that you join him downstairs in the dining parlour.'

A rush of gratification deprived Prue momentarily of speech. But the face of the creature who had brought the news effectually brought her back to her senses. She felt a little sick, but she fought it, trying for an even note.

'Pray inform Mr Rookham that I have the headache. I would prefer to dine here, if you please.'

Mrs Polmont pursed her lips. 'It isn't as I please, ma'am. And if you choose to send back a message of that kind, I'm afraid you must take it yourself.'

Prue gathered her courage together. She would not dignify the woman's jealousy by acknowledging the inference behind her every word. 'What time does Mr Rookham dine?'

'In half an hour.' The features became more pinched. 'I should spend the time in dressing yourself more becomingly, Miss Hursley, or there won't be point in going down at all.'

It was beyond what anyone could endure. Prue's

temper flared. 'You take too much upon yourself, Mrs Polmont! Is it beyond your understanding that Mr Rookham means only kindness? If he sees nothing out of place in a friendly encounter, what call have you to cavil?'

A low laugh greeted this. 'I don't cavil, ma'am. I'm merely warning you. Anyone can tell you're an innocent. There's those as would see you to the slaughter without a second thought. But I'm not of their number.'

Incensed, Prue hit back strongly. 'I am not as innocent as you suppose, Mrs Polmont. But you do your master less than justice to think him capable of that sort of conduct. And if he was, there is nothing in my person to attract him!'

'Does there have to be? He's had no mistress for several years. Men have their needs, Miss Hursley. In the absence of wine, they will take water if they must. And they'll swear themselves blind they don't want it up until the last. Only by then it's too late—for you, ma'am.'

Prue felt herself trembling. 'Why are you doing this? Why do you tell me this?'

'I thought I said, Miss Hursley. I'm trying to help you.'

Yes, as a snake helps its victim! But Prue said nothing more. There was no point. What motivated the housekeeper she could not tell. She wanted only to get away, for the woman made her skin crawl. She took refuge in formality.

'That will be all, Mrs Polmont. I am going to my bedchamber.'

Retreating in haste, Prue hurried away down the corridor. The little parlour had been her only refuge. Now it felt soiled and no longer safe. The housekeeper had no respect for her privacy, and none at all for her position. She had no recourse but her own tongue, for inform Mr Rookham she could not. How could she repeat the substance of the woman's malicious words?

She could ascribe it only to jealousy, but that was insane. Of what had Mrs Polmont to be jealous? It was not as if she could aspire to the position that she persisted in supposing Mr Rookham intended for herself. After all, she was married. Or was she a widow? Not that it mattered. If by his own admission, the master of the house could not find anything to admire in the person of the governess, Prue could scarcely imagine that he might do so in that of his housekeeper.

The remembrance of Mr Rookham caused her to hurry into her bedchamber. Should she after all obey his summons to dinner? For it was a summons! He must know she could not think of refusing. How would she refuse? After what had passed between them today, she dared not.

She had said so to Mrs Polmont, but that was only in reaction to the creature's horrid manner. What if the woman had indeed taken her message downstairs? Prue almost trembled at the thought of Mr Rookham's likely reaction. He would be furious with her, and with good reason. There was no possible justification for what must be construed as an insult.

But when she looked at the contents of her meagre wardrobe, Prue was very nearly tempted to cry off immediately. She would look like a dowd in any one of the few gowns she possessed.

Well, what of that? Had not Mr Rookham made it abundantly plain that he did not find her attractive? It mattered little which gown she chose. Protocol, however, demanded that she at least make a change from the linsey-woolsey she had been wearing since the accident in the pond.

As she made ready, choosing a plain and demure gown of simple muslin—not in the white of a debutante, but of a discreet pale grey—she was unable to drive out of her mind an unpleasant echo.

In the absence of wine, they will take water...

Prue gazed at her reflection in the glass, shadowy in the half-light. A depression settled upon her spirits. She was persuaded that Mr Rookham had not so raging a thirst!

Within a few moments of entering the dining parlour, Prue knew that she had been foolish to consent. The place was lit only by several sets of candle sconces on the walls, and one candelabrum on the table set at that end where the meal was served. There was a chandelier above, but it was not in use. The atmosphere was all too cosy, despite the silent presence of the butler and a footman.

She was shown to a place at Mr Rookham's left hand, and he remained standing until she was seated—just as if she was not merely the governess, but an honoured guest.

He was dressed as she had never seen him, for the evening. Over black breeches he wore a coat of blue cloth, toning with the waistcoat beneath of a silken sheen, and his cravat was tied in a bow. Prue was both flattered and agitated.

He smiled a welcome as he settled into his own chair, and leaned towards her to speak in a lowered tone.

'I was half afraid you would refuse to come. Thank you!'

Prue knew not how to answer, and could only be thankful that Mr Rookham turned away to speak to Creggan. She had never been more glad of the necessity for servants to remain in the room.

The sensation of intimacy was unavoidable. Never in her life had she sat with a gentleman alone at table. Prue was stricken with a dreadful sense of wrongdoing, and in spite of all her courageous refutations, she found the fell words of Mrs Polmont repeating in her ears.

And they'll swear themselves blind they don't want it up until the last...by then it's too late...

Her pulse jumping, Prue busied herself with her napkin as Mr Rookham's glance returned to her face.

Julius watched the play of expression in the girl's features and wondered if he had been a fool. She was undoubtedly nervous. And he must suppose she had deliberately dressed down rather than up! Unless she possessed no more alluring a gown than this? If she had only chosen not to wear that atrocious cap, one might with advantage enjoy the soft brown curls that wisped out secretly from beneath it. And the half-light did her no disservice, setting a glow to her skin.

However, he had not asked her here for adornment! He had issued the invitation on impulse, catching sight of Polmont as he began on his way upstairs towards his bedchamber, where he had subsequently made a much greater alteration than usual in his dress. Or had it been impulse?

Ever since this morning thoughts of Miss Hursley had been hovering at the back of his mind. That ridiculous delusion she had been harbouring had preyed upon him. More affecting had been the memory of the look in her eyes when he had so disastrously rejected it. He had wanted to atone. Was his conscience then to blame for this situation—which was evidently a source of embarrassment to the girl? He must find a way to ease her.

He waited until both bowls had been filled with a sustaining white soup, and then picked up his spoon.

'Will you not begin, Miss Hursley?'

Prue started. So intent had she been on avoiding his gaze that she found herself staring at the contents of her bowl in an effort of concentration. As she fumbled for the utensil, the pressure of her own consciousness caused her to lose her guard.

'Oh, this is absurd! I must surely wake up soon and find that I am dreaming.'

A soft laugh came from her employer. 'Not unless I am dreaming too.'

Her glance found the steely glint of his eyes, and caution vanished. 'Why did you invite me here?'

Julius hesitated. Must she choose this moment for one of her disconcertingly direct questions? What was he to answer when he did not know himself? He opted for prevarication.

'I thought we agreed this morning on…friendship.'

The slight hesitation caused a disturbing hiccup to interrupt Prue's already unruly pulse. She hurried into speech.

'Oh, yes. It is kind of you, sir, to take me up.'

He was nettled. 'Kind? It is nothing of the sort!' He saw withdrawal in her face, and amended his tone. 'What I mean is that the invitation is for my pleasure as much as yours.'

Pleasure! Prue dug her spoon into the bowl. If this was his notion of pleasure, then it was not hers. She was acutely uncomfortable, beset as much by recurring doubt as by the impropriety of her situation.

'How the Duck would frown upon me!'

'I beg your pardon?'

She had been unaware of speaking aloud. Her eyes shifted again from the soup to his face where puzzlement creased his brow. Driven, she attempted to explain.

'We called her that—Mrs Duxford. At the Seminary, you know. She was in charge of us all.'

'Ah, I see. And you feel she would disapprove?'

'Beyond all doubt!'

'The governess dining with the master of the house. And all alone, bar the servants. Yes, I suppose it would be thought shocking by a great many of the tabbies.'

Prue blinked at him, for his tone had been musing. 'Had you not thought of that, sir?'

Julius spooned soup in a meditative way. 'I had not. Since I am rarely obliged to trouble myself about what others might think, I suppose I have grown out of the way of doing so.'

'You are fortunate,' observed Prue, unable to help a feeling of envy. 'But you are a man. It is all so very different for your sex.'

'Very true.'

He was both amused and touched by the forlorn note. But she was relaxing a little. He found a way to encourage her.

'Was she kind to you, this—er—Duck?'

Prue let out an involuntary giggle. 'How odd to hear you call her so! Kind? No, for she was excessively strict. But she was good to us, and always just, I think.'

'An admirable quality.'

'Well, it is important,' she insisted.

'I don't dispute it.'

He laid down his spoon and signed to Creggan to serve the next course. Reaching out to the bottle, he hesitated before refilling his glass.

'Will you take wine? Or is that a thought too daring for a governess?'

Another of her smothered gurgles rewarded him.

'Well, we were allowed a little on a Sunday. Mrs Duxford held to it that we might be called upon to take a glass now and then, and it would not do to draw attention to oneself.'

He paused in the act of pouring the ruby liquid into her glass. 'What, merely by drinking wine?'

'Oh, no. But if one was unused to the taste, one might choke or make faces.'

That quiver came at his mouth, and Prue saw it.

'It's well to laugh, sir, but it is true that one's first taste of wine is not at all pleasant. Did you not find it so?'

'It's so long ago, I can't remember.'

Prue eyed him with sudden interest as he finished pouring her wine. In the muted light of the dining parlour, she saw only smoothness in his face, and tried to remember whether she had noticed any lines there previously.

Mr Rookham caught her gaze, and frowned. 'What?'

'I was wondering how old you are,' Prue blurted out. Heat rose up in her face as she realised what she had said. 'I beg your p-pardon, sir! That was rude of me.'

Impelled by that irresistible look of contrition, Julius leaned towards her. 'Between friends, there can be no rudeness.'

It was softly uttered, and Prue experienced a resurgence of her earlier disquiet. Why must he speak so intimately? She was relieved to find the butler at her elbow, and turned to examine the dish he was offering. Nodding at random, she watched as a portion of collops was placed upon her plate. Stewed mushrooms and green beans followed, but they might have been anything for all Prue cared. They offered an excuse to withdraw her attention from her employer, and thus served her present purpose.

But the relief was all too temporary. The butler and his minion having withdrawn a little, Julius began upon the contents of his plate and resumed the discussion.

'How old do you think I am?'

The grey gaze veered round, filled with consternation.

'Pray don't, sir. I should not have asked you.'

'From the perspective of one and twenty,' he went on, as if she had not spoken, 'as I know you to be, Miss Prudence Hursley, I can well imagine that I might seem a trifle advanced in years.'

Prue blinked, diverted from her dismay. 'Advanced in years? I would not go so far as that, Mr Rookham.'

'Then how far would you go?'

To his amusement, a grimace appeared in her

face. Yet an odd sensation of suspense attacked him as she hesitated. She was going to place him older than his years, he was sure of it. He could not imagine why it should trouble him, but a rise of faint disappointment would not be dismissed.

'If you must have it,' she said at length, 'I must suppose you to be thirty, or a little past it.'

He said nothing for a moment, but the jut of his nose seemed to intensify. Prue eyed his strong features with growing misgiving.

'I have not guessed aright, have I?'

Julius reached for his wineglass. 'You are not far off.' He fortified himself with a sip of wine. 'In fact, I am eight and twenty. Until this moment past, I had been contented with an appearance of it. I now perceive that I must consult my mirror more closely.'

Torn between guilt and dismay, Prue defended herself vigorously. 'Well, you insisted upon my saying it! In the light of day I might not have put it as high.'

'Worse and worse! Surely you know that candle-light is kinder than daylight.'

'Well, I am sorry,' uttered Prue crossly. 'How was I to know that your vanity would be upset?'

'Upset? My vanity is crushed!'

'Then you will have learned a valuable lesson.

Vanity is one of the seven deadly sins, I will have you know.'

'No, you are thinking of pride.'

'Well, vanity is pride!'

'Spoken like a true governess!'

Prue burst out laughing. Watching her, and unable to help smiling himself, Julius experienced a glow of warmth at his chest. She truly was delightful! Without thinking, he reached out and lightly clasped her wrist.

'I promise I will refrain from all pride and vanity, since you so command me, Prudence.'

Her laughter died abruptly. She looked at his hand, where a burning heat seemed to girdle her wrist. The breath was stopped in her throat. Without volition, her gaze rose up and met his own head on. His expression changed.

'What is it? Are you afraid of me still? Don't you see that I like you too much to treat you with less than the respect you deserve?'

The word caught at her senses, and she felt suddenly as if she floated. *He liked her.*

'You smile, but it's true. God knows where it originated, but I feel a kinship with you. A friendship. I say it again, for it is the only way I can describe it.'

Prue had not been aware of smiling. But the

abrupt lift of happiness dimmed. Somewhere deep inside she was weeping. Only the cause of it demanded acceptance. She must take the proffered half of the loaf, for the whole could never be hers.

'Thank you, Mr Rookham. I feel it too.'

She treasured the sudden leaping spark at his eyes. He released her, and took up his wineglass, that engaging quirk upon his lips.

'Then here's to defiance of your Duck, and all her ilk!'

Prue raised her own glass, and drank a little of the wine as she watched Mr Rookham toss back the contents of his glass. His long hair fell back, and she allowed her gaze to dwell for an instant on the powerful jutting profile that had become, inexplicably, so haunting a feature of her waking mind.

It was an effort to maintain her calm for the remainder of the meal. Afterwards she could not remember what they talked of—his gardens, perhaps, and had he not asked her more about her life at the Seminary? If so, she had spoken automatically, for the discovery she had made had delivered her up to a painful yearning that was bursting for expression.

What had Mrs Polmont said? If he could not have wine, he would take water. She had been wrong. Mr Rookham did not want water. And it was Prue who craved wine now, with a thirst that could never be quenched.

The expedition to the woods had as its aim the collecting of wildflowers to be pressed for a work of art. The twins raced ahead, swishing through dead bracken and leaves with hardly a check. Proceeding at a more sober pace, Prue sensibly abandoned any attempt to curb their exuberant spirits, bidding them only to keep within sight. A superfluous request, as it proved; since Prue had had the forethought to provide herself with a basket, the girls returned time and again to canvass her opinion and place each new acquisition into this convenient receptacle.

The moments of solitude placed a severe strain upon Prue's peace of mind, leaving her thoughts at too much leisure. Against her will—indeed, against her express command!—they strayed into that impossible world of her wayward imagination. A place where words were spoken that could never be uttered; where things were done in visions that made her ashamed.

It was all the fault of the housekeeper! Had she not pressed the matter in a fashion that must cause an idiot to understand her veiled references, Prue would never have dared upon such thoughts.

Indeed, it would not have occurred to her to do so—particularly with reference to Mr Rookham. He was so far above her that she ought more appropriately to have yearned after the footman!

But, oh, those fanciful dreams! Ever since that fatal dinner all too short a time ago. Four days? No, five, for it was Wednesday. Six weeks since she came here—a time impossibly short. Yet it had proved long enough to hurl Prue into a lost sea of merging days and hideously troubled nights.

Where had the dreams come from? It was as if Kitty's vivid thinking had invaded her own head. For had it not ever been Kitty who had mooned over the thought of being held in a man's embrace, of being *kissed*?

A wash of heat coursed through her veins, engulfing her in guilty warmth. Fiercely she lashed herself. Prudence Hursley, you are wicked! What would her reverend father have to say to her, could he see inside her foolish head from beyond the grave? Mama she barely recalled. But often and often had she been struck with a remembrance of a stern eye she knew to be Papa's when the Duck had bent upon her one of her more serious frowns.

The thought of Mrs Duxford caused her to blank off the hazy image that haunted her mind. How many times had she given warning? 'Make no mistake. You will be tempted.' And Prue had foolishly thought herself immune.

Heaven knows she wished she had been! It was not as if Mr Rookham was handsome. Kitty would have dismissed him from her mind without a second thought. But Prue was guiltily aware that his attraction had drawn her from the very first. Why, she could not tell. One could not admire the lean rangy figure or the jutting nose. And there was nothing remarkable to recommend him in his dress, which was plain and serviceable. His manner, too, was so apt to be changeable that one could never rely upon receiving the same treatment from him. Indeed, now she thought about it, there was no reason in the world why she should have formed so foolish a *tendre* for the man!

At which thought a hiccuping sob threatened to erupt from her throat, and she was relieved to see the twins flying back, waving flowers of pink and yellow.

'These are pretty, Miss Prue,' said Lotty as she placed one in the basket. 'What are they?'

Prue had been obliged to call to mind all her scanty botanical lore, for the girls had little understanding of English plants and were inclined to disparage the lack of variety in the wildflowers they had found.

'Primroses. Does not your uncle have them in his gardens?'

'Uncle Julius never tells us nothing about his flowers,' said Dodo scornfully.

'Have you ever asked him?'

Both twins blinked at her. Then Lotty grinned. 'He don't like us to plague him, you know that, Miss Prue.'

Dodo was counting the different colours in the basket. 'Six blue, two purple. And only one pink. Look, Lotty, there's too many yellow! Why is everything in England all yellow?'

Lotty instantly disputed this assumption, declaring that green was the predominant colour, which was why England differed so much from the countries they had lived in. Dodo paid no heed, picking out one of many flowers they had collected with a globular head of yellow.

'There's too many of these. What are they again, Miss Prue?'

'Lavender cotton,' said Prue, removing the delicate plant from the child's unfriendly fingers. 'You must not poke it so, Dodo, or it will fall to pieces before we can press it.'

'Who cares? We've got lots and lots of them.'

Lotty frowned disapprovingly at the flower. 'See, that's silly. How can it be called Lavender when it's yellow? Lavender isn't yellow.'

'Very true,' agreed Prue in a placating sort of way, 'but perhaps it is the cotton that makes it yellow.'

'I don't see how. I shall ask Uncle Julius.'

'A very good notion,' agreed Prue, aware of a faint tremor in her voice—and a slight chill in her body.

An abrupt realisation caused her to dismiss all thought of Mr Rookham. She cast a glance at the darkening sky.

'Oh, dear, the sun has gone in.'

How remiss of her not to have noticed it before! That was what came of allowing her thoughts to stray in dangerous directions.

But they had set out on a perfect spring day, warm enough to dare the expedition with only a light covering. The twins had on short cloaks over their usual blue gowns, and Prue had herself ventured forth clad only in the grey Seminary uniform, which had been returned to her refreshed and neatly laundered. It had been a point of courtesy, Prue felt, to resume wearing it, despite finding in herself a newfound distaste for the garments that had received so severe a wetting.

The ominous greying of the clouds mocked her now, threatening a second drenching. The twins, she discovered, had no thoughts to spare for the changing weather. They were squabbling over who had found the most flowers. Prue broke in without ceremony.

'We must start back. I am afraid it is going to rain.'

A flood of protest was nipped in the bud by an abrupt spitting from the skies. Both girls turned up their faces to catch the spots. Prue attempted to steer them homewards.

'Pooh, it's only a drizzle!'

'Look, I can get them on my tongue!'

'Girls, we must get home!'

They consented to walk, but at a crawling pace, stopping every moment as they vied with each other upon the cleverness with which each sought to capture the fleeting drops. Impatience itched at Prue as she cast another apprehensive look upon the lowering clouds.

There was a sudden flash, forking through the sky. Gasping with fright, the twins froze, clutching at Prue.

'Lightning!'

'There is a storm coming!'

Sure enough, a low rumble in the distance rapidly grew in volume, ending in a fearful crack almost above their heads.

Prue's heart was hammering, but her only thought was for the now whimpering twins. She must get them to shelter! Her eyes pierced the woody thicknesses around them. Too many trees. They would be safer in more open country, but she did not know in which direction she should go to find it.

There was another flash, followed almost immediately by the echoing thunder behind. And then the heavens opened.

The girls abruptly broke away, running for the nearest tree. Prue dropped the basket and started after them.

'No! Not under the trees! Come back!'

But she had to seize both of them, forcibly pulling them to a stop. They were crying, but Prue had no time to deal gently with their natural fright.

'Stop it at once! This is no time for tears. You must be strong, do you understand?'

Lotty made a valiant effort to swallow her sobs, but Dodo wailed mightily. Prue took her by one shoulder and dealt her a light slap on the cheek. The child gasped, her tears arrested.

'Ouch!'

Prue nodded, only half aware of the battering rain upon her bonnet and face. 'That's better. Now, follow me!'

Turning, she led them back out onto the path, and once again searched the surrounding area. Within the forest on the other side, she spied a fallen log.

Grabbing the twins, she made for it, as swiftly as she could for the clinging bracken below.

Within a few minutes, she had sat the girls down in a little hollow formed by a dead branch against the trunk, and was busily employed in gathering bracken to form a roof above it. She was oblivious to the intermittent thunder grumbling overhead, as much as to the soaking of the rain into her garments. All her attention was for the protection of the twins. She was panting with effort by the time Lotty from within informed her that it was now relatively dry inside their improvised shelter.

'You better come in now, Miss Prue.'

At which point, Prue became conscious of her sodden state. Would she not take the rain in with her? Besides, she did not think there was room for an adult. Nevertheless, she could not remain here, standing in this downpour as the momentum of the storm grew, whipping at the leaves.

'I will try for another place,' she told the girls. 'Stay there until I come for you.'

Her progress back to the path was distressingly slow, aware as she had now become of her own discomforts. The rain had already soaked through her jacket to the skin, although her layers of petticoats afforded limited protection. They were rapidly gathering moisture, however, weighting heavily about her legs as she trudged through the bracken, assailed by a horrible feeling of *déjà vu*.

But as she emerged from the trees, she heard the sound of fast-moving feet. Straining into the sheeting rain, she spied someone coming towards her. Attired in a bulky greatcoat with a hat upon his head, he looked to be a working man.

Without hesitation, Prue hailed him. He checked. Then catching sight of Prue, he hurried towards her. He was of sturdy build, and, for what she could see under the driving rain, of middle years. His voice was heavily accented in the local burr.

'What be ye doin' out in this, missie?'

'I was walking with the girls in my charge,' Prue told him, loud against the hammer from the heavens. 'We have come from Rookham Hall. Pray can you help us?'

'Is that the master's little 'uns? Twins they be, as I heard.'

'Yes, indeed. But is Mr Rookham your master?'

'I be forester here, and these be his lands, missie.'

Relief flooded Prue. She dashed the wet from her face. 'How far are we from the Hall, do you know?'

'Too far, if you was thinking o' going now.'

He looked up, and Prue realised that the rain had lessened. Was this the end of it? It was apparent that the forester did not believe so.

'Do you think it will come on heavy again?'

The fellow nodded. 'Aye. Seems I'd best take you to the hut yonder. I was going there meself.'

'You have a hut nearby? Oh, thank heaven!'

She led him to where the twins were hidden, and with his assistance, freed them quickly. They eyed him at first askance, clinging to their governess's wet form. But the man only glanced at them, and immediately led the way beyond their little shelter, weaving through the trees.

It was not long before the hut became visible ahead, a rough construction of thorny wood and straw with a thatched roof. But already the rain was thickening again, and Prue was relieved to be able to usher the girls inside and herself get into the dry.

The little hut was dim within, lit only by one small window open to the elements. It was also cold, and as her eyes became accustomed, Prue discovered that the girls were shivering. She was herself excessively wet, but no thought of her own danger entered her head. She turned to the forester, who was busy with a pile of straw or grasses.

'Have you any sacking? I must try to keep the girls warm.'

The forester was ahead of her, indicating where he had already created a bed of sorts, into which he suggested that all three should huddle.

Prue shook her head. 'I am too wet. I shall only make the girls damp, and there is not room enough for three.'

So the twins bedded down in the straw, now hugely enjoying the adventure, and Prue covered them over. The forester did indeed have sacking, which he insisted upon placing around Prue's own shoulders. It afforded little warmth, but she was grateful for the man's kind thought and thanked him prettily as she sank down upon a heap of grasses.

To pass the time, and to distract the twins from a quarrel over whether one of them had stolen straw from the other, Prue offered to tell them a story.

By the time the storm at last ceased, she had been obliged to dredge up half a dozen tales from a wayward memory, and had fallen back upon rhymes and nursery songs. Prue's voice was cracking, and she was shivering uncontrollably. Nothing could have been more welcome to her ears than the forester's considered pronunciation.

'Seems like it's over, missie.'

'Thank heaven!' She moved to extract the twins. 'Pray, would you be so kind as to lead us home?'

With hands that shook, Prue dragged off her ill-fortuned Seminary uniform. Having handed the twins over to a scandalised Yvette, she had made her way to her own chamber, bedraggled and worn.

With her charges safe, she was able to turn attention to her own condition, and found she had barely strength to get herself undressed. How she longed for a repeat of that far-off day when her sodden body had been immersed into a steaming bath. But it was not to be on this occasion, for her situation was unknown this time to the author of that instruction.

The forester had left them at the start of the gardens, and they had gained the house without anyone seeing them, coming in by a side door. Once she had the twins in their bedchamber, Prue had rung for the Frenchwoman, knowing that however furious Yvette might be, she would attend to the needs of her nurslings better than Prue could.

Nevertheless, she had already persuaded them out of most of their wet clothes before the nurse arrived. Yvette had listened in unconcealed fury, black eyes snapping, as Prue had explained their unfortunate predicament. Protesting in voluble French, Yvette had announced her intention of stripping the twins down and huddling them into towels. She then turned on Prue herself.

'Eef you are wise, *mam'zelle*, you also weel take off ze clothes *toute de suite*.'

Advice with which Prue had been in complete

agreement. Leaving the girls to Yvette's competent ministrations, she had made the best of her way to her chamber, and at last discovered her own sorry state. The remembrance of that earlier disastrous wetting could not but obtrude, but Prue shrank from requesting assistance.

For no consideration would she expose herself to the scornful taunting of Mrs Polmont. The house-keeper would not help her without positive instructions from the master of the house. And nothing in the world would persuade Prue to sue to Mr Rookham. What would he think of her?

Not that she was to blame this time, for no one could have foreseen that such an apparently fine day would turn sour so quickly. But he would undoubtedly amuse himself at her expense. To be found once again in this distressingly wet condition? No, he must not know of it.

A sneaking little voice deep down within her conscience belied her. Would he not be angrier for her *not* seeking his help? He would think her foolish beyond permission to suffer in silence, when she knew well that he would insist upon her receiving every possible assistance did he know of her plight. Only she could not let him know it.

How could she tell him that her wits had gone wool-gathering, indulging in such foolish fancies that she had not noticed the changing condition of the weather? She might well have had ample time to return to the Hall had she not been so self-indulgent. Guilt swamped her as she towelled herself dry before the cold ashes in the grate, kicking aside the heap of sodden clothes.

Abruptly, a wave of weakness swept over her, and she staggered blindly to the bed. Falling upon its surface, she gathered the quilt up around her, and for an endless while lay shivering, fighting the dizzying sensation of faintness.

After what seemed an age, she managed to drag herself up and sought under the pillows for her nightgown. Tugging it on, Prue thrust herself under the bedclothes, pulling them up around her shuddering frame.

Chapter Eight

Someone was shaking her shoulder. Prue struggled to open her eyes, which felt unbearably heavy. Like the thick fog in her head which prevented coherent thought.

'Miss! Miss, wake up!'

A pale blurry face appeared above her. Prue found it vaguely familiar, although the features remained unclear. She tried to answer.

'Wh-what is it?'

'It's nigh on five o'clock, miss, and the master is expecting you for dinner.'

Prue blinked bleary eyes. The thought of food made her tired. 'Pray tell him I cannot eat.'

There was a pause, and Prue thankfully closed her aching lids. But a tickle at her nose made itself felt, and she let out a violent sneeze.

The face retreated, and a disembodied voice delivered itself of a sage pronouncement.

'You've caught cold, miss, if you ask me. And no wonder, caught out in the rain like that.'

Prue was struggling with the gathering moistures, hunting desperately under her pillows for a handkerchief. The visitor seemed to divine her need, for she heard rattling and a muttered question.

'Now where does she keep them?'

'In the top shelf, on the right,' Prue uttered, realising that the girl must be searching in the press.

In a few moments one of her supply of cotton cloths—hemmed in Nell's neat stitch—was put into her hand. She clutched it gratefully, and mopped at her nose. But she was possessed of a creeping lethargy, and even this small action was an effort.

'Dearie me,' fussed the face, once more bending over her. 'Seems I'd best fetch Mrs Polmont to you.'

Panic thrust in upon Prue, and she half-rose in the bed. 'No! Pray don't bring her here.'

'Mrs Polmont, miss? But it's her business to look to you.'

Too little mistress of herself to consider her words, Prue thought only of prevention.

'For pity's sake, don't let her come in to me! She will say such things, and look at me in that hideous way she has, and I have not strength to withstand her now.'

There was puzzlement in the girl's tone. 'But someone has to know, miss, as you're not fit. Seemingly Mrs Polmont ought to tell the master.'

With an effort, Prue managed to sit up. She recognised the maid now, the same who had helped her on the last occasion. She reached out to her as a name floated into her head.

'Pray don't tell him, Maggie. Or if you must, send to him by Creggan rather than Mrs Polmont.'

'I suppose I could ask Jacob to do that. He's the footman, miss.'

'Yes, do so, if you will. But say only that I have a little cold in the head and will keep abed until morning.'

'If you say so, miss.'

Was there doubt in the voice? She could not tell. It was superseded by a new thought forcing its way into her sluggish mind.

'The girls! Are they all right?'

'Merry as grigs, miss,' replied Maggie, laughing. 'It'd take more than a bit o' wet to put them two out of frame!'

Relieved, Prue sank back upon her pillows. 'Does Mr Roo—does the master know about them being caught in the rain?'

'That Frenchie went and told him.' The maid hesitated, frowning. 'Now I think of it, seemingly she never said nothing about you, miss, for the master ain't asked after you. Only he sent for you to come to dinner.'

There was no question of going down to dinner. Prue knew she could not even stand up. She was vaguely aware that there was another, more cogent, reason why she should not go.

'You must make my excuses, if you please.'

'Very well, miss. And shall I bring you something up? A little broth, perhaps? They do say as you should feed a cold.'

Prue shook her head. 'I feel cold, but I am not hungry, only thirsty.'

The maid tutted in sympathy and promised to bring up a jug of lemonade. Then it went quiet and Prue deduced that she must have left the chamber. But a pattering sound came to her ears, and next moment Folly landed on the bed. Mewing at her, he trotted up to the pillow and thrust an investigative nose into her cheek.

Prue brought out a wavering hand to stroke him, but was taken with a fit of shivering which sent Folly retreating to the end of the bed, where he sat, the green eyes bewildered.

'Poor mite,' she murmured regretfully. 'I'm so sorry.'

And then a wave of heaviness engulfed her head. Prue was aware only of this, and shivers that intermittently attacked her from head to foot. She felt feverish, and although a little dribble of moisture had to be dealt with from time to time, it was not at all as if she had a cold. It was excessively uncomfortable, but Prue took a morbid satisfaction in what she conceived to be a fitting punishment.

Had she not been so stupidly engaged upon daydreaming, she would not have been caught in the rain. Her only consolation lay in having taken sufficient care of the twins to ensure that they were not similarly suffering. That would have been infinitely worse to bear.

Once or twice she heard Folly's plaintive mew, and tried to open her eyes. But the kitten was not on the bed, and she had not strength to pull herself up to discover his whereabouts. When she at last heard the door opening, she made a heroic effort to secure the animal's welfare.

'Pray—whoever it is—take the kitten to the girls. They must look after him for me, for I cannot manage—'

'Do stop fretting, miss,' came from the same young maid who had come up before. 'I'll take him to the kitchens, for I daren't for my life put him in with that Frenchie.'

Disturbed by the disembodied voice, Prue raised her head and blinked across the room. The maid was on her knees.

'What are you doing?'

'Laying down wood for the fire, miss. The master's orders. There's a hot brick on the way, too, and what the master calls a "toddy".'

Prue's eyes pricked, and she had recourse to her handkerchief—and not on account of the moistures. Had she not known it? He would order whatever he could for her deliverance. He truly was the kindest of men. Oh, how she wished she had never come here!

Maggie's features popped into view above her, sporting a cheery grin. 'If you ask me, miss, the master has a soft spot for you. He come down to the kitchen himself, only to tell Mrs Wincle how to make this toddy. And then I'm blowed if he doesn't stay and insist upon making it himself!'

This intelligence almost overpowered Prue. She sniffed dolefully into her handkerchief, hoping desperately that Maggie would attribute her distressed state to nothing more than her illness. Apparently she did, for her features became solemn again and she tutted.

'In a bad way, aren't you, miss? Are you thirsty? Here, you'd best take a little of this lemonade.'

Prue gulped gratefully from the proffered glass, and her head cleared a trifle. She felt the maid tuck the bedclothes more securely about her.

'Thank you.'

'It's no trouble, miss. Is there aught else I can do for you? Are you warm enough?'

'I should be, but I keep shivering.'

'Dearie me, don't say you have a fever. You look downright peaky, and that's a fact.'

Prue crumpled the handkerchief in her hand. 'It's only that my head feels so hot.'

Maggie's face vanished and Prue closed her eyes. In a moment, she felt a coolness at her brow.

'I've wrung out a cloth in your basin, miss.'

The relief was immediate, and Prue sighed her thanks.

'Now then, pet, let's take care of you.'

A protesting mewl and the sound of a softly closing door gave Prue to understand that Folly had been removed along with the maid. He would be safe with Maggie, she thought thankfully.

Presently she drifted, losing track of time. And then there was movement at the side of the bed and a sudden sensation of heat. Her head was raised, and someone was bidding her drink. Warmth was at her lips, and she sipped upon a taste strongly sweet, with an afterkick that made her cough.

'What is that?'

'Don't ask questions!' said a peremptory voice. 'Just drink it and be thankful. In a very short time, you will be sleeping like a baby.'

Prue forced her eyes open. It could not be Mr Rookham! Only it was. His face was a shadow against the candle glow in the background, but she could see the outline of his ragged hair and the glitter of his steely eyes.

In her semi-dreaming state, Prue had no defences. And no will against the force of him, right up there above her where he should not be.

'Drink,' he said again.

'Must I?'

'Come now, it is for your own good.'

Obediently, Prue sipped again, and this time found the tang less strong. She struggled up onto her elbow, and tried to take the glass into her own hand. Her fingers came into contact with his, and a buzzing warmth slid into her head.

'You should not do this.'

She was unaware of having spoken, but a soft laugh floated between them.

'It would shock your Duck, I dare say. I shall

remain, however, until you have drunk all of my medication.'

So saying, he urged the cup once again to her lips, and Prue perforce had to partake of its contents. She managed a few more mouthfuls before weakness overcame her. Her fingers dropped away and she sank back onto her pillows.

'No more, I pray you.'

There was a moment of hesitation, and then he set the cup down upon her bedside table.

'Very well. You have probably taken enough to do the trick, but I shall leave the rest here. If you wake in the night, drink it all down and I guarantee you will sleep again.'

Prue felt the bed shift as his weight was removed from the side. A sensation of loss attacked her. To hide it, she retreated further under the covers.

'Good night, my poor Prue.'

It was softly uttered, and Prue's heart swelled. There was movement in the room. Then the door latch clicked, and she was left to silence and a feeling of aching loneliness.

Having been out for his usual morning's exercise on horseback, Julius was partaking of a late breakfast. Digging his fork into a substantial helping of ham that accompanied a couple of poached eggs on the platter before him, he turned his attention to his butler, who was pouring him out a cup of coffee.

'Creggan, have you news of Miss Hursley's condition this morning?'

The butler shook his head, laying down the coffee pot. 'I have not been informed, sir. Would you wish me to institute enquiries?'

'No, don't trouble. I will go up myself.' Something in Creggan's immobile features made him add a rider. 'I ought, in any event, to check those imps are none the worse for wear.'

Now why had he said that? He watched Creggan shift to the dresser and slice bread from the fresh baked loaf. Why must he account for his movements to his own butler? Was it unnatural in him to wish to know how the governess fared? Yes, of course it was! But then Prudence had become, by degrees—or was it leaps and bounds?—much more than a governess. He counted her a friend, and it seemed the most natural thing in the world to have gone in to her last night with his potion.

Only Prudence had herself deprecated his presence—even at a moment when she was obviously unwell and not herself. Strictly speaking, it was the height of impropriety to be in her bedchamber at all. But then Miss Hursley was not a debutante, nor he a raw youth of fashion. There were no gossips here, and no question of compromise. Yet he must feel himself at fault to be making excuses to his butler!

He accepted two of the proffered slices of bread, transferring them to his side plate and spreading on butter with a lavish hand. He sipped at his coffee in a meditative way.

It was not the first time he had been in her room, he recalled. There had been that other time with the episode of the frogs. But there had been every excuse on that occasion. Who could blame him for investigating the cause of a scream? And no man of honour would refuse his assistance in such a case on the score of impropriety. Besides, the governess had been decently clad in a dressing-gown, and had not been in bed.

Here his conscience smote him. He had known she was in bed last night, and there had been no perceived excuse for his entering her bedchamber only to give her a drink. Any one of the female servants might have acted as his deputy. Only no-one could have ascertained to his satisfaction the true nature of her condition.

Annoyed to find that the matter had been of so much importance to him, Julius attacked an egg with such ferocity that it shot off the plate, spattering yolk across the pristine whiteness of the covers.

'Hell and damnation!'

He half rose from his chair, but Creggan moved smoothly in, armed with suitable implements.

'Allow me, sir.'

Julius reseated himself, taking a moody swig of coffee as he watched the butler remove the offending egg together with the worst traces of its ravages. He regarded the remaining contents of his breakfast platter with a jaundiced eye.

Before he could make up his mind whether or not to instruct Creggan to remove it, an interruption occurred. The door opened, and Julius briefly saw the disgruntled features of the nurse Yvette before the butler moved to intercept her.

A brief muttered colloquy—Creggan attempting to prevent the woman's entrance, he made no doubt!—was enough to inform him that unusual circumstances must lie behind this unprecedented move. He intervened.

'Let her come in, Creggan.'

The butler stood aside. With a sinking heart, Julius watched the advance of the fierce little Frenchwoman. Not for the first time, he was struck with a passing pang of sympathy for his nieces. They were abominable minxes, but it was a trifle hard on them to be under the rule of this diminutive tartar.

'Eet ees as I sink, *monsieur*,' began the black-eyed female in her cross-grained tone. 'Ze *enfants*, zey 'ave now zees cold in ze nose.'

'Ah, have they?' replied Julius mildly. 'Are you keeping them in bed?'

'In bed, yesse. *Naturellement*, I make *tout ce qu'on demande* for make zem well. But zees I do not come to say. I come of zees *gouvernante* zat I weesh to complain, *monsieur*.'

Julius became conscious of his own stiffening, and a spark ignited in his breast.

'Yes?' he enquired dangerously.

His manner had no apparent effect upon the nurse. Her eyes snapped with anger. 'She 'ave take zem in ze rain! *Je me demande*, why? 'Ave she not ze room for teach zem? Yesse, she 'ave ze room. You 'ave give her ze room, *monsieur*. She 'ave use ze room, I ask myself? *Mais, non*! She 'ave not use ze room. She take zem in ze rain! Why, and again why? *Mais, qu'elle est folle*!'

Even had he wanted to, Julius was given no opportunity to interrupt this rapid speech. As it was, he found himself unable for several moments to utter a word. Not because he had nothing to say, but because he was obliged to reject every utterance that sprang to his mind as being wholly out of context and proportion to the event.

Everything in him urged him to jump to the defence of Prudence Hursley. He wanted to berate the nurse for daring to criticise her. To tell her, in his iciest tone, that the governess was worth a dozen of the nurse; that her charges would undoubtedly give Miss Hursley the preference, was their opinion to be canvassed; and that it would be the worse for her if one further word of disparagement was to cross her lips.

His whole reaction was ridiculous, and he knew it. Worse, it argued a partiality that far exceeded the reality of his feeling towards the girl. And further, it could not be denied that there was justice in the complaint.

The nurse was waiting, a frown gathering between her black orbs. Julius pulled his wits together.

'I shall come up and see the twins shortly. You may confine yourself to your duties, Yvette, and—er—leave the other matter in my hands.'

Surprise flickered for a moment in the nurse's lined features. She gave a nod, and bobbed a curtsy.

'I weel prepare ze *enfants* zat you come, *monsieur*.'

He watched the woman march out, and let his breath go as Creggan closed the door behind her. The butler caught his eye as he came across to the table.

'More coffee, sir?'

Julius pushed away his plate. 'Thank you, yes.'

Creggan raised an eyebrow, and the faintest note of sympathy entered his voice. 'French, sir. Excitable nation.'

A glimmer of amusement broke through Julius's inner tension. 'Just so.'

He took up the refilled cup and sipped at the hot liquid. Creggan removed his half-empty plate without comment, and he was thankful for the man's discretion. Not that he supposed the butler to have any clue to his chaotic thoughts. The irrational anger had stilled, thank God! But it had left him with some uncomfortable reflections.

By no stretch of the imagination could it be argued that Prudence Hursley was a suitable preceptress for his nieces. They clearly liked her—as who would not?—but whether they were learning anything useful was debatable.

He had seen them at battledore and shuttlecock; he had found them listening to fairy tales; and only the other day he had caught the governess making daisy chains while the twins were flying a kite. Indeed, as far as he could see, the three of them spent most of their time in idle pursuits out of doors—like yesterday! What in the world had Prudence thought to teach them on such an excursion? Botany, perhaps? If so, it was unlikely to be of the least use to their intended future. It was all of a piece, and he truly did not know if he could in conscience recommend that Trixie keep the girl on.

There was a sneaking suspicion at the back of his mind that it would suit him better if his sister let Miss Hursley go. He ought to banish it, for his needs were not in question. The trouble was that he liked the governess too much for his own good. If Trixie kept her, he would be bound to see her— and that in circumstances which would preclude his enjoying the freedom with which he was wont to address her. Which would be unfair to her, after all that had passed between them. Her departure to another post, where he need not encounter her at all, might be the kindest solution.

Curiously, this neat disposal of the problem left Julius with a feeling of dissatisfaction. He suppressed it, and rose from the table with the intention of going to visit his nieces.

But as Creggan was about to open the door for him, a whispering commotion on the other side drew his attention. An irritated frown entered the butler's face and he plucked open the door. Behind it, Julius spied the bulky form of his cook, with a maid at her back, peeping over her shoulder.

Creggan's shocked disapproval was patent.

'Mrs Wincle!'

'Begging your pardon, Mr Creggan,' began

Wincle with a determined air, 'but see the master I must, and see him I will!'

Another domestic complaint? It was one of those mornings, Julius decided resignedly. He intervened before the butler could gather himself to reject this unprecedented invasion.

'Come in, Wincle.'

The cook bustled in, rubbing her hands on her apron. The maid hung back, eyeing Creggan doubtfully, but Wincle caught at her sleeve and drew her into the room. Much to Julius's amusement, she then waved pudgy fingers in the butler's face.

'Private this is, Mr Creggan, if you don't mind.'

It was plain that the butler objected mightily, but Julius was too intrigued to give this any weight. He signed to Creggan to withdraw. Wincle watched until the door shut behind him, with a meticulous care that showed the man's disgust, and then turned at last to her employer.

Julius moved back to the table and leaned negligently upon the back of a chair. 'What is it, Wincle? I imagine it must be a matter of moment.'

Wincle nodded, her ruddy features suffused with concern. 'I don't rightly know as it is, sir, only there's something going on as I don't hold with, and that's a fact.'

Her manner struck him as indignant rather than

portentous. Which might explain why she had not made her approach through Polmont in the customary manner.

'Very well, Wincle, what is it?'

'It's Miss Hursley, sir. Leastways, it's her as is affected, and it ain't nowise what you'll like to hear.'

A sharp pang of fear sliced into Julius's chest. He straightened up and rapped out a smart command. 'Go on!'

Wincle hesitated, however, fiddling with her apron. 'Seemingly, it's Maggie here as ought to tell it to you, sir. She it is who's been tending her.'

Julius eyed the maid, whose cheeks became a trifle flushed. 'How is Miss Hursley this morning?'

The maid looked distressed. 'She's bad, sir.'

A hollow opened up inside his chest. He felt his voice go hoarse. 'How bad?'

'I can't say, sir, only she's that hot with the fever, and tossing and turning. And—well, sir—'

The maid hesitated, wriggling a little, and it was plain that she had more to add. Impatience warred with anxiety. Julius curbed his tongue with difficulty, and tried for a calm he was far from feeling.

'Just tell me, if you please.'

'She ain't in her right mind!' broke from the girl in a rush.

Julius experienced a short, but hideous feeling of dread. And then common sense reasserted itself.

'You mean she is delirious?'

The maid looked puzzled. 'I don't rightly know, sir.'

He tried another tack. 'What makes you think she is not in her right mind?'

Again the girl hesitated, but Wincle nudged her sharply.

'Go on and say it, Maggie.' She turned back to Julius. 'She come and told me in my kitchen, sir, and I couldn't reconcile it with my conscience not to come to you straight.'

Julius frowned. 'Why didn't you go directly to Polmont?'

The maid looked even more reluctant. 'Well, see, that's it, sir. Miss didn't want me to tell Mrs Polmont. It were the same last night, when she begged me as I shouldn't tell her. But I thought as you'd wish to know as she were ill, sir, and I said so. But Miss said as Mrs Polmont would say horrid things to her, and so I told Jacob instead so as Mr Creggan could tell you, sir.'

Julius began to feel confused. 'I don't understand. Is this all your reason for supposing Miss Hursley to be out of her right mind?'

'It weren't last night's to-do, sir,' butted in Wincle.

'Only this morning, when Maggie finds Miss Hursley so bad, she tells Mrs Polmont straight, and no nonsense. And Mrs Polmont goes up to Miss Hursley's room, with Maggie following—'

'And that's when the commotion started!' finished Maggie, evidently losing her diffidence. 'The second miss spied her, she starts off a-cryin' and a-wavin' of her hands. She calls to me to save her, and I don't know what besides!'

'Well, what besides?' demanded Julius, appalled.

'I don't know as I rightly remember, sir,' said the maid unhappily. 'It were all such a muddle!'

'Well, I remember,' stated Wincle stoutly. 'Leastways, I remember what you told me when you first come down to my kitchen.' She turned back to Julius, and he saw real trouble in her plump face. 'Seemingly, she's afeard of what Mrs Polmont might say to her. Maggie told me just what she said. "She'll say as I done it a-purpose," she said. "She'll make me think the worse of him," she said. "She'll say as he come in the night to me for evil, and I know as he done it to be kind." That's what Miss Hursley said, sir.'

Julius stared at the woman, feeling benumbed. If the suspicion burgeoning in his mind had any substance, then his housekeeper had a trifle of explaining to do. That Prudence was experiencing a species of delirium he could not doubt—and that her illness had run to this extreme was a matter demanding his urgent attention. But just at this moment he was too dismayed for action by the intelligence contained in this odd little history.

'What Maggie thought, sir,' pursued Wincle, 'was that Miss Hursley was speaking of the devil. She thought as how Miss didn't recognise Mrs Polmont.' A grim look settled in the cook's face. 'Only I don't think to put me faith in devils and such. If you ask me, the only devil in the case is very much alive, and is doing something—I don't say as I know exactly what!—as I don't hold with nohow. Interference, I call it. And it ain't got nothing to do with Miss Hursley's illness!'

Startled by his cook's evident perception, Julius could think of nothing to say. It was otherwise with the maid, who was staring blankly at Wincle.

'You never said nothing to me, Mrs Wincle!'

'No, and I wouldn't neither, you and your devils. If ever I met such a nodcock! She's out of her right mind—I don't think!'

Which timely reminder jerked Julius out of his abstraction. Whatever had been going on, as his percipient cook put it, would have to wait. What he must do at once was to get Prudence urgent medical attention.

He seized the handbell from the table, and rang

it fiercely. 'I will send at once for the doctor. Thank you, Wincle. And you too—er—Maggie. You did right to warn me, and you may safely leave me to deal with the matter. Ah, and, Maggie…?'

'Yes, sir?'

'I rely upon you to serve Miss Hursley until she is up and about again.'

'I'll do my best, sir. I've relit the fire already.' The girl looked distressed again. 'I only wish I'd gone in earlier, for it must have been out for hours and it's my belief, sir, as miss were mortal cold in the night. I'm afeared she were wandering out of bed, for her limbs was like ice, sir.'

Every word threw Julius into deeper anxiety. There was now nothing in his head bar the necessity of instant succour. He dismissed the women, who bobbed curtsies and withdrew, almost colliding with Creggan in the doorway. He could not, reflected Julius wryly, have been far away.

'Tell Beith to ride for the doctor immediately, Creggan. It is a matter of the utmost urgency! And when the fellow arrives, send him straight up to Miss Hursley, if you please.'

A few moments later, he was racing up the stairs two at a time, all thought suspended save the one all-consuming need to find out for himself exactly how Prudence fared.

* * *

The voice calling her had a familiar ring. Prue tried to answer, but it was difficult to make her tongue obey her command. She could vaguely see, as through a long tunnel in the distance, a wavering face. She had tried to keep her eyes closed, for the strange shapes that danced in her vision disturbed her.

'Prudence! Do you hear me?'

He was a long way away. It was like drowning, she thought. Yet she must reassure him. She reached up through the murky tunnel, and felt her fingers caught in warmth.

'She hears me, I think.'

A thought thrust at Prue's consciousness. He ought to be warned. Only she could not grasp the meaning of what she would say to him. That it concerned him very nearly she was certain. It was a thing he must not do. She struggled to express it.

'You must be careful.'

Stillness and silence ensued. Prue peered through the tunnel and thought she spied him there. Far away. That was safer.

'Stay there. You must not come any closer.'

A face shot into focus above her. The wrong face. It was wide-jawed and bloated, with a fuzzy wig that stuck out at the sides. It must be got rid of at once! She waved frantic hands. Or thought she did.

'Pray, Mr Rookham, take it away.'

The face vanished, and her hands were captured. His voice came, soothingly. 'There now, my poor girl, don't thresh so.'

Prue clutched his fingers. 'You are too close!'

She felt him disengage his fingers and her hands were laid down upon the coverlet. 'Prudence, listen to me. The doctor is here to examine you.'

'I don't want him.'

She spoke from a hazy desire that he should himself stay with her. Not close, which was dangerous, but there. She would have liked to tell him so, but somehow she felt it was forbidden. She did not know why.

There was a cough above her. 'If you will allow me, sir.'

The face reappeared. Prue turned her eyes away, and encountered a black figure standing on the other side of the bed. It was tall and thin, with a beaky nose.

'You have a face like a parrot,' she told it.

Laughter rang in the room. Was it laughter? She could hear a murmuring sound. It grew in volume in her head and she had to close her eyes. Vaguely she heard snatches of speech about her.

'Is it a fever?'

'There is an apparency of fever. But this sort of confusion of mind betokens a different disorder, I believe.'

'Like what?'

'Overlong exposure to the elements, sir, can give rise to just these sort of symptoms. She has been too long chilled.'

Chilled? Who was chilled? A memory came. The twins! Were they safe? Thrusting against the immense lassitude that possessed her, Prue shoved open her eyes again.

'Are they ill? I tried to keep them safe.'

The murmuring ceased. Prue cast about the faces above her and found the one she sought. She reached up and her hand came in contact with an arm. She clutched at it.

'Tell me, pray. Oh, I am so very much to blame!'

'Nonsense!' The tone was bracing. 'They are none the worse for wear.'

Another voice spoke. 'I don't know how you can say so, sir, when you know well—'

'Be silent, Mrs Polmont!'

Prue shrank from the anger, withdrawing her hand and digging herself down into the bedclothes. Then the heaviness overtook her head again, and she heard no more.

* * *

Prue's eyes opened upon surroundings that looked a degree more familiar. Nor did the shape of things seem out of true as they had done before. She was conscious of warmth about her, but when she moved her legs, they felt stiff and unwieldy.

Her movement brought someone to the bed. She recognised the young maid. Maggie smiled at her.

'You look a degree better, miss. Now do you feel cold, for I'm to fetch you another blanket if you do.'

Prue yawned. 'No, I am quite warm.'

She felt a hand reach under the covers and pat at her skin through the nightgown.

'Well, you do feel warmer, I'll say that.' Was it relief in the tone? 'Would you like a little water?'

Prue felt her head raised and drank of the glass that was put to her lips. The cool liquid did much to free her mind of cobwebs. And then a pressing need made itself felt.

'I must get up!'

'On no account, miss! I'd be afeard for my post if I let you.'

But she tutted when Prue explained more clearly, and fetching the pot from under the bed, bustled to assist Prue to make use of it. The whole operation, for which she was obliged to rely heavily on Maggie's support, demonstrated her extreme weakness, and Prue was only too glad to slide back under the covers.

'That's done with,' said the maid with satisfaction. 'Now, do you think you might take a morsel to eat?'

A faint sensation of hunger surfaced at the thought of food. Only Prue was not sure she had strength left to manage eating.

'I do not know if I can.'

'I've orders to try you, so we'll see, shall we? It won't be nothing heavy. A bit of chicken breast, or plain broth, the doctor said. Mrs Wincle will have seen to it.'

Prue watched the maid move to the fireplace where she yanked on the bell-pull. She became aware of daylight in the room, and wondered how long she had lain here.

'What time is it?'

'Nigh on three o'clock, miss. You've been asleep for hours and hours.'

'But I remember people here—talking. That was surely not long ago?'

Laughter trilled out of the maid as she came back to the bed. 'Lordy, miss, that were this morning when the doctor was here.'

Only Prue remembered someone other than the doctor. She did not make the enquiry. She could not ask that. It would be too dreadful if she should find she had been dreaming—if he had not been here at all.

The maid was disposed to be chatty. Prue let the words wash over her, attending little to what was said.

'It's mighty chilled you were this morning, miss, and no mistake. But I've kept the fire going, and what with the extra quilt and hot bricks, not to mention the doctor's potion as he give you to make you sleep, it looks like we done the trick.'

Feeling that something was required of her, Prue tried to find a suitable response. 'It is kind of you.'

Maggie's laughter trilled again. 'It ain't nothing of the sort, miss. Setting aside I've me duty to the master, there's such a thing as common feeling.' A friendly wink closed one eye. 'And I ain't the only one of the household as is struck with it neither!'

Her attention caught, Prue stared up into the girl's cheery features. What was she meant to understand by that? Too weak to be fully mistress of her own tongue, she put a faintly apprehensive question.

'Whom do you mean?'

A chuckle escaped the girl's lips. 'Let's see now, miss. There's Mrs Wincle for one. Took up the cudgels on your part, she did, and bearded the master. I shouldn't have dared, not without Mrs Wincle's say-so!'

'Took up the cudgels?'

Prue's heart skipped a beat. What in the world had been said? Against whom had the cook taken them up?

A knock at the door prevented any reply to this.

'That'll be Jacob with your meal, miss.'

She disappeared from sight, and Prue heard the opening of the door, the clink of crockery, and a man's low tones. Then the latch clicked and Maggie was back, bearing a tray.

'Now, I'll just set this down, miss, and make you ready so's you can eat.'

The tray disposed of temporarily, Prue struggled against her weakness as the maid helped her to sit up. She was obliged to hold on to the girl's shoulders as the pillows were banked behind her, and she sank back against them with a sigh of relief.

'Now, then, shall you take the tray on your knees?'

Prue shook her head slightly. 'I do not think I can.'

'Then I'd best bring the plate to you and hold it.'

In the event, Maggie was obliged actually to feed Prue, for when she tried to dip the spoon that was given into her hands, her fingers trembled too much to keep it steady.

The maid tutted, and took matters into her own hands. It was silly to be unable to feed herself, but there was nothing Prue could do but give in to the situation. She was comforted by the cheerful mien of the girl, who kept up a running commentary throughout.

'There now, open up, miss. And in it goes. That's it, swallow it down. We'll soon have you back in trim, miss. Another one for luck, as my old mum used to say. There it goes, miss. I've the next all ready for you. It's light broth, this is, miss. Made special, I can tell you, for Mrs Wincle is that worrited for you. Here's another. Down it goes. Smells good, don't it, miss? Mushroom and herbs, I'd say. And I'd not be a bit surprised if she didn't put a touch of cream in too.'

The gentle flow of inconsequent chatter lulled Prue's mind, and she obeyed in an automatic way the presentation of the spoon. But at length the effort of swallowing proved too much. She waved the spoon away.

'No more, I pray you.'

The maid tutted again, returning the spoon to the bowl. 'Well, I'll not fuss, since you've had near half of it. I'll let you rest, and then we'll try a bit of chicken.'

Prue wanted to protest, for the thought of eating anything else demanded more than she felt she could give. But she said nothing, feeling herself indebted to Maggie.

She should not be lying here, accepting this service as if it was her right. She ought to be up about her duties, teaching the girls. Only her body was forcing her to abandon all pretensions to normality. She supposed, in a vague sort of way, that she would presently find herself sufficiently recovered to resume the usual pursuit of her days. But for now, there was a curious balm in this enforced inactivity, as though with the suspension of her body's motion, her mind was able to rest. Was her mind so much in need of rest? She had a memory of troubled thoughts, but at this present it was too far away to matter.

'Now don't you go off to sleep again, miss! I'll not answer for the master's wrath, if I let you drift off before I've got a bit more substance down you.'

Prue pulled herself back into consciousness. The master! That was it. Mr Rookham had been here, she knew he had. It had not then been a dream. He had cared enough to come to her!

Elation warmed her breast, and she made no demur when the maid produced a plate and plonked on the edge of the bed again with a determined air.

'Now, you'll take a little of this chicken, miss. It's ever so tender, straight off the breast.' A small portion of white meat speared on a fork appeared in front of Prue's face. 'Come now, open up. I'd like fine to report to the master as you've eaten well.'

The thought of pleasing Mr Rookham so wrought upon Prue that she opened her mouth at once. It was only as she chewed at the soft meat that it dawned on her that Maggie had taken a great deal for granted. Was that what that wink had implied? Had she noticed—had the cook done so?—that there was a friendship between herself and the master of the house? Or was there a different construction put upon it?

A part of her mind cleared. She remembered the housekeeper's warnings. The comfortable blanket that had enwrapped her began to dissipate, and reality floated in.

As if on cue, the door opened. From her raised position in the bed, Prue's eyeline was perfectly placed to note the entrance of the black-garbed figure herself.

Chapter Nine

The maid was heard to mutter under her breath, but Prue was unable to decipher what she said. A pulse was rising in her breast, and she could feel the beat of her own heart as Mrs Polmont approached the bed.

'What are you doing, Maggie? Surely Miss Hursley can feed herself?'

Prue was holding her breath, but she saw the maid look the woman straight in the eyes.

'She did try, Mrs Polmont, but she's too weak.'

The fork was once again at Prue's mouth, only the churning in her stomach made her reject the thought of food. She shifted her face away.

'No more, I thank you.'

From the other side of the bed, the housekeeper addressed her. 'You'd best eat. We don't want you malingering here any longer than you must.'

Prue saw the maid's eyes flash, but the girl pursed

her lips tightly together. She presented the fork again. Prue shook her head.

'Take it away, Maggie,' said Mrs Polmont. 'You may go now. Take the tray back to the kitchen.'

The maid had risen, but she stood her ground. 'I'm to stay and nurse Miss Hursley, ma'am.'

The pinched look became more pronounced, and the woman's eyes glittered dangerously. 'Are you questioning my orders, Maggie? Take the tray away.'

'I ain't questioning nothing, ma'am. Only the master himself told me as I was to nurse her.'

Mrs Polmont's brows rose. 'Did I say you weren't to nurse her? Take the tray to the kitchens. You are entitled to a break, and I say you are to have one. Come back in an hour.'

Prue looked from Maggie's mutinous features to the tightly drawn face of the housekeeper. Her conscience smote her. She could not be the cause of dissension among the domestic staff. She put out an unsteady hand towards the maid.

'Do as she says, if you please. I am much better, so you need not fear to leave your post.'

The maid gave her a swift, conspiratorial smile. Then she collected the tray, and left the room. The housekeeper held the door for her, and shut it carefully behind her. Prue braced herself as she turned. The woman's tone was bitter.

'Already it begins.'

Bewilderment rose up. 'I don't understand you.'

A sour look settled about Mrs Polmont's mouth. 'Don't you?' She crossed to stand by the bed again. 'You think to usurp my position, is that it?'

Prue stared at her. 'Are you mad?'

'I don't mean as housekeeper. I thought at first you were an innocent, but I perceive my error now.'

Annoyance mingled with the puzzled apprehension. 'I have not the remotest notion what you are talking about.'

The housekeeper laughed, a rasping sound. 'And you so clever, Miss Hursley! I was fooled at first, but I see through your scheme now. Only the most determined assault could encompass such a dangerous ploy.'

The woman's words began to take on the quality of a nightmare, making no sense. Prue shrunk into her pillows, weak all over again.

'I do wish you will not speak in riddles. What is it you are trying to say to me? Of what do you accuse me?'

'Don't play the innocent with me, miss, for it won't work any longer.' Her tone had sharpened, striking heavily into the room. 'Chilled from the rain? Yes, and prettily played, I must say. Did you choose it because of his reaction on the last occasion? I see what you hope to gain. Worming your way into his affections! You have ambitions beyond what one might have expected, have you not?'

As the meaning behind her words began to penetrate, Prue could only stare at the creature in the blankest astonishment. She supposed her to be scheming to attach Mr Rookham. How little the woman knew! What, did she imagine Prue had dared to think the utterly unthinkable?

'You mistake me completely,' was all she could find to say in her own defence.

The housekeeper gazed down her beaky nose. 'Can you deny that your own affections are engaged?'

Prue could not. Nor had she power to make a refutation that she knew to be a lie. The pulsing pressure of her heartbeat caused a tremble to start up again in her limbs. She tried to speak, to make an attempt to defend herself.

'That h-has n-nothing to d-do with the c-case.'

'Nothing,' agreed Mrs Polmont drily, 'except in impairing your judgement. You see in him what you want to see, but I know him better. He might have taken you as his mistress. But a wife?' A coarse laugh came rasping from her throat. 'Mr Rookham is too set in his ways, too comfortable in his bachelor establishment. He will not wed you. No, Miss Hursley, you are aiming at the moon. I rule the roost here. You will not take that from me, I promise you!'

Nausea was adding to the discomforts Prue was already experiencing. The woman had shown her hand. How blinding was her jealousy! Prue was unable to help the words that tumbled from her mouth.

'You are wrong, so very wrong. I had no thought of such a thing. Nothing could be farther from my mind than to suppose I should be offered such a position. Nor to scheme for it! As if I could, even had I wanted to.'

Mrs Polmont's expression did not change. 'Say on, Miss Hursley. I am wise to you now.'

Prue sighed wearily. 'I think your jealousy has maddened you, Mrs Polmont. There is no use talking.'

'I have said my say. Take heed. Your schemes can only end in disaster for yourself.'

Irritation flared. 'You need not say so! My life has been already overtaken by disaster, if you only knew. I have no anticipation either of felicity or any future happiness.'

A faint look of surprise showed in the house-keeper's face. She looked as if she would speak again. But a rapping on the door brought her head whipping round. It opened and, with an intensity of relief, Prue saw that the newcomer was Mr Rookham.

* * *

For the first moment or two Julius had no attention to spare for his housekeeper. Such a wave of sensation struck him at the sight of Prudence sitting up, that he had eyes only for this as he approached the foot of the bed.

She looked better, thank God! A trifle pale, perhaps. Those limpid eyes of hers were all too vulnerable, large in her white face. Her hair was tumbled, falling pell-mell upon the white linen bedgown at her shoulders.

Julius experienced a tug of attraction that had nothing to do with friendship. Hastily he broke into speech.

'I am glad to see you so much improved. Have you eaten?'

There was a constriction in Prue's throat, but she answered as calmly as she could. 'I have had some broth. Oh, and a trifle of chicken.'

A frown entered his face. 'How much chicken?'

Prue looked away from him. 'Sufficient. Truly, I am not hungry.'

She had been relieved to see him. But it immediately became oppressive to have him there while the housekeeper was in the room. Everything the woman had said rose tauntingly into her mind. She could not but acknowledge that her conduct might well appear suspect. What if Mr Rookham shared Mrs Polmont's opinion?

Julius found his eyes turning upon the house-keeper, standing silent by the side of the bed. He could see nothing in Polmont beyond her familiar assured calm. Yet he could have sworn he had heard her voice raised as he had never heard it before. He was careful to give no sign of his thoughts.

'Where is the young maid? I gave orders that she was to attend Miss Hursley.'

There was only the usual prim manner in Polmont's response. 'I gave her leave to take a respite, sir. She will return presently.'

'In that case, I will keep Miss Hursley company for a space. You may go.'

A movement in the bed drew his eyes, but Prudence was not looking at him. Her fingers plucked restlessly at the covers, and his chest tightened. Had there been an altercation?

Polmont had not moved when Julius glanced back at her. A cynical devil prompted him, and his tongue became sharp.

'What is it, Polmont? Do you fear to leave Miss Hursley unchaperoned in my care?'

He watched with satisfaction as her lips pursed tightly together. But she clearly dared not venture upon a retort. He softened his tone.

'I do not intend to remain for long. And if I should be tempted to overstay my time, I have no doubt you will speedily send Maggie up to play propriety.'

Dismayed, if guiltily triumphant, Prue watched her tormenter drop a curtsy and withdraw, pointedly leaving the door ajar. There would be no quarter after this! In not a little trepidation, she turned furtive eyes upon her employer.

Mr Rookham was staring frowningly at the open door, as if lost in thought. With an abruptness that startled her, he turned with a curt question.

'Has that woman been troubling you, Prudence?'

Prue bit her lip, looking quickly down at the coverlet. She must refute it at once. Only her tongue seemed not to wish to obey her.

'I don't—it is not—'

'It is not something of which you may speak freely, is that it? Well, never mind.'

The sudden fierce look vanished, and Mr Rookham smiled as she glanced up again. He perched on the bed and took one of her hands between his fingers, feeling them.

'You are much warmer. They were like ice this morning! You gave us all a great fright, I can tell you.'

Prue felt herself melting. 'I am so sorry.'

He released her fingers. 'For God's sake, don't

apologise! I am eternally grateful to you, Miss Hursley.'

Unable to believe she had heard him aright, Prue blinked dazedly. 'I beg your pardon?'

Mr Rookham grinned. 'Yes, you heard me correctly.'

His perspicacity was uncanny. Prue sank numbly into her banked pillows. 'I don't understand you. After I was so stupid as to remain out in the woods in a storm? I should have seen it coming. Only I was—' She broke off, realising to where her incautious words were leading.

A warm hand was laid over one of hers. 'You could not have done so. It blew up out of nowhere, and took us all by surprise. I was caught myself, out in the gardens.'

Prue's heart lightened. Then she had not been too much at fault. She felt the hand removed from hers, and her spirits drooped a little. But she had yet a question.

'The girls, Mr Rookham. Have they taken any harm?'

'You asked that this morning, but I dare say you don't remember.'

She thought he hesitated, and her heart dimmed the more as a memory stirred. 'She spoke of it! They are ill too, aren't they?'

'A trifle of sneezing and coughing, but nothing to concern you. The doctor saw them this morning, and his diagnosis was sanguine. Yvette has kept them in bed for today.'

Dismay flooded Prue. 'Oh, I am so sorry, sir. I should never have taken them into the woods.'

An odd expression flitted across his face. 'Why did you?'

'Go to the woods? Oh, we were collecting flowers—and we have lost them all.'

'Botany. I guessed as much.'

Prue let out a laugh. 'Botany? Indeed, no. I have no knowledge of botany. It was for a work of art. You may press them, you know, and then create a picture.'

'I see.'

Julius said nothing further for a moment. A work of art! It was all of a piece. Who but Prudence Hursley would think of such a thing? He recalled the pin-cushions shaped as hearts. Her sensibility was clearly incurable. The thought caused a resurgence of that warmth that had attacked him upon setting eyes on her earlier. A misplaced feeling! There was nothing remotely sensual in her now.

'Why did you say you are grateful to me?'

He almost started at the sound of her voice. Those wretchedly disarming eyes were fixed upon him in a look compounded of puzzlement and pleading. She was pathetically in need of reassurance. He could at least give her the satisfaction of knowing that she had done something right.

'Lotty and Dodo told me what you did for them. They are fond of you, but don't run away with the idea that they had any thought of praising your presence of mind. I do so wholeheartedly, but the twins were only bent upon recounting their adventure. Through which, let me tell you, it is plain that you acted purely from an instinct to preserve them, and without the slightest thought for your own safety—which is exactly what I should have expected from you!'

'But what else could have I done? Pray don't scold me, Mr Rookham, for I could scarcely have done less.'

He laughed out. 'Scold you? Goose! I am trying to thank you. How in the world would I have explained it to Trixie, if her daughters had become seriously ill—as you did?'

Her features creased with distaste. 'Not seriously. I am well now, I promise you. Indeed, I should hope I might resume my duties tomorrow.'

He rose abruptly, and Prue quailed at the look in his face. 'You will do no such thing! You will remain in bed until the doctor sees fit to release you. And then, if you are yet in need of rest, you will stay quietly in your parlour until your health is fully recovered.'

'But—'

'Don't argue with me, for my mind is made up!' he snapped. 'As for the twins, they can survive without schooling for a few days. It will be nothing new in their lives.'

Prue eyed him in silence, disturbed by his sudden outburst. Why he should have been angered by her desire to get back to work, she could not imagine. Unless he thought she was merely being foolish? She sought for a way to placate him.

'I will do as you wish, Mr Rookham. But I cannot think that I will be laid up for long.'

'Then you know little of what you have been through,' he retorted.

She watched him shift away a step or two, and thought he took a deep breath, as if to steady himself. When he spoke again, she was glad to find his tone to be more moderate, although the look in his eyes quite frightened her.

'You could have *died*, Prue. Our doctor here is a countrified fellow, but he knows his business. Had you not been warmed a little last night—despite the fire giving out so that you became chilled again— you might have slipped away by morning.'

Prue stared at his face, struck more by what she saw there than by what he had said. There was a quality to it that was—yes, haunted! Her heart began a rough tattoo in her bosom, but she dared not formulate, even in thought, the implication that hovered at the edge of her mind.

'You look at me as if I am mad!' A faint laugh escaped him. 'I am, perhaps. At least I am maddened by the horrible thought that, had I not grown tired of my own company and sent to you to come and dine with me last night, no one would have known anything about your condition.'

The sense of this penetrated and Prue's unruly pulses subsided. So that was it.

'Oh.' Sighing it out.

'Is that all you can say?'

She swallowed. 'What would you wish me to say?'

Disconcertingly, he came back to perch on the bed again. His fingers caught at her cheek and lifted her face.

'You little goose! Do you think so little of me that you did not ask for help? In heaven's name, girl, don't you know me by now? You could not have supposed I would have let you suffer!'

Prue's throat tightened, and she shook her head.

'Then why didn't you send to me?'

There was exasperation in his voice, and tears

welled at Prue's eyes. She tried to blink them away, but in vain.

Julius saw them, and instantly cursed himself. He released her, catching instead at her hand. 'Don't cry! I'm a clod, Prue. I should never have said anything. I never meant to carp at you—not now.'

She was shaking her head, as if in denial, but it was obvious that she could not speak. Julius let her go and dived a hand into his pocket for his handkerchief. Bringing it out, he abruptly recalled a letter that had come for her that morning. He passed over his handkerchief, and then reached into the pocket of his sober blue frock-coat for the letter, his attention on Prudence as she stemmed the flow. What had possessed him to bring all that up? He had been shocked at the doctor's dire pronouncement, but thought he had overcome it. He had in no way intended to throw it at the girl's head in this stupid fashion. Had he lost his wits?

She was sniffing, and the redness was receding at her eyes. Relieved, he gave her a rueful look.

'Forgive me, Prudence. I should not have spoken of it.'

'N-no, pray, it is my fault. I knew that you w-would order everything for my c-comfort. And I did not mean to say anything, it is true. Only perhaps I would have done, had I any inkling how bad I was. But the weakness overcame me before I could think of asking for help.'

Her words served only to increase his irritation with himself for having brought up the matter. But he contrived to speak without showing it.

'Besides which, I don't doubt you had your attention wholly on the children.'

If only she had done, thought Prue dolefully, recalling the silly argument she'd had with herself about whether she should throw herself upon Mr Rookham's generosity. She prevaricated.

'Well, I had given them up to Yvette by then. But I was quite mistress of myself, you see, until I had removed my wet clothes. And suddenly, I felt faint, and could by no means do more than crawl into my bed.'

A perfectly charming smile creased his mouth, and her breath caught. 'You are fully absolved. But you will understand why I am anxious that you should preserve your health. I should hate to be obliged to give an account of myself to your formidable Duck!'

A weak laugh greeted this sally, and Julius relaxed a trifle. Feeling that he had atoned a little for his hasty temper, he held out the letter.

'I meant to have given you this at once, but I was distracted. My apologies.'

She took the sealed note from him and looked at the inscription. One of those rare joyful smiles lightened her features. Julius was conscious of disappointment. Nothing he had said had brought that ray of sunshine to her face!

'It is from Nell. Oh, thank you so much, sir!'

'Don't thank me,' he responded, aware of gruffness in his speech. 'I am only the messenger.'

Her face dimmed a trifle and Julius regretted his tone. 'Your Seminary friend, is it not? I had best leave you in peace to enjoy it. Indeed, it is time and past that I departed, before I set the household by the ears. It is a good thing there are none but servants to see me here.'

Was that a faint blush on her cheek? Her words belied it, and there was no consciousness in them.

'Be sure that I attribute your presence to nothing but kindness, Mr Rookham.'

Did she, indeed? He wondered if it was merely that. But he shied off from discussing the matter further, and made haste to change the subject.

'Is there anything I can do for you? Would you care for a book to read? Are you perhaps hungry or thirsty?'

'Oh, no! I mean, there is no need to bestir yourself, sir. I cannot have you wait upon me! I am grateful for Maggie's help, and—'

'But I wish to serve you!' he interrupted, putting an end to this agitated speech. He gave her a quizzical look. 'You must know that I shall do just as I choose, no matter what you or anyone else may think.'

Yes, she did know! And just who did he mean by 'anyone else'? As if there could be any doubt! Reflecting that it was as well that the housekeeper had not heard anything of their conversation, Prue sought in vain for something to say over the disastrous pulsing in her veins.

Mr Rookham was eyeing her in that teasing fashion that had always the power to melt her. Movement at the door caught in the periphery of her vision, and with mixed feelings she saw that Maggie was hovering in the doorway.

'Ah, your nurse is back,' said Julius easily, feeling himself relieved at the excuse afforded him to leave. Not that he had been in any way held here by anything other than his own will, but he badly needed time for readjustment.

He beckoned to the maid, and then looked back at the patient. 'I shall leave you now, Miss Hursley, and will hope to hear that you have eaten better. Send to me if there is anything you need.'

'There is nothing. And thank you.'

She looked woebegone, clutching tightly to the letter that had so briefly changed her mood. Had his incautious words upset her more than she had allowed to appear? But he could ask nothing more in front of the servant, who was busily tidying the bedclothes.

He turned and made for the door. Her voice caught him just as he was about to walk through it.

'Mr Rookham!'

Prue watched him check and turn, enquiry in his face. She had nothing to ask of him! She had only wanted to stop him leaving her. Frantically searching her mind, she found a much needed excuse—which would itself bring balm to her lonely spirit.

'Folly. I would like to have him here, if you please.'

He nodded. 'Certainly. I will arrange it.'

And then he was gone. With a heavy heart, Prue gave herself up to the ministrations of the maid, and found, with a catch at her bosom that, together with Nell's letter, she was still clutching Mr Rookham's handkerchief.

With fingers that trembled slightly, she tucked the square of linen under her pillow, and turned her attention to the welcome missive from her friend.

Standing before the fireplace in his library, Julius held his hands to the warmth and rubbed them briskly together. It had been dull and misty since the storm and the air was chill. His eyes strayed to the bell-pull again. How many times had he looked at it? The matter could not be put off for much longer.

There was a feeling of expectancy in the house. Or was it his imagination? It appeared to him that the staff walked on eggshells in his presence. He had caught the tail-end of sidelong looks, as if there might be an answer in his features to the unspoken questions that fluttered in the atmosphere about him. Whatever had been said or hinted at had rapidly spread, even to his gardeners!

Not that he had ventured these two days upon an excursion to the treillage, where the men were working. But Hessle, who pursued his trade in all weathers—and made his minions do likewise, poor devils!—had come to him with a query earlier. Even Hessle, dour martinet as he was, had cast an odd glance or two his way. It was unsettling, to say the least.

He had meant to tackle Polmont yesterday, but—not to put too fine a point on it!—his nerve had failed him. It was ridiculous, but he was reluctant to broach the subject. It could not be avoided for long. For one thing, an official complaint had been laid by Wincle. For another, he was certain he had walked smash into a wrangle when he had discovered the housekeeper in Prudence's bedchamber yesterday.

And then what had ensued between himself and the governess had put him into such a state of confusion that he knew not how to tackle the matter. Which was, he decided, at the root of the problem.

Julius turned from the fire and paced restlessly to the windows, staring blankly at the unresponsive drizzle beyond.

How was he to deal with Polmont, when he did not know himself what he felt about Prudence Hursley? He had liked her from the first. On those few occasions he'd had an opportunity to increase their acquaintance, she had grown on him. Her extreme sensibility was both endearing and exasperating, and the effect upon him of that particular look in her eyes was disastrous. Could that alone justify the seizure of shock that had attacked him upon hearing the doctor pronounce her to have been so close to death?

He had felt himself freeze inside, a latent horror stopping the breath in his throat. It had been an appalling moment. And surely it had been that which had caused him to fly off the handle with the girl? An angry frustration had attacked him, that she took so little care of herself. He knew it had been born in her by consciousness of her lowly position. The little goose thought so badly of her own worth!

Julius thought a good deal better of her than she

did herself, that was certain. Only was he prepared to stake his future upon that foundation?

There, he had said it at last. Useless to deny that it had been growing at the back of his mind. Festering, he might have said, for it was like a sore that one tried desperately to ignore, but which refused to heal.

The cold came in at him through the glass of the long window, and he crossed back to the fireplace. As if compelled, his glance dragged back to the bell-pull. Hell and damnation! Let him quiet the house at least, if he could not quiet his own mind.

He seized the cord and tugged upon it. He would see Polmont and settle that nonsense once and for all. It was plain to him now that those earlier fears expressed by Prudence had their origin from this source. He recalled that when she had herself driven a wedge between their burgeoning friendship, he had wondered if another tongue had been responsible for the fears she had expressed.

The door opened to admit Creggan, and Julius turned.

'Send Polmont to me here, if you please.'

Was that a glint in the fellow's eye? The butler looked too impassive to be true as he bowed assent and withdrew.

Even with the moment upon him, Julius had no

notion what he was going to say to the woman. Should he accuse her outright? Question her? No, pointless. She would affect ignorance. He would have to be more subtle than that.

The trouble with Polmont was that she had been here since his father's time. Julius could not say that he cared for her, but she was quietly efficient and ran the house precisely to his satisfaction. His mother had trained her well, for his father had been just such another as Julius was himself. A hedonist, Mrs Rookham had called him. Not that either he or his father had been devoted to pleasure. But he pleaded guilty to a selfish desire to do just as he wished upon every occasion. And it was this comfortable existence that was threatened by the exasperating female lying above-stairs!

The door opened, and the familiar black-garbed figure entered. Julius crossed to the desk. Polmont moved into the room and dropped her prim curtsy.

'You sent for me, sir?'

Abruptly, Julius was swept with a rush of anger. It came apparently from nowhere, and he was obliged to curb it with the tightest of reins. There was no longer any difficulty about what he would say to her.

'Are you happy in my employ, Polmont?'

To his intense satisfaction, a look of alarm leaped

into her face. She veiled it quickly, but her eyes held a frightened expression. Her voice was faintly hoarse.

'I have been happy in this house for many years, Mr Rookham, as I am sure you know.'

'Until recently, I take it?'

Her hands came up, and her fingers twisted together. Her cheeks paled, and a vibrant note crept into her words.

'What has been said? She has poisoned your mind against me, has she not?'

Julius stiffened. 'How could that be, Polmont? Of whom are you talking?'

The eyes glanced away from his, and he saw a sliver of tongue slip out to moisten her lips. Her fingers tightened, one upon the other.

'I spoke without thinking, sir.' Hard, and metallic.

Julius was silent for a space. An instinct was urging him to dispense with her services forthwith. But justice and fairness had ever been his watchwords. The woman had been in her post for too many years to be dismissed upon a whim. But a warning might be heeded.

'I should be loath to spoil your record here, Polmont. You have given satisfactory service, and my mother valued your work, I know.'

He saw at once that he had judged it amiss. Her

chin came up, and her eyes glittered. At her waist, her fingers remained entwined, but they stilled.

'I was ever fond of Mrs Rookham, sir. It was by her wish that I continued to serve you. But I am bound to state that if I am to remain in your employ, conditions would need to be right.'

Fury simmered in Julius's breast. It was no longer a question of Prudence Hursley's protection. How dared the woman threaten him?

'I think you had better explain that remark, Polmont.'

She seemed to struggle with herself. For a moment she met his glance, but her courage evidently gave way. She looked down, and her response was a mutter.

'If I cannot run the household, sir, as you would wish, then perhaps it would be better for me to leave.'

'What I wish,' stated Julius curtly, 'is that my housekeeper should extend the same courtesy towards other persons in my household, however situated, as she does to myself. Is that too much to ask?'

The black eyes flashed up again, and for an instant Julius saw malevolence there. It was swiftly gone, but the image of it stayed in his head.

'I will endeavour to give satisfaction, sir, to the best of my ability.'

That was in her usual calm manner. Did she mean it? Julius doubted it, but his own reluctance to push it further surfaced. Until he knew his own mind, let him maintain the status quo—or a semblance of it at least.

'Very well, Polmont, you may go.'

Was that triumph in her look? She curtsied and went out. Julius's stiffness relaxed. One thing was clear. If there were to be a change in his circumstances, he would have to be rid of the housekeeper.

What that would mean in terms of the change in his personal life he shoved to the back of his mind. He did not want to think about it. Not now. He was dragging himself into unnecessarily deep waters. He felt sure that time would resolve everything, and he need do nothing about it.

Seating himself at his desk, he attempted to apply himself to work. It was no use trying to improve upon his design for the Rockery, for he knew he had not the concentration. But there were letters enough demanding his attention, and he settled to this task for a time undisturbed.

When the butler once again entered the room, Julius did not notice until the man was before his desk. A soft cough drew his attention.

'What is it, Creggan?'

The butler held out a salver, upon which lay a sealed missive. 'This has just arrived by courier, sir. From London.'

Frowning, Julius picked up the folded sheet and looked at the inscription. 'It is my sister's hand. Is the messenger awaiting a reply?'

'No, sir. He has departed about his business.'

Julius broke the seal. 'Very well, thank you.'

He heard the door close as he began to run his eye down the sheet. When he reached the end, he sat staring at the paper, a creeping paralysis seeming to overtake his mind.

Trixie was to be married, and he would have no further need of a governess at Rookham Hall.

Prue lifted her arms so that Maggie could drop the linsey-woolsey gown over her head. Once inside the stifling folds, she closed her eyes against the prevailing weakness that yet had power to overtake her. But as her head came through the neck of the gown, she was obliged once more to dissemble. Not, it would appear, very successfully.

'Are you sure you're well enough to get up, miss? You still look right pale to me.'

Prue tried to sound reassuring. 'It is bound to be difficult at first, for I have been abed nigh on three days. My legs are a little uncertain yet, that is all.'

She must get back to work! It was Saturday, and she need only teach the twins for the morning, and then she might rest again. It could not be worse than lying here with nothing to do but think as she had done these last two days. Nell's letter had provided but temporary relief, glad though she had been of her tidings. For Nell had after all been requested for that position in a gothic castle, and had written almost upon the point of setting out.

Prue was in two minds. On the one hand, it was fortunate that no less than two females, each engaged ahead of Nell, had apparently taken one look at the place and turned instantly for home. On the other, she could not help but feel a trifle apprehensive on Nell's behalf, despite the determinedly cheerful tone of her letter. And Kitty, Nell wrote, still held out for a better life, and so Mrs Duxford had meanwhile insisted upon her teaching deportment and dance to the younger students in order to earn her board.

Poor Kitty. Though perhaps she was better off where she was, among those who understood and loved her. Heaven knew what dread unhappiness and disillusionment might have been in store for her! Though she could scarcely have been more unhappy than Prue herself.

No, she must not think in that way. It was excessively stupid of her to be mooning over Mr Rookham's absence! What obligation had he to come anywhere near the governess? For no consideration would the governess take him up on his insistence that she send to him for anything she might need. Why, he had probably forgotten by now that he said it. Besides, he had faithfully discharged the one request. Folly—frolicking about the chamber at this moment with a paper ball with which she had provided him—had been her constant companion from that day.

No, she expected nothing from Mr Rookham, though she was guiltily aware of stowing that handkerchief he had loaned her in a secret place, for fear that Maggie might find it and whisk it away. Surely she might hold just this one thing for a keepsake?

Maggie was doing up the buttons with a brisk hand, and Prue tottered. The maid caught her.

'Steady! Are you sure you ain't doing this too early, miss? It don't seem right to me. And what the master will say, I'm sure I don't know.'

Panic gripped Prue. 'Pray don't tell him, Maggie!'

The maid gave the gown a tweak or two, setting its folds. 'I don't see as how I can avoid it, miss, for he's bound to ask after you. What am I to say?'

Lie! thought Prue frantically. Then common sense returned. She could not expect the girl to risk her position. Only she could not bear it if Mr Rookham was to feel himself obliged to visit her again—merely to order her obedience.

'After all, the doctor said yesterday that I may get up today, if I felt inclined.'

'Yes, and it's what I told the master,' agreed Maggie, adding firmly, 'and it were the master who said as I were to make sure you were ready before you did get up.'

'But I am ready,' protested Prue.

Her unruly legs belied her, so that she staggered a little and was obliged to plonk down upon the bed again. Folly promptly left his play and leapt up beside her. Maggie threw one arm akimbo and shook an admonitory finger.

'There now, what did I say?'

Prue caught the maid's hand. 'Pray, Maggie, help me! He has not been to see me since that dreadful day, and I cannot bear to give Mrs Polmont an excuse to say that I am malingering in hopes that he will.'

It was the first time she had abandoned pretence before the maid. But in the distressing absence of Mr Rookham, she felt Maggie to be all the friend she had—apart from Folly. The kitten was butting at Prue's side, and it was absently that she stroked him.

The maid's eyes had softened, and she was shaking her head. 'Dearie me, miss, you are in a state! Now don't you worrit yourself over Mrs

Polmont, for I know for a fact as the master seen her yesterday in his library.'

Prue's fingers stilled on the furry back, and she stared at Maggie, apprehension warring with the misery that had attended the long lonely hours during which she had waited in vain—secretly cradling that handkerchief!—for Mr Rookham to come and see how she did.

'What did he say to her?'

'That I don't know,' said the maid, crossing to fetch Prue's hairbrush from the top of the press. 'Mrs Wincle thinks as how the master must have warned her off, for she's not come next or nigh you, now has she?'

This could not be denied. Prue submitted without protest to the dragging of the hairbrush through her untidy curls, allowing the kitten to slip from under her hand. Disgusted with the activity on the bed, Folly jumped to the floor and settled by the fire.

Preoccupied as Prue had been with the absence of another, she had taken little notice of the particular relief afforded by the absence of Mrs Polmont's punitive descents. Had she indeed been discouraged?

'Has she said anything to you?'

Maggie giggled. 'She ain't speaking to no one, save as she must to give orders. As for her and Mrs Wincle, they're at daggers drawn, as you might say. Mrs Polmont ain't been near the kitchens, and Mrs Wincle swears as she won't set one foot inside Mrs Polmont's parlour door. It's Mr Creggan as has been passing between 'em, for I know as both of 'em been inside his pantry at different times, talking and talking.'

Prue could only be glad that Maggie was too busy about the dressing of her hair to be able to see her face. She was sure her shock and distress must show. How dreadful to be the cause of such dissension in the household!

'Oh, dear, what have I done?'

She was unaware of having spoken aloud until Maggie set aside the hairbrush, and gathered up a handful of pins.

'Don't you fret over what you done, miss! It's Mrs Polmont as ought to be a-fretting. Mrs Wincle says as how the master will be rid of her, for he won't put up with it, she says. Not if things go as how she thinks they will.'

Prue stared up into the girl's face above her, hardly feeling the pins as they dug into her scalp, firmly attaching her locks in neat bands at the back. There was a hush in her mind, for the cook's prognosis was suddenly of immense importance.

'What do you mean, Maggie—how things go?'

Chapter Ten

The maid pulled back, giving her a sly wink. 'I ain't at liberty to say, miss, but I can tell you this. Mrs Wincle ain't the only one of us as seen it. Nor she ain't the only one to wish for it neither. In fact, the only one of us as wouldn't be right pleased, I reckon, is Mrs Polmont.'

There could no longer be the slightest doubt about what the girl meant. Prue's heart thumped painfully in her chest. Had the entire domestic staff seen into the fervent longings of her deepest dreams? Was it not then only Mrs Polmont who supposed her to have schemed to attach the master of the house?

Only if Maggie were to be believed, it could not be her intentions that were meant—but *his*. Her pulse steadied and a lump came into her throat. Oh, but they were all distressingly mistaken! Could they not see that a man who had any such intention would have come in to her as she lay abed?

She had dared to hope that perhaps his reticence was meant to deter Mrs Polmont from any further complaints of her conduct. But he had seen the housekeeper himself, and still he had not come! She must face the truth. Mr Rookham's care of her sprang only from friendship, just as he had always averred. There was no deeper feeling, and she must not indulge herself with that forlorn hope.

Maggie stepped back. 'There, that's done.'

'My cap, if you please, Maggie.'

The girl made a face. 'What do you want to go a-wearing of that thing for? It don't look pretty, and it makes you look old, miss.'

'Nevertheless, I must wear it.' She tried to smile. 'You forget, Maggie. I am the governess.'

The maid grunted. 'Yes, and a deal more besides.'

'Pray don't let your imagination run away with you. I believe…' Her voice failed, and she tried again. 'I believe Mrs Wincle is mistaken.'

Maggie eyed her, uncertainty in her face. 'Well, and if she is, there's no harm in prettifying yourself a little.'

Prue snapped. 'Yes, there is. Great harm. I will not be other than I am! If you will not give me the cap, then I shall fetch it myself.'

Forgetting her weakened state, she thrust herself up, and was obliged to catch hold of Maggie for support. The maid tutted, but thankfully refrained from crowing in triumph.

'Steady, miss! Sit down, do. I'll fetch the cap to you, since you wish for it.'

A few moments later, suitably attired in the concealing cap, Prue made her precarious way to the schoolroom, leaning heavily upon Maggie's arm.

The twins, to Prue's relief, were far more recovered than their governess herself. While she sat at her desk, she could remain reasonably steady. Thinking to make the morning easier on herself, she had persuaded Lotty and Dodo to write an account of their adventure in the forest. But she had not bargained for the effort required in doing nothing, while their pens scratched laboriously through that day's events.

Prue felt herself sinking, and made a praiseworthy effort to pull her body upright. Folly, who had frisked along beside her to the schoolroom, was now asleep upon her lap. She had nothing to do, therefore, but to keep her seat—a task which she would never have believed could cause her so much difficulty.

Her head felt light, her body heavy. The backrest

of the chair was hard, and she had to hold on to the arms for support. Perhaps she had been foolish not to remain in bed.

On the thought, the schoolroom door opened. Mr Rookham stood upon the threshold, thunder on his brow.

Prue's heart did a double somersault, and she jumped in her seat. Dislodged, Folly let out a yelp and leapt away to the safer area by the window. The twins jerked round.

'Uncle Julius!'

'You gave me such a fright!'

'We're writing about our adventure, Uncle Julius.'

'You can read mine later, if you like.'

Brought up short, Julius bit back the hot words that were hovering on his tongue. His nieces were looking at him in sudden doubt and perplexity. He clamped down on his bursting spleen.

'Pray continue. I only came for a word with Miss Hursley.'

His eyes turned to Prudence and, with a resurgence of anger, he saw that she had risen. But her arms were resting heavily on the desk before her, and it was obvious to the meanest intelligence that she could barely stand.

He went to his nieces. 'On second thoughts, you may take a break for a few moments.'

'But, Uncle Julius, I've just reached the bit where—'

Dodo was rising with alacrity. 'Come on, Lotty.'

'But I'm in the middle of—'

Impatience seized Julius. 'Out, I said!'

Lotty's dark brows rose in surprise, but she got up in haste and followed her sister from the room.

Julius turned just in time to see Prudence come out from behind the desk. She took a single pace and sagged. He sprang forward and caught her, lifting her bodily into his arms.

'You little goose, Prue! Didn't I tell you to rest?'

Prue perforce caught at his coat. The sensation of being swept off her feet had made her ridiculously light-headed, but her pulses were rioting and she could not get her breath.

'Oh, pray s-set me down!'

'By no means! I am taking you back to bed.'

'Oh, no, pray! Oh, Mr Rookham, *pray* let me down! I can perfectly well walk, I promise you.'

There was so frantic a note in her voice that Julius felt compelled to do as she asked. He set her gently back on her feet, but kept an arm firmly about her shoulders.

'L-let me sit for a moment.'

He guided her to the desk, and reached out a hand to tug the chair out into the open. 'Here. Gently, now.'

Prue sank into it, catching at the arms. Her breathing was shallow, and dizziness swam round her brain. His presence alone would have thrown her into dismay. But to be caught up into his arms in that fashion! She felt as if she would never recover.

A plaintive mew caught Julius's attention, and he looked down to find the kitten pawing at the hem of Prue's gown. Swiftly, he leaned down and picked Folly up, absently stroking the animal as he stepped away from the chair. Moving to the window, he deposited the kitten on the sill, where it sat upon its haunches and peered up at him.

He shifted back into the room, and glanced down at Prue's bowed head. All thought of Folly left his mind, and he gave tongue to his driving thought.

'If you only knew how furious I am with you!'

She cast him a fleeting glance, but she did not speak. Goaded, he continued.

'I have a matter of import to tell you, which is why I came up. You cannot imagine the shock upon seeing that you were no longer in your bed!'

Prue felt herself trembling, but the dizziness had passed. She dared to look him fully in the face. 'But I had to get up! I could not lie abed forever. And the girls need me.'

'To Hades with the girls!' He thrust impatient

hands into the air. 'What is more important? Their education or your health?'

'But I am better, I promise you,' pleaded Prue.

'Do you take me for a fool? You may be better, but you are as weak as that defenceless kitten of yours. Only wait until I get hold of the witless maid who helped you to dress!'

Prue's hands clutched the arms of her chair. 'You must not blame Maggie. I begged her to help me. And if she had not, I would have dressed myself.'

'Then I can only say that I wish she had refused you, for if one thing is more certain than another, it is that you would not have had the strength to dress yourself.'

Silenced, Prue gazed at him with a good deal of resentment. It was bad enough that he had stayed away from her. Now he must needs come marching in, scaring her out of her wits, and proceed to lose his temper!

The hawk features were pronounced, and he glared back at her with every evidence of dislike. Prue looked away. Seeing Folly, she chirruped at him and snapped her fingers. The kitten mewed, but remained where he was—in safety? Prue could not blame him.

Mr Rookham's voice came again, its tone only slightly moderated. 'If you must get up, at least make use of your parlour. I have had a day-bed put in there, which you would have known had you a grain of common sense.'

Curiously, this unwarranted scold had the effect of raising Prue's spirits a little. Forgetful of all that had passed, she hit back strongly.

'I don't know why you should accuse me of a lack of common sense, merely because I have no knowledge of it! How was I to guess what you would be at?'

Her attacker did not soften. 'Goose! I told you at the outset that you should rest in your parlour, did I not? Had you gone there, as you were ordered, you would have found the day-bed. However, it is not too late. I will take you there now, and you may settle yourself upon it.'

'And what about the girls?' demanded Prue.

'Forget the girls!'

'But they ought to finish their writing. You have no notion how difficult it is to get them to do any at all. But they were interested enough to begin, and—'

He interrupted without ceremony. 'Very well, if you insist upon them completing the project, I shall deal with them myself.'

Prue stared at him blankly. 'You?'

A sudden grin lightened his stormy features. 'Why not? Do you suppose the task will prove beyond my capabilities?'

'No, but—'

'Then there's an end of it. Now, come!'

Before she could make any further protest, Prue found herself drawn up from the chair. She held back.

'Folly!'

'Have no fear. I have no doubt the wretched creature will follow you.'

Half-carried in Mr Rookham's strong embrace, Prue was hustled willy-nilly along the corridor towards her little parlour, where he lowered her on to the day-bed. It had been placed facing the fire with its scrolled end in the window embrasure so that she might enjoy the view.

A scratching sound, together with an indignant mewl, sent Julius to the door, cursing. 'Get in, then, you misbegotten scrap!'

Prue threw him a reproachful glance, and called a welcome to the kitten. 'Come, Folly!'

Julius watched the animal trot over to the day-bed and jump up. He flung away and tugged violently on the bell-pull.

'We'll have Maggie in to see to you.' He crossed to the desk and picked up one of the volumes he had provided for her use. 'Have you read these? Shall I find you others?'

A trifle overwhelmed, Prue shook her head.

'Thank you, but I have scarce had time to get through one volume.'

'Then you can take time now,' he said curtly.

Recalling something he had said, Prue dared a question. 'What was it you wanted to speak to me about, sir?'

She thought his face changed. He turned to replace the volume he had taken out, and seemed to make a business of straightening the books. At length, he turned to her.

'It can wait. We will talk of it later, when you are truly better.'

He remained with her, saying little, but shifting restlessly about the small chamber until Prue began to feel utterly disturbed. She kept her attention on Folly's determined attempts to tread into her stomach, purring in loud content. Prue was almost glad when Maggie arrived in answer to the bell, and Mr Rookham at last made for the door, turning to impart a few final instructions to the maid.

'Make sure she rests. And feed her up, for God's sake! She is beginning to look like a scarecrow.' He glanced back at Prue. 'I will bring the twins' efforts for you to look over.'

And then he was off, leaving Prue feeling as if a whirlwind had come and gone. But her desperate heart betrayed her, rising with a sneaking hope.

* * *

It appeared that Lotty and Dodo were by no means impressed with the change. Two pairs of dark eyes stared blankly upon Julius where he stood in Prudence's place at the desk.

'Well? What is the matter?'

Lotty recovered herself first. 'You can't teach us, Uncle Julius!'

'No, 'cause you're not a governess,' stated Dodo, adding her mite.

'I am not going to teach you,' Julius told them flatly. 'I am merely acting as Miss Hursley's deputy while you complete your writing.'

The twins looked at each other, and then their frowning glances returned to his face. Reluctantly amused, Julius preserved his countenance, merely waiting for what they might find to say next. It was Lotty again who put the question.

'Can you help us with the spelling then?'

'Miss Prue always helps us with the spelling,' put in Dodo, parrot-like.

Julius raised his brows. 'Do you suppose I am unable to spell as well as Miss Prue?'

Lotty frowned. 'No, but you'll have to write it on the board for us.'

'Then we copy it out ten times so's we remember.'

He picked up a piece of chalk. 'Very well. What word is it that you need?'

Both girls broke into giggles, and he eyed them in some dudgeon. 'Now what is the matter?'

'You don't tell us now.'

'You wait 'til we're finished.'

'Then you read it, and then you put the spellings on the board.'

'Don't you know, Uncle Julius?'

"Course he don't know, Dodo! He's our uncle, not a governess.'

'But Mama knows how to teach us. Why shouldn't Uncle Julius know?'

But their uncle had reached the end of his rope. 'Enough! Sit down, the both of you, and start writing at once!'

Thus adjured—and rather to his surprise—both girls sat down and drew their sheets towards them. He watched with reluctant interest as Lotty chewed at the already mangled feather of her pen for a while, obviously deep in thought. Dodo had not hesitated, but immediately dipped her pen in the standish and began to carve out letters on the paper.

It struck him that they wrote with fluency, their hands rounding carefully. He shifted away from the desk, intending to see what progress they made.

Instantly, both heads shot up, and the twins put protective arms about the edge of their papers.

'You can't read it yet!' burst from Dodo.

'Miss Prue always waits until we're finished,' explained Lotty. 'She says she don't want to make us nervous, so she never looks over our shoulders.'

'You have to go back to the desk, Uncle Julius,' insisted Dodo. 'We can't write if you watch us.'

Julius ostentatiously reseated himself, throwing up his hands. 'Behold me! Now write, if you please.'

The pens began scratching again, and Julius's mind wandered. How Prudence could bear to sit and watch this laborious exercise was beyond him. No wonder she chose to vary the tedium of her days! Were he obliged to sit here day after day, he might also seek for ways in which to lighten the load. Or was it for the sake of the twins that she invented games involving daisy chains and woodland wanderings?

He was obliged to admit that he had hardly expected this easy a return to a dull writing task. What had she said? That it was difficult to get them to write? Yet they had consented to continue without a fight. Was it because he ordered them? Julius did not think so. Despite all his misgivings, it was plain that Prudence had made progress.

When he was at length permitted to read the effusions presented to him at the end of another half hour or so, he was astonished to discover how much improvement had been made in the twins' English. Search how he might, he was unable to discover more than half a dozen spelling errors. And the writing was relatively neat, with few splotches.

He had seen their efforts before Prudence came, and the change was remarkable. In so short a time too. And he had been disparaging in his mind, believing her to be as inept as she thought herself.

The dilemma that had been presented to him loomed the larger. How was he to tell her? What excuse could he now present to her, when he explained—as he must—the content of his sister's letter?

There was no excuse, he realised. He must give her the truth. That she would be bitterly disappointed, he could not doubt. For himself, there was—there had to be!—relief. It was what he had himself predicted, and he must be glad of it.

Feeling that the sooner the deed was done, the better, Julius chose to broach the matter later that day. Taking with him the specimens of the twins' writing efforts, he betook himself to Prudence's parlour after partaking of a light luncheon.

Opening the door softly, he found her dozing on the day-bed, an open book in her lap. From the window, a shaft of rare sunlight filtered, playing over her face. There was no sign of the kitten.

Julius stood looking down at her, his thoughts

unsteady. There was that about her pose that he found infinitely appealing, but he was determined not to yield. He was upon the point of deliverance, and though he itched to lean down and kiss that pale face, he knew it would be madness to give in to the impulse.

Prudence Hursley and he could not deal together. It was only a passing fancy. He could not subject himself—or her, if it came to that!—to a lifetime of regret. Better to let her go.

What he ought to do was to go to town for a spell and find himself another mistress. He had been too long alone, and that was not good for a man. He must not let himself be tempted to uproot his whole existence merely for the sake of a whim.

The whim opened its eyes and blinked up at him in a dazed fashion for a moment. Then the grey orbs widened and Prue started up.

'Mr Rookham!'

He held up a hand and stepped back. 'Stay where you are! I had no intention of disturbing you, and you looked exceedingly peaceful.'

Prue smothered a yawn. 'I feel peaceful.'

Or she had, she reflected. But a tattoo had begun pattering in her veins, and her chest had tightened. She tried to steady it, feeling relieved for the comfortable scrolled end of the day-bed at her head. At least she need not attempt to sit or stand in his presence, which gave her a decided advantage.

'Where is Folly?'

'With the girls. They took him for his feed at luncheon.'

She watched Mr Rookham take the straight chair by the desk and turn it, placing it at the foot of the day-bed. He came to her and held out two sheets of paper.

'Your charges have done well.'

Prue took the proffered sheets with an automatic gesture, but her scanning eyes took in little of the matter written upon them. From the periphery of her vision, she saw him seat himself in the chair so that he faced her. The flurry of her heartbeat increased. He looked as if he meant to remain for a space. Prue did not know whether she was glad or sorry.

'I was surprised at how few spelling mistakes they made.'

She tried to concentrate her mind upon the sheets she held in her hands, but the letters were nothing but a blur. She blinked to focus her eyes, and brought the papers closer. Seeking to prevaricate, she threw out a remark at random.

'Their spelling is better, it is true.'

'So I perceive. I congratulate you.'

Prue glanced up at him. 'It is little enough.'

His eyes became fierce. 'But it is something. Don't belittle yourself so!'

She swallowed. 'If you are pleased, I must be thankful.'

Julius got up abruptly, and took a hasty turn about the room. Hell and damnation! He had known it would be difficult. Only he had not bargained for her agonizing humility. Had forgotten it! Pleased? Nothing could please him but that she went away from here. Far away, so that he could resume his former comfortable existence!

Prue eyed him with growing trepidation. What had she said? He was angry again! Did he mean to attack her?

But to her relief, he returned to the chair, almost throwing himself down. Prue pretended a studious examination of the papers, reading swiftly words that made little sense in her head.

'For God's sake, put those down!'

He regretted his tone immediately, for her hands dropped and a look of dismayed reproach entered her face. Julius leaned forward and twitched the papers out of her hands, laying them upon the desk. When he glanced at Prudence again, he found her with her hands over her face. Remorse swamped him.

'I beg your pardon! Pay no heed to me, Prue!'

Her hands came down, and he saw a smile waver. 'I am only a little tired, sir.'

'And my brutish manners are making you feel worse! Accept my apologies.'

A gurgle escaped her, and her features lit abruptly. 'If I do, I dare say it will not be long before you are scolding me again.'

He was obliged to laugh, despite a sudden sensation of deadness in his chest. 'You are probably right.'

A silence fell, and Prue eyed him with a quickening at her breast. Why was he so moody? There was a deep frown between his brows, making the hawk-look of his jutting nose stand out. Abruptly, a great sigh swept out of him and he leaned forward, resting his clasped hands upon his knees.

'Prudence, I don't know how to tell you, but I must.'

Shadows gathered in the corners of her mind. 'Tell me what, Mr Rookham?'

He hesitated, his eyes raking her in a manner that made her feel as if he probed to her very depths. Then he brought it out flat.

'My sister is betrothed. She writes that she wishes to take the twins upon a visit to her prospective husband's estates.'

The pit of Prue's stomach seemed to vanish. Then she must leave here! She must leave him. It was finished.

She did not know that she spoke. 'When is it to be?'

'Soon. A week or two only.'

'So soon?'

Her chest had hollowed out. She did not know that in her eyes was all the emptiness she felt.

Julius could hardly bear to look at her. He could no more doubt the reason for her evident despair than he could doubt his own attraction to her. For the first time, he acknowledged that he had known it all along. Had guessed it! And it was his fault. What had he done, blundering his way into her affections without thought for the consequences?

He recalled a remark she once had made. About regretting the intimacy of this unorthodox friendship when she must in the end move on.

For a breathless moment, he toyed with the notion of throwing caution to the winds—only to make her some reparation. But a deeper knowledge told him that it would be a greater wrong than that he had already committed. Unless he could offer her his whole heart, he had no right to offer her anything at all.

The dreadful news had sunk in, and Prue's shock began to recede. In a way, it was a comfort. To know that she must go from his vicinity. It would hurt, but less than to live with the dreadful uncertainties and unbidden hopes that must attend her here.

She sought for a neutral note. 'Well, I shall be sorry to leave here, Mr Rookham. Where is it that we must go?'

We! The moment had come. He could no longer avoid the issue. How hard it was to say it!

'I am afraid it is not as simple as that, Prudence.'

Dear God, the dread effect of those vulnerable orbs! He wished she would not look at him. Or that he had not chosen her little parlour where there was no possible way for him to avoid her gaze. There was enquiry there, and it was hard indeed to be obliged to say that which must inevitably deal her the harshest blow. And he would see it in her eyes!

'What do you mean, Mr Rookham?'

His intent upon softening the news fell apart. There was no way to soften it. He only hoped his voice did not come out as harshly as the words he must say.

'Trixie has engaged a governess of her own choice in London. I am sorry, Prudence, but your services will no longer be required. You must find yourself another post.'

Prue lay on the day-bed, the *Morning Post* spread neglected across her lap, gazing at the sunlit grounds outside. At her feet, Folly slept, a splash of multi-coloured warmth stretched out in the sun's rays. She had been resting here all through Sunday and again on Monday, forbidden by Mr Rookham from resuming her temporary duties.

Temporary—a horrid word! She had known from the first that it might be so. Only she had not bargained for a double loss, the greater of which gnawed like a hungry rat within. All hope was abandoned. Had he intended to offer her a different future, then would have been his opportunity. He had not taken it.

Nor had he so much as mentioned the departure in prospect on those two brief visits he had made to her parlour—only, so he said, to ensure that she was obedient to his orders, and was not behaving like the goose he knew her to be. Prue was forced to recognise that he was reconciled to her going.

She had wept it out now, there in the secret confines of her lonely bedchamber. Shock had held the grief inside through those first hideous moments. And there had been that in his face, when he had told her, which had its own balm. Prue had known then that he cared—only not enough. He must not be made to feel in any way to blame for what he could not help.

After all, she had told herself, when he had left her—he had stayed but a moment, thank the Lord!—what she'd had from Mr Rookham was a great deal more than she had ever looked for, or deserved. Who was she to bay for the moon?

But the tears had wetted her pillow half the night. With the result that she had slept overlong upon the Sunday, leading Mr Rookham to decree, when he heard of it, that she must spend a further day of rest. It was ironic, Prue thought, that Mrs Polmont was not now—when she might have had reason—at pains to accuse her of malingering!

The housekeeper had been in once or twice, and the obvious triumph in her features told Prue that she was in possession of the news. But no one could have accused her either of neglect in her duties or of incivility. It was to Maggie that Prue was indebted for her knowledge of how the rest of the household had taken it.

'Mrs Wincle is fair rattled, miss. She keeps on saying as she'd never have thought it, and it's all a great mistake. "Mark my words, Maggie," she said to me, "we ain't heard the end of it nohow. I seen what I seen, and I know what I know," she said to me.'

Even the austere butler was inclined, according to the maid, to 'wait and see'. As for Maggie herself, it was the severest trial to Prue to be obliged to listen to her veiled doubts and attempts to bolster Prue's own hopes.

'Don't take it so hard, miss. There's time yet. As

I heard it, that there Mrs Chillingham ain't nowise coming to fetch them twins this side of May. If you ask me, there's them as will change their minds afore that day comes!'

It did not take a genius to work out that the maid's elusive 'them' was in reference to Mr Rookham. And May—as if she was not herself counting down the hours, never mind the days!—was less than two weeks away. Since such conversations could only give her pain, Prue refrained either from encouraging Maggie or arguing with her. Her solution was to find things for the maid to do in order to be rid of her.

'If you will be so kind, Maggie, as to fetch me the daily journal when Mr Rookham has finished with it, I shall be grateful.'

Not that the maid had let the request pass without comment. 'I'll fetch it to you, miss, with pleasure. But if you was meaning to look for another position, I'd not waste your time. You ain't going to need one, not according to Mrs Wincle.'

It should have consoled her to know that she had well-wishers among the domestics. But the truth was that though this support was kindly meant, its effect was merely to rub salt into the wound.

Sighing, she took up the newspaper and scanned the advertisements. There were several, but only two for which she might be thought suitable. With a heavy heart, Prue read the requirements more closely. Knowledge of the globes and the French tongue? Yes, she was on safe ground there. Some artistic ability. That would depend upon how much was needed. A lively personality? Well, that must rule her out at once! She was more dead than alive, and she could see no diminution of this condition in the foreseeable future.

Perhaps Mrs Duxford would be able to help her. She had written to her old preceptress yesterday, with the hope that if she was unable to secure a position immediately she might at least return to the Seminary. She would have to pay her board—all the old students did so when they stayed—but there would be considerable comfort in the company of Kitty, and she would hear news of Nell. Only it must depend upon whether there was room. If the Seminary was full, she would have to take a lodging until such time as she found herself another place.

The prospect was uninviting, but not as chilling as it might have been in other circumstances. Numbed as she was by the greater evil, Prue was able to contemplate this possibility with equanimity. Nothing could be worse than her removal from Rookham Hall.

She had just begun to read again the less likely

advertisements when the door burst open to admit the twins, in a state of high indignation. Folly woke with a start, and sat blinking green eyes as they dashed up to the day-bed.

'Miss Prue, the most dreadful thing!'

'Uncle Julius just told us that Mama wrote to him, and—'

'Mama won't let us keep you!'

It was beyond what anyone could endure. Prue dissolved into tears.

Julius regarded his nieces with a deliberate calm that in no way reflected his state of mind. His will to resist, which was unshaken, stood him in good stead.

Lotty was frowning heavily. 'Uncle Julius, don't you understand?'

'She's *crying*,' repeated Dodo for the fifth time.

'Yes, I heard you.'

'Then what are you going to do about it?' demanded the more percipient of the pair. 'You have to do something!'

Julius raised his brows. 'Why?'

Dodo glared up at him. 'Last time you were as cross as crabs!'

'Yes, and you said you was going to beat us,' averred Lotty feelingly.

A faint smile was drawn from him. 'Are you in any way to blame this time?'

"Course not,' scoffed Dodo. 'You told us it, Uncle Julius. You said Mama got us another governess.'

'But we don't *want* another governess,' insisted Lotty. 'And Miss Prue don't want to go neither. She wants to stay with us.'

Julius was aware of a tremor inside himself, but he suppressed it. 'Did she say so?'

'She said she don't want to leave here, not really.'

'Yes, and she cried and cried,' stated Dodo again.

Lotty turned on her. 'She didn't, you noodle. She started, and then she stopped herself. And she said we wasn't to pay no attention.'

'Then why are you doing so?' demanded Julius.

'Because she—'

"Cos we want you to tell Mama to keep her for us,' cut in Dodo impatiently.

'Mama will do it if you tell her, I know she will,' averred Lotty in persuasive tones.

Julius turned away from them and went to the window. He could do it, there was no question. Trixie might have engaged another female, but he was fairly certain he could persuade her to change her mind. Were his own desires out of court, would he, in all conscience, feel justified in recommending Prudence Hursley for the post?

He had thought not, but it could not be denied that his nieces were much improved. He had been impressed with their writing. Once he began to think about it, he had realised that their manners and deportment had also adjusted for the better. And they liked her.

From behind him, he caught whispers. There was a drag at his chest which he attempted to ignore. But its message could not be gainsaid. He was convinced that Lotty and Dodo were motivated purely by their own wishes. That Prudence had wept afforded them all the excuse they needed to demand his aid. But they did not know why she wept! Nor could they judge of the need for this highly desirable parting.

If it was to his advantage to be freed of the tie, then it was essential for Prudence. Nothing could be worse for her than a continued sojourn among members of his family. A clean break was the kindest measure.

As for the twins, they would recover soon enough. And their welfare was far less his concern. They had a mother to care for their future. Prudence Hursley's future was in his hands—temporarily.

He turned. Two pretty faces watched him expectantly. He gave a comprehensive shrug and spoke with finality.

'I cannot help you, children. Your mama has other plans, and there the matter ends.'

To his relief, the girls accepted this. They pouted a little, and threw him darkling looks, but surprisingly argued no further.

That evening as he sat at dinner, plagued by the poor appetite that had attended him for several days, the reason for their reticence was borne in upon him with stunning force.

He had just waved away untasted a dish of white veal escalopes, garnished with slices of lemon, fried mushrooms and forcemeat balls, when the footman, who was serving him in place of Creggan on his evening off, was called to the door by a furtive knock.

Julius, lost in his own thoughts, paid no heed. His hand reached out for his wineglass, and, finding it again empty—had he not refilled it only a moment or two ago?—took up the bottle and splashed a further measure into his glass.

He was tossing it back when the footman approached him, bearing a folded billet. The fellow looked doubtful, but held it out.

'The maid Maggie brought this, sir. It appears that it was sent by the young ladies.'

Julius looked at him blankly. 'You mean my nieces?'

'I believe so, sir.'

Now what were those little minxes up to? Was this another attempt to persuade him to intervene with his sister? He unfolded the paper. Its missive was roughly penned, but its message was plain.

Dear Uncle Joleos
We have kidnap Mis Proo and we won't let her go nohow til you tell mamma to keep her.
love Lotty and Dodo.

Julius was on his feet. 'Outrageous! Have they run mad?'

'Sir?'

He became aware of the footman's startled features. He had not known he had uttered aloud. A curse escaped him, and he addressed himself unthinkingly to the servant.

'It must be a ruse. A jest! I am persuaded they cannot mean it.'

But already he was throwing his napkin to one side along with the fateful note, and grabbing up one of the candelabra set upon the table. A few strides took him to the door, and he seized the handle, slamming it open. It did not take him many minutes to make the journey into the wing given over to the Chillingham family, but he crammed into them every pent-up frustration of the past few days.

The devil fly away with the girl! This was all her fault. Had she not shown them a laxity of discipline that was bound to redound upon them all? Persuade Trixie of her suitability, indeed! Were it open to him to do it, he would not. A more foolish and hopelessly inadequate female for the purpose could not be imagined. She had done nothing but set his household by the ears from the moment she arrived. With the result, if you please, that the entirety of the domestic staff—with one notable exception, whose stupidity equalled only the governess's own—had convinced themselves of her imminent advancement to the rank of mistress of the house! A more insane, ridiculous, and utterly futile notion he had never encountered. Willingly could he strangle the wench!

Yet his emotions, upon entering her bedchamber without the preliminary of knocking on the door, only to discover it empty, took a violent turn in the opposite direction.

God in heaven, but she was not there! He stood for a moment, blank with shock. Then his senses bid him go at once to her parlour. It was early yet. She might be dining.

But as he traversed back along the way he had come, Julius experienced a rising dread that threatened every moment to choke him. The parlour was dimly lit by a single candle on the mantel, and one sweep of the ones he held showed it to be as empty as her chamber, but for the tray upon the table.

He entered quickly and lifted one of the covers. The meal was intact. He caught sight of Folly on the day-bed, standing and blinking in the sudden light.

It struck him poignantly to see the animal alone in here—as if Prudence had deserted it.

But it was the twins who had sent the note. Was he so much a fool? They must have her in their room!

He went out, shutting the parlour door upon the kitten, and once more sped along the corridor towards Prudence's bedchamber, stopping short at his nieces' door. He turned the handle and found it locked. Fury ripped through him and he rapped smartly on the wood.

'Lotty! Dodo! Open this door at once!'

A smothered shriek of fright emanated from the other side. Then an urgent whispering broke out.

Julius banged fiercely on the door.

'You will open this door immediately, or I shall break it down, I promise you!'

Behind him, he heard the opening of another door, and quickly turned his head. A shadowed form, too small in stature for Prudence, erupted rapidly down the corridor, emitting a flood of French.

'*Mais, qu'est-ce qui ce passe? Ah, c'est le maître.* What ees zees zat you do, *monsieur*?'

Julius did not bother to answer. 'Have you a key to this door?'

Yvette jumped. 'Eet ees lock?'

'Those minxes have locked themselves inside, yes. Why have you not a key?'

'I 'ave ze key. I weel fetch.' She hurried away.

Julius once again thumped upon the wood. 'Dodo and Lotty, you are in big trouble! Have you Miss Hursley in there?'

There was no other reply than a hushed squeaking, as if the twins had fallen into argument. A thumping of footsteps overlaid it, and he turned to see that several of his servants were hurrying down the corridor towards him from the main house, one of them bearing a candle.

'Oh, sir!' came frantically from Maggie. 'I never knew as the wicked little things would do such a thing! I swear I never knew what was in that note! They give it me when I come for their supper tray, sir.'

Behind the maid, he spied both the footman, who lighted the way, and Wincle. What, was his entire household roused by this event?

'For heaven's sake, go away, all of you! Things are bad enough as it is.'

No one obeyed him, and the cook pushed through. 'Do you let me at 'em, sir! I'll give them kidnapped!'

'Wincle, for the lord's sake, go away! And take the rest of them with you.'

To his intense irritation, Wincle planted herself firmly in the corridor, arms akimbo, determination in her chubby features.

'I ain't going nowhere, Mr Rookham, not if my post depends on it. To think them naughty creatures would play such a trick!'

Before Julius could again request them to depart, a mutter of French was heard, and Yvette had rejoined the party.

'I 'ave not ze key, *monsieur*. And why? Because zees *enfants* have stole heem!'

'Stolen the key! Mercy me, whatever will they think of next?'

'Wincle, take this and be quiet,' begged Julius wearily, handing over the candelabrum.

'Seems to me,' said the cook, ignoring this request, and passing the burden to the maid, 'as Jacob here ought to smash the lock for you, sir.'

Julius glanced at the brawny young fellow who had remained bashfully in the background. 'That is the first sensible suggestion anyone has made. However, let me have one last try before we resort to such extremes.'

The cook pushed her way to the door. 'Let me, sir.' Setting her face to the keyhole, she bellowed through it. 'Now see here, young sauceboxes! You've to open this door double quick, or it'll be the worse for you. Here's the master ready with a stick to beat you, I'll be bound. Now, are you going to open this door, or are you not?'

So sure was Julius that Prudence was held in the bedchamber that a measure of calm had returned to his mind. He could not but be amused at his cook's direct methods.

For a moment it appeared that she was to be as unsuccessful as himself, for all that emanated from the other side of the locked door was a desperate conference conducted in excitable undertones. The watchers outside waited in silence, and then Wincle rose from her bent posture.

'Well, sir, I never did! Seems as if it's determined they are, and no mistake.'

But then the key turned in the lock, and the door was cautiously pulled inwards. Two scared faces peered out, and a cacophony burst forth among the servants.

Yvette herded the girls back inside, voluble in complaint, while Wincle and Maggie broke out scolding. All that concerned Julius at that precise moment was to find Prudence. Without ceremony, he swept his way into the bedchamber and cast a quick glance around. Unless she was under the four-poster bed which the twins inhabited, the governess was not there!

Then they must have locked her up in a different room. He turned wrathful eyes upon the miscreants, who were now huddled in the bed, clad only in their nightgowns and clutching each other as they shrank away from the nurse's shrill complaints. Wincle had given over scolding in order to express her astonishment to her colleagues. In no mood to be trifled with, Julius took command.

'Silence! Quiet, all of you!'

His voice, cutting across the babble with that authority they all recognised, stopped the noise dead. Julius trod across to the bed, and the nurse gave way before him.

In the relatively dim glow of the available light, the twins looked excessively white. It occurred to Julius that they had frightened themselves as much as anyone else. He sat on the bed, and addressed them with all the mildness they might have expected from Prudence herself.

'I dare say you did not intend to cause such a stir, but what you have done is very silly indeed. Now, where is Miss Prue? Have you shut her up in some other room in the house?'

The girls exchanged a glance, and then looked at him again, shaking their heads. Julius tried again, his tone almost conversational.

'She is still not fully recovered, you know. If you have truly kidnapped her, as you say, it could be very dangerous for her.' He softened his voice the more. 'Now, are you going to tell me where she is, or do I have to resort to measures I had much rather not undertake?'

Lotty gasped. 'You mean to beat us?'

Dodo's face crumpled. 'I told you he would!'

Julius waited. Behind him the silence was total, although he could feel the suspense in the air. He wondered if the servants believed he would actually do it.

Dodo was whimpering, but Lotty dug her sharply in the ribs with her elbow. 'Stop it!'

'But he's g-going to beat us!'

Lotty bit her lip, and her dark eyes met her uncle's. Julius remained perfectly still, holding her gaze. For a moment, the challenge held. And then the girl sighed out a defeated breath.

'She's in the forester's hut.'

Chapter Eleven

For a moment, Julius did not take in what Lotty meant. The utter impossibility of it prevented belief. And then it sank home. A hollow opened up inside his chest. He hardly knew that he spoke, wholly unaware of the flat menace of his tone.

'You left her in a hut in the forest, after she has been as near death from exposure as makes no matter? What are you trying to do, kill her outright?'

He saw horror leap into both pairs of eyes. And then they were wailing.

But Julius had no time to deal with their distress. He was up, wholly ignoring everyone but his footman.

'Jacob, go and find Hessle and meet me outside the west door in five minutes. Tell him to bring torches, and get on a coat and good boots yourself.'

He turned next to the maid, who was staring

open-mouthed at the sobbing twins. 'Maggie, isn't it?'

She was alert to him in an instant. 'Yes, sir?'

'Have quilts and a hot brick ready, and a fire in her chamber. Tea—hot and plenty of it. And then a cup of warm milk. Mrs Wincle will help you. Now, go!'

He did not wait to see whether he was obeyed, but snapped smartly out of the twins' room, and headed for the main house and his own chamber, driven by a haunting image of Prudence's face, deathly pale on her pillows.

She was relieved that she had not ventured forth without the thick Seminary cloak. Huddled within it, with the hood up, Prue had buried herself inside the heap of straw, just as the forester had buried the girls that earlier time. The intense cold she had felt at first had faded, along with hunger and the wakeful thoughts that had plagued her.

At first she had done nothing but rail against her own stupidity. How could she have been so blind? Why could she not have seen through the trick the twins had played upon her? Well did she know their fund of ingenuity, their ability to act a part! Only it had not occurred to her, lost in her own despair, that they would use so dreadful a ruse to try to get their own way. After she had expressly forbidden them to act in the matter, too!

'It is not for you to decide, my dears, and we must all be content with the situation.'

'But you ain't content, Miss Prue,' had protested Lotty.

'You cried!' Dodo had accused.

Prue had not known how to defend herself, for the true cause of her distress had little to do with the twins. She had temporized.

'That is partly because I am still a little unwell, and my nerves are shaky.'

Four dark eyes had stared at her. Lotty had frowned, but it was Dodo who had put her finger on it.

'But you was *sad.*'

'Yes, and so are we!' claimed Lotty.

Gathering them into a warm embrace, Prue had thanked them, but her will had not altered. Mr Rookham must not be troubled in the matter.

'Naturally I am sad to leave you both, but you must not try to get your uncle to interfere. I had not expected to remain with you for long, for your future was uncertain. Your uncle told me so at the outset. Your mama must be the best judge of what will suit you.'

She had thought that the twins had accepted her dictum. They had looked at each other with that sort of conspiratorial signal they seemed always to understand between them, and she had heard no more of it. Until, that was, Dodo had come to her parlour in a frenzy of panic.

'Lotty has gone to the forest! I told her not to, but she wouldn't listen to me nohow. She said as she was going to run away to the hut, and not come back until Uncle Julius said you could stay with us!'

Shock had made Prue abandon her usual caution. Had it been excitement in Dodo's dark eyes, rather than the fright for which she had taken it? The child had played her part only too well. Prue had been thankful that she was now steady upon her feet, for the thought uppermost in her mind had been a determination to fetch Lotty back before Mr Rookham caught wind of the matter.

She had gone as quickly as she could to her bed-chamber, in order to don suitable footgear and throw on the woollen cloak over the linsey-woolsey gown. Dodo had refused to remain at home. Instead, suitably clad in a duffle coat, she had frisked at Prue's side in an inexplicable state of high glee— which was all too readily explained now!

It had not taken long to reach the forest, for the way had been clear. But it had been another matter finding the hut. Prue had begun to entertain fears that they might not do so before the light failed. By the time they had rediscovered the fallen trunk which had served for the twins' first refuge on that fatal day, Prue had found herself flagging. Her breath had shortened, and she had felt considerably less stable upon her feet. But the need to find Lotty had kept her on the move.

By good fortune—or pre-arrangement?—Dodo had apparently recognised landmarks that led them in the right direction. The hut had come into sight at last, and relief had swept through Prue's veins. It had been short-lived.

The door of the hut was latched, with slots either side into which the forester was used to place a bar to prevent the door accidentally flying open. But the bar had not been there.

Prue had called for Lotty as she lifted the latch and peered into the gloom beyond. No sound had come from within, and she'd had no hesitation in pulling the door open and pushing into the hut.

Before she well knew what had happened, the square of light behind her had disappeared as the door had been thrust to. Plunged into relative darkness, Prue had whirled about, alerted to the sounds of a whispered conversation and a clump and thud that signalled the barring of the door from the outside.

She had not recognised it for what it was at once,

but upon reaching for the door, it had soon been borne in upon her that she had been locked in. She had called out to the culprits in no uncertain fury.

'What in the world are you doing? Dodo? Or is that you, Lotty? Have you barred the door? What do you mean by it?'

Lotty's voice had come through to her, a trifle muffled by the thickness of the thatched walls.

'It's all right, Miss Prue. We won't keep you there long.'

Shock had ripped through Prue's chest. 'Keep me here? Have you run mad?'

"Course we ain't!' had come Dodo's shrill response. 'And when Uncle Julius says he'll tell Mama to keep you, we'll let you out again.'

Prue's mind had blanked of all notions but the horrifying fact. The twins were holding her to ransom!

She had barely heard Lotty's furious protest to her sister. 'You wasn't supposed to say it, noodle!'

'It don't matter. It's better if she knows, then she won't be scared in there.'

'Scared? Don't you know her better than that? Miss Prue ain't scared of nothing!'

But Prue, coming a little to her senses, had been altogether swamped with fear. Not at the thought of being left alone in the confines of the forester's hut. But at the notion of what Mr Rookham's emotions might be upon hearing of this latest escapade! The effect upon him was all too likely to be the opposite of that which the twins intended.

If anything had been needed to prove to him how unfitted she was to be in charge of two such enterprising imps, this must truly suffice. Who but a confirmed ninnyhammer would have fallen into so obvious a trap? Oh, she was altogether the goose he called her!

This self-critical state of mind had been superseded by a slow gathering of realisation of the even more critical state of her body. Prue had tried in vain to witness the departure of the twins through the cut-out window. She could hear them, but they had been making away from the other side of the hut. As she had remained standing there, railing at her own inadequacies and gazing profitlessly into the unrelenting forest, the light had begun to fade.

With it, the chill of evening had seeped bit by bit into her consciousness. And then her legs had almost given way, and dizziness had wreathed her brain. She had caught at the window's edge, tugging at her breath. Lord, let not her frail and weakened frame betray her now!

The thought of Mr Rookham's wrath at finding her health once more endangered, had made her seek for a way to extract herself. Waiting only for the dizziness to recede, she had embarked upon a tentative exploration.

The window was both too high and too small to afford her an exit. The door opened outwards, and she could by no means pull it in the opposite direction, as she had discovered when she tugged mightily at its stubborn bulk. The thatch at the walls, when she had tried to penetrate its woody interior, had proved obdurate against her failing strength. And she could scarce reach the roof, which in all likelihood was as stiffly firm as anything else in the place. Why in the world could the hut not have been tumbledown?

It was clear that there was to be no escape. But it would not be from neglect of herself that Prue became once again bereft of her body's warmth, she had determined. And she had burrowed into the straw, there to shiver for some little time, and await what must be an inevitable rescue. She had soon begun to feel the pangs of hunger along with the cold.

Time had dragged. And at last lost meaning. By now the cold had numbed her, and she lay in a semi-conscious state, between waking and dreaming. Drowsily she wondered whether the twins had dared to carry out their plan. Suppose their nerve failed them? They would never find their way here in the dark. In that case she was doomed, for she did not think she would survive the night.

The thought, floating through her mind, afforded an unexpected balm. She had not thought of dying, but had not Mr Rookham said she had been near death? Well, if it came, she would embrace it. There could be no pain in death, for she would not be there to feel it.

A faint pang smote her for the realisation that she might die without seeing him again. She could not forget him, for she carried his image in her mind—and death, be it never so cruel, could not erase it. Only she would have liked to see him just once more. To gaze upon the steely eyes and the jutting nose, even if there was fierceness in his looks. To hear again the sound of his voice, whether teasing or wrathful.

'My poor Prue!'

Yes, or gentle. So gentle his touch, his fingers at her cheek. Was that a sigh she heard?

'She is cold, but not as icy as the last time. Hold the torch closer!'

Brisk. He was ever brisk, she recalled.

'Prudence, look at me!'

Commanding he was. Even in the shadowed face as it hung over her, the dark locks falling forward in a halo of light that surrounded his head, she could see the strength of command.

'She is barely conscious.'

'Shall I carry her, sir?'

'You keep hold of the torch, Jacob. Prue, listen to me! I am going to lift you now.'

Lift her? But was she not in bed? She was floating in the air. Warmth was close at her side. Only she had not strength to prise open her eyelids to find its source.

'Keep that door open!'

A murmuring assailed her ears, and a sense of motion. Her arm was awkwardly placed and she flailed in an effort to pull it in. There was a reeling in the air, and a flare of light at her eyes.

'Stay close before me. I will follow your light. Hessle, you lead the way ahead.'

What strange bobbing of that flare in the darkness? Then it was gone, and she rolled her head into the warmth.

'Prudence, are you awake?'

It rumbled at her ear, and a small corner of the mist lifted. Prue's awareness heightened. There was something she must say to him. Her voice was not as strong as she wished.

'I knew you would find me.'

'I could wish it had been sooner.'

He had heard her. She recognised an undertone of anger, and remembered what she must tell him.

'If I died, it was not for want of care. I tried, Mr Rookham. I did try.'

She felt his hold tighten, and there was a rough-ness in his tone. 'I know. You did well, Prue.'

But had she died? She thought perhaps she was still alive, although the strangeness of his advent had all the makings of a dream. She no longer understood why she had spoken in that way. Nor could she think what it meant, that he should be carrying her. If that was what he did?

'Where are you taking me?'

'Home, and to bed.'

Then it must be a dream. Not all her waking longings had dared to take her to this. A trembling awoke in her breast.

'Poor girl, you are cold!'

A faint gurgle escaped her. 'No, I am lost in the wonder of it. I have never allowed myself to dream this far before. A kiss, perhaps. But your bed!'

An odd quality in the silence, in the way he held her, arrested her attention. An effort of will thrust her eyes open. Above her she noted the dark shadow of his jawline. She wanted to touch him, but her fingers were unavailable. One arm was tucked tightly out of her reach. With an effort, she managed to throw up the other from where it hung, landing with a thump at his chest. He looked down.

'Mr Rookham, I shall not object to it.'

She was abruptly aware that she must have been

in motion, for everything became still. His features were visible to her. A blaze at his eyes thrilled her, and the guttural note in his voice had a meaning that spoke to her depths.

'You don't know what you are saying, Prudence. But I beg you to keep mum, for we are not alone.'

Then she must be obedient to his wish. She snuggled into his chest, and thought she heard it pumping. A savage rhythm that stirred the blood in her veins.

The motion resumed, lulling her into sleep. When she next became aware, there were hands at work upon her clothes, and a muttered conference above her head.

'Do you turn her, Mrs Wincle, while I pull off the gown.'

'Never you fret, Maggie. I'll hold her up and you can tug it off straight.'

Prue found herself in a sitting posture, firmly held against a cushioning support. It did not seem worthwhile to protest, and she submitted to the drag of her clothing. Before long she found herself tucked into a cocoon of warmth, where she lay blissful and undisturbed for a while.

'Has she had anything to eat or drink?'

The new voice penetrated, where the others, un-

ceasing and unnoticed, had become part of the surroundings. Prue tried to come up out of the fog of
lethargy. Her head was lifted, and something
placed at her lips.

'Drink.'

As he commanded, so she must do, she knew that
much. She complied as best she could, swallowing
down much of whatever it was that he presented.
At length, she was permitted to stop.

'Good girl.'

Prue's head was laid down again, and she sank
back into the slough of forgetfulness. When she
woke again, her mind was more alert, although she
could not yet fathom whether what she saw was
dream or reality.

In a pool of light near the still-burning fire, Mr
Rookham sat in an armchair, his cravat loosened
and his chin sunk upon his chest. His legs were
stretched out, his arms slack as in sleep.

'Would he remain in my room? Why is he there?'

She must have spoken aloud, for he started
awake, sitting up in a bang. His eyes searched
towards her, but perhaps there was not light enough
for him to see that she was awake.

'Why are you there?'

He stood up and came across, his figure blocking
out the light so that he became a silhouette. He sat

on the bed, and bent towards her. His features sprang to life against the glow behind.

'How are you feeling?'

Prue was swept with a rush of affection. She struggled to pull her arms out from under the covers that held her tightly enclosed.

'You should keep in the warm,' he warned.

But she paid no heed. Her hands came free. Without hesitation, she reached up to his face, pulling him down. She pressed her lips to his cheek, and drew him close, entwining her arms about his neck. His face was warm against her own, and she sighed in content.

'Julius…'

He shifted in a convulsive movement, and Prue found herself caught up in an embrace so tight that the breath was stopped in her chest. It eased after a moment, and she gasped for air as his face came away, hovering over her own. A husky whisper reached her.

'You impossible creature, what have you done to me?'

Then there was sensation, inexpressibly pleasurable, and utterly outside the scope of her wayward imaginings. His lips gentled hers, so that his warm breath mingled with her own. She heard him groan, and felt the pressure at her mouth intensify. A spark ignited within her, and a rush of blood to her head made her glad that she was safe in bed where she could not fall.

The kiss grew too rich to be borne, and she caught at his hair with her fingers, as if she would hold him off. But a treacherous hand caressed her throat, and the lips travelled to her cheeks, her brow, and down again to her mouth.

'There is no turning back now, my sweet,' they murmured, and then took her mouth anew.

'But I have no strength,' she uttered when she was able.

He lifted up and she saw his eyes, a glitter in the shadows. A faint laugh came.

'I was rather forgetting that.' A defeated sound sighed out of him. 'Then it must wait—much to my chagrin, believe me! But I warn you, my patience is by no means inexhaustible.'

Prue was moved to laughter. 'That I had noticed, sir.'

She saw his smile, and reached up wavering fingers to touch his face in wonder. So excellent a dream. How real it felt! She ran her finger down the length of his jutting nose. He kissed it as it reached his mouth, and then sat up.

'You had best sleep, my Prue. Tomorrow we will arrange everything.'

Obedient to his will, she closed her eyes. With the morning light, she awoke to normality, bar a little stiffness of the joints. There was nothing in her head to guide her as to the night's event, although she recalled something of the forester's hut. As for her dreams, she knew nothing of them, except that they had encompassed Mr Rookham—and a sensation that it saddened her to lose.

This happy state of ignorance lasted only until Maggie arrived with her breakfast on a tray.

'There now, miss, you look ever so much better.'

Prue struggled to sit up. 'Better? What in the world do you mean, Maggie? I have been better for several days.'

The maid's jaw dropped. 'Don't say as you can't remember! Lordy, miss, and you setting the house by the ears!'

The tray was laid across Prue's knees, but despite a ravenous feeling of hunger, she scarcely noticed. She stared at the girl, bemused.

'Was it not then a dream? I had thought I was in the forester's hut.'

'And so you were, miss. Them naughty twins told the master as they'd kidnapped you and they wouldn't nowise tell him where you was. They soon thought better of that, I can tell you. And the master went after you straight and brought you home. Nigh gone you were, miss! Mrs Wincle and me was that shocked to see you. I don't wonder you don't remember it all, now I come to think on it, for you was bare awake and he had to carry you all the way!'

Prue blinked dazedly at the contents of the breakfast tray, as images swam into her mind. Dodo's excited face. The open maw of the hut's dark interior. A vague outline of Mr Rookham's features—at the oddest angle!—and a sensation of being held, of her head buried against a strong chest so that she heard his heartbeat.

A wave of warmth attacked her, sending shivers up her limbs. She grasped at the edges of the tray upon her knees.

'Maggie, pray move this, for I am afraid I will upset it.'

Tutting, Maggie picked up the tray and transferred it to the corner commode. She poured tea and brought the cup across.

'Here, you'd best drink this while it's hot. I'll fetch a buttered oatcake to you when you're ready.'

Prue was none too sure that she was capable of eating, despite the rumbling emptiness of her stomach, but she took the cup and sipped gratefully at the refreshing beverage. After a moment it dawned on her that the maid was eyeing her in a manner both searching and smug. A horrid feeling of apprehension invaded her.

'Why do you look at me so?'

Maggie raised innocent brows. 'Who, me, miss? Don't know what you mean.'

It would not do. 'Pray don't trifle with me, Maggie. What is amiss?'

The maid looked conscious. 'I don't know as I'd say anything were amiss exactly.'

Prue was not in the least comforted. What had happened? Was it to do with last night's events?

'If there is something I should know, pray tell me without roundaboutation.'

'Seemingly it's the master should tell you. Leastways, if you don't know already. Which the whole household wouldn't believe, if I told them 'til I was blue in the face!'

Alarm triggered a series of thumping palpitations in Prue's bosom. She clutched the cup with fingers that quivered uncontrollably.

The maid leaned forward and removed it from her dangerous grasp. 'You'll have it all over the quilt in a minute!'

As the girl set the cup down on the bedside table, Prue reached out and gripped her arm. 'Tell me, for heaven's sake!'

Maggie patted the hand and perched on the bed.

'There, miss. There ain't no call for you to fret. Why, it's the best thing as could've happened. It's fair rattled Mrs Polmont, o'course, as was only to be expected. But Mrs Wincle went dancing all round the kitchen table, she's that pleased! Only Mr Creggan said as how it weren't seemly as we should all be talking on it with nothing said. But, I ask you, miss, what was anyone to think when the master insisted on staying all night in your chamber?'

A vision popped into Prue's horrified mind. Mr Rookham—there in the chair by the fire! And then came a wash of heat as a memory—was it a memory?—slid into sight. He had kissed her!

She heard a murmur in her mind. *There is no turning back.* Oh, what had she done? What had she led him to? Hazily she recollected having been caught by a trick laid by the twins. Which must be why he had been here in her room. It must be her fault. Had he not been here, he would not have been tempted.

An urgent need assailed her. 'Where is Mr Rookham now?'

'Abed and asleep, miss, for I'll warrant he was that tired. The kitchen maid found him when she come in to make up the fire.'

'Asleep in the chair?' Hushed, and desperate.

A coy look settled upon Maggie's features. 'Well, he were on the bed, miss.'

'What?'

The maid tutted. 'Not *in* it. Though that don't make no difference, Mrs Wincle says. It ain't nowise seemly, and he's bound to see you right.'

Prue's veins pulsed unevenly, and her voice was unsteady. 'That is n-nonsense. I am nobody, after all, and he has been in my room b-before.'

'But not all night,' argued the maid. 'And you've no need to fret over what Mrs Polmont says neither.'

'What does Mrs Polmont say?' As if she needed to ask!

'As how you meant for to make the master marry you. I wish you'd heard Mrs Wincle! Ooh, she did go for her, she did. A right argy-bargy they had, I can tell you. Mr Creggan was afraid as they would come to blows. And everyone joining in, one way or t'other— some saying as he must, others as he won't neither. What with Mrs Polmont declaring as she'd march out of the place, and Mrs Wincle telling her "good riddance", you never heard such a carry-on, miss!'

Appalled, Prue could only gaze at her. How had it come to this? Was it her indulgence in daydreams that had led her to such a pass? Oh, that she had never come here! Indeed, it were better she had never been born than allow Mr Rookham to sacrifice himself. And only to quiet the ravings of a collection of servants? She must not let it happen!

She sank back against the pillows. 'Pray, Maggie, leave me, if you will. I need to be alone for a space.'

'I don't wonder, miss.' She got up from the bed. 'I'll leave the breakfast things, for I'd hate to face the master this time, if he thought as I'd neglected your needs.' With which, the maid took herself off.

Food was essential, or Prue knew she would never carry out her intention—but it must wait. Hardly had the door closed behind Maggie, than she threw aside the covers and shifted gingerly to her feet. She found herself reasonably steady. Heaving a sigh of relief, she made at once for the press and extracted her grey Seminary uniform.

With waking had come remembrance, and a feeling of intense relief. The thing was done! He need no longer expend all that wasted energy in a futile attempt to maintain the status quo. Recalling the sweet innocence of that fatal tender kiss, Julius experienced a surge of a like sensation to that which had led to this liberating surrender. The thrill of possession!

But it was not akin to the need which had kept him tied to his mistress for so long. This was entirely different. To have guessed at her emotions was one thing. To be the recipient of a demonstration of affection, born from a state of mind that had shaken off all inhibition, had proved altogether irresistible. And it had sealed the future with a final recognition of what he felt himself.

He leaned to tug at the bell-pull to summon his valet. Then stretching luxuriously, he settled his hands behind his head and gave himself up to thoughts of Prudence Hursley.

These readily led him to the realisation that there was much to be done—and quickly!—to secure both her reputation and her happiness. The sooner the formalities were dispensed with, the better for both of them. How soon things could be managed must be a question for the local vicar. Yes, he had best write to the fellow immediately!

He had not eaten before seeking his bed in the early hours, but his valet had the forethought to bring up coffee, accompanied by a plate of broken meats and fresh baked rolls. Partaking of this late breakfast in his bed, Julius revolved plans in his head, which persisted while his valet assisted him at his toilet.

His attention concentrated little on what he was doing, Julius allowed himself to be dressed in his usual buckskins and a frock-coat of mulberry cloth. The sight of his well-cut attire in the mirror served only to remind him that something must be done about Prudence's wardrobe. That must begin before the ceremony. What might she choose were she given a free rein? He would have to accompany her, if only to ensure that she set no store by expense—which she was bound to do.

He looked forward with pleasurable anticipation to see the effect upon her of all this intended generosity. Julius dared swear she would try to dissuade him from it. Well, she would not succeed. It must be his delight, let alone his duty, to shower her with all that a female ought to enjoy, and of which she had hitherto been horridly deprived.

Desire urged him to seek her out immediately. Instinct charged him to set in train his schemes before he went to her. Prudence must not suffer the slightest doubt or qualm as to his intentions. Better to present her with a *fait accompli.*

Accordingly, upon leaving his bedchamber, Julius headed directly for his library with the intention of penning a note to be taken round to the vicar directly. Upon opening the door, he was brought up short by the sight of a cloaked figure before his desk, that turned as he entered. It was Prudence herself.

He started in, letting the door slide shut. 'You are up! Are you well enough to—?'

He fell silent as he took in her appearance. She was dressed for a journey! She had on a black bonnet, and under the cloak, which hung open, he caught sight of that hideous grey ensemble in which she had entered his life. She looked both startled and guilty. Julius felt his chest cave in.

'What in Hades are you doing?'

She swallowed, and her glance avoided his. 'I am going away.'

'Going away?' Blank with incomprehension. How could she be going away? An object drew his eye, and he saw a squat portmanteau set down a little before the desk. His guts went solid on him. 'Oh, dear God!'

'Pray, Mr Rookham—'

Julius snapped. '*Mr Rookham*—after last night! Have you run mad, Prue? What have I done to deserve that you should fly from me?'

'Nothing, upon my honour!'

She shifted back, huddling her arms into her chest. It was then borne in upon Julius that she was clutching the multi-coloured kitten. He strode forward.

'Hell and damnation, you *are* trying to leave!'

Prue shifted swiftly, putting the desk between them. There was a dull thudding in her bosom. Why had he to come in just at this moment? She had thought herself safe for another hour or two. It was, she had ascertained, barely eleven o'clock. Was he made of iron that he could survive on so little sleep?

He had halted at her strategic retirement, baffled. The last thing he wished was to make her afraid! With an effort, he moderated his tone.

'Why, Prue? What has prompted you to this?'

How was she to tell him? She had written it all in the letter which she had come to deliver. But it was a very different matter to say those words to him in person.

Prue dared to look at him, and found the hawk-look pronounced. Her heart skittered.

'Oh, pray don't look at me in that accusing fashion! You are angry, but—'

He flung out a hand. 'Not that!' A wry smile curved his lips. 'Upset, perhaps, and a trifle hurt.'

A wash of distress flooded Prue, and she cradled Folly closer as he began to wriggle. 'I don't mean to hurt you, sir.'

Julius flinched. 'You do so every time you address me with that repressive formality.' He saw the kitten squirming in her hold. 'I wish you will put that wretched animal down!'

Recognizing the futility of holding on to Folly for the present, Prue bent and released him. He immediately began upon an investigation of the library. She watched him a moment, and then turned back to encounter the steely eyes of Mr Rookham. A great sigh escaped her, and she sank into the chair reserved for his use, burying her face in her hands.

Julius eyed her in silence. The sensation of shocked disbelief had abated, and he was able to think more clearly. It occurred to him forcibly that there were practical barriers to this intended flight besides his own objections. Had Prudence considered them? He voiced his instant thought.

'You must know that I cannot let you go like this, even was I willing for you to leave.'

She shook her head, but her face remained hidden from him.

'Did you think to walk out of the place just as you came in, with a portmanteau and that wretched cat under your arm? After everything that has passed? Where in Hades had you in mind to go?'

Her hands dropped, and the bleakness in her face twisted his heart. Yet it distanced him, curbing that instinct to go to her and overbear whatever barrier it was she had set up against him.

'I am going back to the Seminary.' Prue saw with pain the puzzlement enter his eyes. Did he suppose she wanted to go? She drew a steadying breath. 'Mrs Duxford, I know, will let me stay there for a day or so. Or perhaps longer, while I search for a new appointment.'

Julius wanted to consign Mrs Duxford to hell, and her Seminary with her. But he fought down the rise of frustration.

'And how did you propose to get there?' he asked curtly. 'You don't even know if the stage runs today. And don't try to make me believe that one of the servants told you, for they would have come to me at once.' A hideous thought occurred to him. 'Have you looked to Polmont for this scheme? She is the only one of my household who would be willing to aid you to leave me!'

Her eyes flashed suddenly. 'Mrs Polmont? Have you run mad? I had rather die than seek her aid!'

'Then how—'

'I don't know how!' she threw at him. 'I only knew I must go—and that as speedily as p-possible.'

Prue felt her voice crack on the last word, and tried desperately to hold back the rising tears. She reached out her hand for the letter she had set upon his desk, scrunching it with her fingers.

'Is that for me?'

She nodded. 'There is no point in it now.'

Julius watched her tuck the screwed-up paper somewhere in the recesses of her cloak. He was tempted to seize it from her, in the hope of quelling the desperate question bursting in his head. Instead he let his tongue work for him.

'You have not yet told me why, Prue. After last night, I thought—'

Her eyes flew up, luminous now. 'That is just it, sir. Last night is exactly the difficulty.'

It was like a blow in the chest. 'Then your memory must be mightily at fault!'

She struck her hands together. 'But I don't remember! At least, I have a few hazy images.'

Julius stared at her, conscious of an abrupt lifting of his spirits. If she did not recall what had happened between them, what had been said—? Dear God, had he so quickly forgotten her condition? Had the whole been dreamlike to her in her semi-conscious state?

'Forgive me, Prue! Finding you here has made me stupid.' He dropped into gentleness. 'But I remember if you do not, and I shall find ways to remind you.'

Prue's veins began to pulse unevenly. She gazed across the desk at his softened features.

'You remained in my room all night, did you not? The servants are all talking of it.' Her fingers twisted together. 'I thought it better to remove from here, so that you need not feel yourself obliged to—to—' She could not say it!

But Julius laughed. 'Obliged to! Don't you know me better than that?' There was tenderness in the

steel eyes, but determination too. 'There is no obligation, Prue. Yet I have every intention of
marrying you.'

Her heart took a bound, and her eyes searched the
strong features. But she resisted the more.

'You cannot! I will not let you sacrifice yourself!'

Julius moved swiftly. Before Prue knew what he
would be at, he had come around the desk, and
caught her up from the chair, grasping her strongly.
There was fire in his gaze.

'You goose, Prue! Sacrifice? I wish for nothing
better!'

Her pulses were rioting, but she held fast to the
obstinate certainty in her head. She was unaware
that her hands crept up to his chest, unaware that
she used his given name.

'It is not possible, Julius. You are saying it only
to relieve my guilt. Oh, I know that I dreamed—
and perhaps some of it was real—but you *could* not
want me. I have known it all along.'

Julius tried to draw her closer. 'Then you have
been wonderfully mistaken all along!'

To his chagrin, she held him off. But those impossible eyes had that pitiable look, and his heart melted.

'If you will look at me in that fashion, my darling
goose, you will induce me to kiss you.'

The endearment was almost too much to bear. As

he moved his head to suit the action to the words, Prue quickly put her hand up to his mouth.

'Don't!'

Julius caught her fingers instead to his lips and held them there. Her bones jellied as she felt the warmth and softness of his kiss upon her skin. His gaze was altogether too close, and infinitely tender.

'My sweet Prue, how can I convince you?'

Her eyes pricked, and only half knowing what she did, Prue curled her fingers about his hand. A little more, and he would induce her to abandon her determination. It must not be! Urgency engulfed her, and she pulled away from him, breaking the contact.

'Pray don't try, Julius. You see, I know that you care for me—I had realised it a little while since.'

There was a catch in her breath, and a simple air of sincerity that gave Julius pause. A chill of apprehension seized him.

'But?' he prompted.

Prue nodded. 'Yes, there is a but.'

A sad little smile wavered on her lips and pain entered his heart. 'Go on.'

'You did not care enough, Julius. I was forced to know it, or you would have taken the opportunity—it offered more than once!—to ask me before. Only now, when your hand is forced, you feel obliged to it.' Her eyes filled. 'I had rather bear to live without you than to marry you upon those terms!'

His heart twisted. Julius pulled her gently into his arms. He felt her resist for a moment, and then sink helplessly against him. Julius cradled her, touched by the valiant stifling of her sobs.

How little had he thought upon her lowly opinion of her own worth! His hand played up and down her back, stroking her into quiet. He made up his mind. Nothing would serve him now but truth.

The comfort of his embrace was both balm and agony for Prue. She had said it all—more than she had penned in the letter. He had forced it out of her. She clung to him, as if she knew it to be her last moment in the haven of his arms.

Julius did indeed release her, but only that he might instead fold her hands within his own. She gazed up into his face and found a rueful gleam in his eyes.

'My darling girl, you don't understand at all. Yes, I did hesitate, that I admit. But it was not for lack of feeling. I have loved you—I don't know for how long!—only I thought I loved my untrammelled life the more.'

Prue blinked dazedly. 'I don't understand you.'

'That's what I said,' he retorted, releasing her hands and tugging instead at the ribbons of her bonnet. 'I wish you had known my mother. She would have told you how selfish I am, just like my father. Here I have carved out an existence in which I have no one to please but myself. I believed—or tried to!—that nothing must be allowed to change that.'

A faint stirring of hope had risen in Prue's bosom. She paid no attention to the removal of her bonnet, and no more than glanced at it as he threw it aside upon the desk. Her attention wholly concentrated on his words, she searched for ways to refute them, in the unacknowledged desire that he should overbear her protests.

'You are making this up.'

A smile touched his mouth. 'I only wish I was, for it scarcely redounds to my credit.'

'It is another ploy to try to disabuse me.'

Julius laughed, and his finger reached out to stroke her cheek. 'I would I might disabuse you! But I cannot. For what you perceived was precisely what I was attempting to prove in myself. That I did not care enough.'

He saw her lip tremble, and into the grey eyes crept that vulnerable look of uncertainty. His heart filled to bursting. Just so had he early been made captive, on that very first day. His fingers quivered as he reached out, clasping her face between his hands.

'Only I had not bargained for the way a hopelessly sentimental female had inveigled herself into my very soul, so that I can no longer call it my own. And, God help me, I don't even wish to!'

Prue read the truth in his eyes. They blurred in her vision, and a sigh of pure happiness rolled out of her, along with the tears. She felt his fingers at her cheek, brushing them away. Next instant, his lips were against her own—a delicious warmth that sprang remembrance in her mind.

'Oh, Julius,' she murmured breathily, and felt herself caught up into that same crushing embrace that filled her sudden memory. No dream this! Her heart soared.

She felt herself released a little, but desire hungered at her mouth in a kiss so explosive that Prue became wholly lost in sensation. By the time she was at last permitted to come up for air, her head was swimming.

'Oh, dear,' she uttered breathily.

The hawk features glared down at her. 'Is that all you can find to say?'

Something between a gurgle of laughter and a gasp escaped her. 'What do you expect me to say?'

Julius felt her sagging, and held her closer. But he maintained the steely look, his nose jutting dangerously.

'A declaration of love would be a start! Followed,

perhaps, by an endearment to indicate how much my sentiments are reciprocated.'

Prue wound her arms about his neck. 'But you know I reciprocate them.'

'Knowing and hearing are two different things. I warn you now that I shall expect frequent assurancɛs—both verbal and otherwise.'

She gazed up at him in a trifle of uncertainty. But that telltale quirk came at his lips and Prue let out a sigh of relief. 'I was afraid you truly meant it.'

His most enigmatic look appeared. 'I most assuredly do mean it. Last night, let me remind you, I had no need to request it.' One of his supporting arms left her, and his fingers caught at her face, lifting her chin. 'Well?'

It was softly uttered, and Prue's unruly pulses skittered into life again—in anticipation of his kiss, and faintly apprehensive.

'What was it I said last night?'

Julius could not forbear a smile. 'Oh, no. You do not get out of it so easily, my Prue. You must start anew.'

'But I don't know what to say!'

He leaned down and brushed her lips with his. 'Say what you feel.'

The touch of his mouth upon hers caused such a flutter within her that Prue could not bear him to withhold the kiss any longer.

'I had rather show you,' she breathed, and drew him down again.

The tender yielding of her mouth to his shot Julius through with renewed passion, and the tease he had begun went right out of his head. When at length he commanded himself to call a halt, he could scarce contain his elation at the spontaneous declaration that whispered from her lips.

'I do love you, Julius—quite desperately!'

Prue found herself rewarded with yet another kiss, so full of passionate need that she could barely stand. Presently, she was seated side by side with Julius in one of the window seats, his arm firmly about her. Folly, discovering that his chosen companion had sensibly placed herself in a suitable position to provide him with comfortable accommodation, promptly jumped into her lap.

'I might have known your wretched beast would spoil the romance of the occasion!' complained Julius.

'Poor Folly.' Prue stroked him as he curled up in his customary fashion and began to purr. 'He has become used to having me to himself.'

'Indeed? That will soon be remedied.'

'Oh, pray, Julius, don't say I must let the twins take him, for I could not bear it! I am excessively fond of them, but—' She broke off, struck by a sudden thought. 'Julius, I shall be their aunt! Will they mind?'

'On the contrary, they will be delighted. Indeed, it would not much surprise me if they attempt to beg off any further scold by claiming that our union is solely due to their tricks.'

'Well, in a way it is,' argued Prue, petting the kitten. 'And perhaps they will not mind leaving Folly with me.' She turned anxious eyes upon him. 'As long as you don't mind it?'

But Julius was fingering the grey stuff of her Seminary uniform. 'What I do mind is this hideous garment foisted upon you by your Duck. I wish you will remove it.'

'What, now?' gasped Prue, shocked.

'Goose! I meant later. And I give you fair warning that I shall throw the thing on the fire!'

Prue gurgled. 'That is excessively improvident of you, Mr Rookham. I am sure there must be some deserving creature who would be glad of it.'

The hawk-look appeared, and he eyed her bodingly. 'Do you wish to know what I'm going to do to you, if you persist in calling me "Mr Rookham"?'

'Oh, dear, did I do so?' asked Prue guiltily. 'I dare say it may take me a little time to accustom myself to the change.'

'Accustom yourself fast, or it will be the worse for you!'

As he chose to kiss her again upon the words, Prue was unable to reply suitably to this unfair command. Besides, the kiss was most enjoyable, and she was obliged to keep Folly secure with one hand. And then her attention was distracted, for as Julius spoke of an immediate wedding, Prue bethought her of the housekeeper.

'Oh, dear, Mrs Polmont! She will be more than ever disposed to scold me!'

A grim look settled in Julius's face. 'You need not trouble your head about Polmont, my sweet.'

Prue turned in the seat and caught at his arm. 'Julius, you don't understand. She will be as mad as fire and say that I have entrapped you.'

'I think not.'

There was an inflexible look in his face, the steel in his eyes pronounced. Consternation engulfed Prue, and she laid tense hands upon the ball of fur in her lap.

'What do you mean to do? Julius, I cannot be the cause of her losing her employment.'

'You are not the cause. She has dug her own grave.'

'But—'

'Hush, Prue,' he urged, catching one of her hands up into his. 'You will have nothing with which to reproach yourself. Do you suppose me to be so unjust? I cannot allow her to stay, but she has given long service in my family. Therefore I will not dismiss her, but instead pension her off.'

Prue's face lit. 'Oh, yes, that will be an admirable solution.' Then a dreadful thought occurred to her. 'But who will do the housekeeping for you?'

Julius grinned, tightening his hold about her. 'Once I have a wife, I will have no need for a housekeeper.'

Aghast, Prue gazed at him. 'But I know nothing of housekeeping!'

'Then you will learn.'

'Julius, pray don't rely upon me,' begged Prue desperately. 'You know I shall only make a goose of myself.'

A teasing look crept into his eyes, and his lips quirked. 'On second thoughts, perhaps it is not such an excellent notion. I should hate to find myself reduced to eating a diet of vegetables, only because you cannot bring yourself to order the execution of a pig or a chicken.'

Prue bubbled over. 'I am not quite such a goose, sir.'

He laughed, and brought her fingers to his lips. 'Don't trouble your head over it. Wincle is fully capable of continuing her duties without supervision. As for the rest, with Polmont gone, I am sure you will find the entirety of the staff more than willing to assist you to learn your way about.'

She relaxed again, her fingers absently seeking for the kitten. 'And may I keep Folly?'

'You may do just as you please, my far-from-prudent love. With one notable exception.'

Prue looked at him anxiously, for his expression had turned serious. 'What is that, sir?'

He caressed her cheek. 'You must promise me faithfully never to risk your life in any more daring rescues.'

'I shall do my best, Julius, but I cannot possibly promise.'

Julius groaned. 'Then I foresee a future dogged by frantic attempts to keep you firmly under my eye.' A gleam entered the steel eyes. 'Which brings to mind the matter of the horribly long and tedious days before we can be married. Since you obviously can't be trusted even at night, I fail to see how I am to quiet my conscience unless—'

'You propose to sleep in my room again?'

His mouth hovered over hers. 'Preferably not in that excessively uncomfortable chair.'

The implication sent a sliver of heat racing through Prue's veins. She swallowed with difficulty, and her voice was a trifle hoarse.

'Well, if you do not mind sharing with Folly…'

A soft laugh floated between them. 'Since he was instrumental in bringing us together, I suppose I must bear with it.'

But the kitten, apparently recognising that there were moments when his presence could well be dispensed with, obligingly jumped off Prue's lap. And since she was wholly occupied in answering the intense fire in the lips of her betrothed, Prue quite failed to notice his temporary absence.

* * * * *

1/21	41	61	81	101	121	141	161	181
22	42	62	82	102	122	142	162	182
3	43	63	83	103	123	143	163	183
4	44	64	84	104	124	144	164	184
5	45	65	85	105	125	145	165	185
6	46	66	86	106	126	146	166	186
7	47	67	87	107	127	147	167	187
8	48	68	88	108	128	148	168	188
		69	89	109	129	149	169	189
		70	90	110	130	150	170	190
		71	91	111	131	151	171	191
		72	92	112	132	152	172	192
		73	93	113	133	153	173	193
		74	94	114	134	154	174	194
			95	115	135	155	175	195
			96	116	136	156	176	196
			97	117	137	157	177	197
			98	118	138	158	178	198
			99	119	139	159	179	199
			00	120	140	160	180	200

201					
202	276	291	306	321	336
203	277	292	307	322	337
204	278	293	308	323	338
205	279	294	309	324	339
206	280	295	310	325	340
207	281	296	311	326	341
208	282	297	312	327	342
209	283	298	313	328	343
210		299	314	329	344
211		300	315	330	345
212		301	316	331	346
213		302	317	332	347
214		303	318	333	348
215		304	319	334	349
290		305	320	335	350